Disrespectfully Yours

Disrespectfully Yours

Raynesha Pittman

www.urbanbooks.net

Urban Books, LLC
300 Farmingdale Road, NY-Route 109
Farmingdale, NY 11735

Disrespectfully Yours

ISBN 13: 978-1-64556-181-1
ISBN 10: 1-64556-181-X

First Trade Paperback Printing February 2021
Printed in the United States of America

10 9 8 7 6 5 4 3 2 1

*This is a work of fiction. Any references or similarities
to actual events, real people, living or dead, or to real
locales are intended to give the novel a sense of reality.
Any similarity in other names, characters, places, and
incidents is entirely coincidental.*

Distributed by Kensington Publishing Corp.
Submit Orders to:
Customer Service
400 Hahn Road
Westminster, MD 21157-4627
Phone: 1-800-733-3000
Fax: 1-800-659-2436

Dedicated to those of you who try hard to keep drama out of your lives but love to read it in the pages of my books. Thank you for allowing me to entertain you.

Prologue

Meagan's foot pressed the gas pedal to the floor, but her Mercury Bobcat refused to go over seventy miles per hour. She despised driving the 1980s heap of junk, as she liked to call to it, but it was a graduation present from her boyfriend, William, and that made the ten-year-old pile of scrap metal on wheels priceless. Baby girl was in love, and that was all that mattered to her. Everything within her arm's reach could go up in flames and transform into the pits of hell, and she would welcome the devil into her personal space with a smile. As long as she had William burning alongside her, neither their location nor their situation mattered.

He was the boss, her boss, that is, and the owner of the diner where she worked. He was a fair employer, though sometimes too demanding, but he never asked his employees to take on a task he hadn't already tackled first. William had the focus of an expensive camera, and when he locked that focus on a target or task, he didn't detach from until it was picture perfect. It had taken him years to perfect the craft of cheating on his wife and getting away with it. Now that he had, he was fucking a variety of women, and to his surprise, Meagan was still one of them. With the poise only a true "in denial" pedophile could have, William had taught her how to mix business with pleasure. And being spread eagle on the desk of this forty-year-old man, who had once sung alto in the same youth choir as her mother, excited the meaty space between her nineteen-year-old thighs.

Why should Meagan give a damn about William being married to the woman her mother forced her to call Godmama? There wasn't any DNA bonding them, and if it wasn't for her mother's longing for the sister she never had, Clara, William's wife, wouldn't be a factor in her life at all. That small piece of candy-coated bullshit she fed herself was enough to keep the fling she was having with her godfather going.

Meagan's young age had betrayed her, as it enabled her to confuse love and William's thirst to lay pipe in her fountain of youth. The genuine feelings she had for this older man spilled out into everything she did, and she was ready to have William all to herself.

"He loves me . . . He loves me not," she chanted while she tore each petal off the rose until she was down to the final petals. With a sigh that released all the doubt that destroying this once healthy flower had created in her mind, she screamed, "He loves me!" And there was nothing that could convince her otherwise.

The day had finally come when all their sneaking around, lying, and hiding their love from the world would finally pay her dividends. William had heard her heart-breaking pleas to be his one and only, and he was going to give his wife her walking papers, with Meagan sitting front-row center to witness it. He had it all planned out and had told her where and what time it would go down. At 11:30 a.m. in his restaurant, the same place where their love story had begun, he would break one woman's heart and mend another's.

The plan was for him to meet his wife and her best friend/godsister, Rita, who also happened to be Meagan's mother, for lunch to share some life-changing news. He had told his wife that the news was about his diner, but he really planned to ask Rita for Meagan's hand in marriage while he handed Clara divorce documents all in the same breath. He had gone over his plan with Meagan every day that week, and although he had given Meagan that Saturday off to prepare for their engagement announcement, she was headed to the restaurant to help her man with the early morning rush. She had been too excited to sleep last night, and William hadn't been there to hold her and put her to sleep, as she had grown accustomed to. But she understood that he had been obligated to play husband one more time to a wife he hadn't loved or desired in years.

William was a walking dreamer with a pocketful of goals. He intended to achieve each one, and whenever he had shared those dreams with Clara, she'd shot them down like she was playing a game of *Duck Hunt* on Nintendo. She even had had the nerve to laugh at his short-term goals when he'd failed to reach them, like that annoying brown dog would after missing a duck. His words had no effect on his wife anymore. He was days away from opening his first restaurant, just shy of two hundred miles away in Atlanta, Georgia, and he didn't want to carry Clara's country-ass baggage to the big city with him. It wasn't Clara's words that had encouraged him to venture beyond Albany, Georgia. It was his goddaughter's. From the time Meagan was a small child with pigtails, she had made it clear that she thought the world of him, and this had become even more evident to William when she came of age.

Meagan had begged her godfather to escort her to her high school prom and had lied about not being able to secure a date. She had been beautiful with her honey-toned skin and her overly curvy body for a minor, but the bifocals she'd worn and the thick train tracks of braces across her teeth had made her story believable. It hadn't been until the prom was over that William realized he'd been bamboozled by the closest thing to a child his wife's unwanted hysterectomy would allow him to have.

"You know, everyone else is going out to eat or to make out now. Maybe we should find something else to do too. It's bad enough I had to ask you to be my date. I'd hate to say I turned in early too." Meagan threw out the fishing line, but there wasn't enough bait on it.

"Nope. I'm done for the night, Georgia Peach. Your goddaddy hasn't danced that much since the night I married Clara. But if you're hungry, we can swing by the diner, and I'll whip you up a fried pork chop sandwich and a shake before I take you home."

"Yes, thank you. You're so perfect, Goddaddy. I hope I marry a man like you when the time comes," she said, staring out the passenger-side window into the peace of the mid-spring night.

"You will." He laughed. "Because I'll be right there to scare the hell out of the guy you bring home and make sure he treats you even better than I do."

"You can't expect him to stay after you do that," she said in between giggles.

"Then that's even better. You can focus on your education and then your career. I know you said you want to go into business administration, but you really should look into modeling."

"I keep telling you that a pretty face doesn't go with fat on the waist, Goddaddy. That's like wearing white after Labor Day at an all-black party."

"Yeah, well, I keep telling you the rules are broken and a magazine would be foolish to pass up your beauty over a little baby fat. Chubby is cute on you, and I have a bullet for the first person who disagrees with me."

Blushing, Meagan stared deeper into the night sky until she could see a vision of their faces in the moon. Then she said, "Thank you. I love you so much."

"And I love you too, Georgia Peach."

It wasn't long before they made it to the restaurant, and while he cooked, Meagan set the table in a nontraditional manner. Instead of arranging plates, napkins, and utensils, Meagan used her naked body as the centerpiece and wrapped the thin plastic tablecloth around her stomach to hide its grotesque shape. When William entered the dining area, the sandwich hit the floor and the shake followed behind it.

"What the hell are you doing? Put your clothes on now!" he spat, his voice full of anger, as he averted his gaze.

"No. If you want me to put my clothes on, look at me, dammit. Look at me without seeing your fucking goddaughter, like the way I look at you."

"Hell no, you are my goddaughter, my minor goddaughter at that. I used to change your shitty diapers and bathe you. I know what you look like naked, so get dressed right fucking now."

She got off the table and approached him. He was still gazing over his shoulder, trying hard not to look at her nude. When her breasts rested against his chest, she pressed her hardened nipples into him.

"Did my titties feel like this when you used to bathe me?" she asked. Her smile was wiped off her face as fast as it had appeared when his open hand slapped her cheek. She screamed out in pain.

"I'm sorry, baby, but you left me no choice. I've noticed your stares at me, but I was hoping they weren't *those* kinds of looks. I don't know what's got into you lately, but you need to slow your roll. This shit right here is sick. You're my daughter, my Georgia Peach."

"You mean *who* has gotten into me, not what," she managed to say between sniffles.

"What's that's supposed to mean?"

"It means that I'm far from being a virgin, and I need a real man to please me. I thought it was you, but I guess I was wrong. I'm seventeen years old, and seventeen-year-old boys' dicks don't do shit for me. I like my dicks twenty-five or better."

William's jaw dropped.

"Don't look shocked about the shit. Everybody knows I'm getting big, grown dicks but you. Take me home. You've wasted enough of my time, old man."

William grabbed her by the throat and locked his hands. It took every ounce of sanity he had in him not to choke her until the fire in between her thighs went out permanently.

"Whose grown dicks have you been getting? I'll kill him. Do you hear me? That pervert is a dead man walking!" he screamed as he continued to ring her neck.

"I . . . can't . . . breathe."

After releasing her, he walked over to the bar and took a seat while she dressed and cried. He couldn't believe how the night of charity work had turned out. Not only had he disciplined her for the first time in her life, but he had also found out abruptly that his Georgia sweet peach no longer had her core. And to make matters worse, she had her underage eyes set on him. William was so lost in his thoughts that he didn't realize Meagan was outside in the car, waiting on him, until she blew the horn to hurry him up. He took her home in silence and couldn't wait to get to his own house to find out what was really going on with her from his wife.

"That little bitch was fucking Charles," Clara said while puffing on her extra-long cigarette.

"Charles? Like in her mama's ex-boyfriend, Charles?"

"Damn right, that Charles. Why do you think he's an ex? Rita caught that little bitch on her knees, with a mouthful of him, when she was thirteen. Then she caught the ho in the garage, having sex with Mr. Evans, when she was fifteen. Now you know the truth on why his drunken ass went to jail. If you weren't that little slut's goddaddy, she'd be drooling over you too."

"Why didn't you tell me any of this before?" He snatched Clara's pack of cigarettes off her TV tray and lit one. He didn't smoke, but the urge he felt now was too strong to ignore. William didn't continue speaking until he had inhaled and exhaled the menthol twice. "I would have killed those niggas over Meagan. I thought you said Rita left Charles because he was beating her ass?"

"That was part of the reason, but when she found out Meagan had been seducing him, Rita sent his ass packing. We know how crazy you are over that little girl, and I couldn't lose you to the jailhouse over that tramp doing exactly what she saw her mama doing. You remember how Rita was back then. Don't forget about how many secret trips to the abortion clinic we took her on before she got pregnant with Meagan. Hoes breed hoes, and you can't save that girl, so don't try to."

The cigarette wasn't strong enough to soothe the anger he was feeling at the men taking advantage of his goddaughter's youth. He took a seat at his minibar and made himself a stiff drink. He swallowed the cup of brown liquor with a loud gulp, which didn't go unheard by his wife.

"What made you ask me about Meagan tonight, William? Oh, hell no . . . ," she said while sliding her feet into her house slippers and standing up. "I know that little slut bitch didn't try any shit with you at that prom of hers, did she? I'll beat her ass."

"Sit down. You know I wouldn't let you touch a strand of hair on my Georgia Peach. I asked what was going on with her, because I caught her making eyes at some of the chaperones at the dance. Damn. You and I both know she plays the innocent little girl role when it comes to me."

"Yeah, she does, but the bitch is three months away from turning eighteen, and if she thinks you're next on her list, she has another thing coming." She took another puff on her cigarette as she regretted encouraging Rita to teach her goddaughter the game they had played for so many years with the men in their city. Meagan was gorgeous and like a cup of ice water to the thirsty men in their little city. If she didn't own a tenth of the beauty Meagan possessed and never knew what broke felt like, she was sure that Meagan could bring home the cash cows, and as her second mother, she'd help her milk them dry.

After emptying the smoke from her lungs, Clara concluded, "But in the meantime, I don't want you around her unless she's working at the restaurant. I know you. You'll make it your business to try to save the bitch. She can't be saved, trust me."

"I'm not going to try to save her, but if I find out who has been touching my Peach, that nigga will need the saving."

William kept his word to his wife and didn't try to save Meagan. Instead, he started bending her over every chance he could get once she turned eighteen. A part of him thought that if he pretended to love her and provided the attention she was seeking, he would be saving her from turning into her mother. The other part of him felt like if she was going to fuck older cats, why shouldn't it be him? What he hadn't expected was to fall in love with her within a year's time. He wasn't faithful to Clara and hadn't been for years. When her support for him and his dreams had left, so had the faithfulness of his dick, but he had never thought he'd yearn to leave his wife for a new start with his nonbiological child.

But Meagan had played her role. She had catered to all his physical and mental needs, and she had goals of her own, unlike his wife. Meagan was making moves to turn her dreams into her reality, while Clara had reached her life's goal of living off him.

William knew riches in life would unfold for them both if they stayed together and worked at it together, as a team. When he had shared his dreams with Meagan, she hadn't let him leave them on her dorm room's pillows. With the help of one of her professors, Meagan had written the proposal for his restaurant's expansion and had applied for the grants he needed to make it happen. Thanks to her, he hadn't had to apply for a business loan, because the money he had received from the grants was more than enough to open his new location. There wasn't a doubt in his mind that Meagan would be on his arm at the red ribbon cutting for his hot new Atlanta spot. It was final.

Meagan pulled into her normal parking space in front of the restaurant at 6:30 a.m. and smiled at the lit sign, which read WILLIAM'S DINER She had looked up at the neon-colored sign all her life, and no matter what was going on, those simple words would always bring a smile to her face. William had been the only father she'd known and the only man in her life who hadn't sexually abused her after pressuring her to consent. She had freely given him access to her cookie jar; he had never tried to crack it open on his own. It was amazing how something as simple as his name could bring her peace.

From the front of the diner, Meagan could see the lights on in the kitchen, but William's car wasn't parked outside. Maybe I beat him here, she thought as she turned her key in the door. The alarm was disabled, which meant he had definitely been there and had left. She placed her bag that held her engagement outfit on the bar and made her way into the kitchen. The smile on her face grew when she noticed William's keys on the countertop, next to his jacket. Without thinking, she ran through the kitchen to his office, and there he was, pants around his ankles, stroking in and out between two legs that belonged to a lazy bitch who couldn't keep them up on her own.

Meagan couldn't believe he was fucking his wife, Clara, in the same place he normally fucked her, but what could she say? Clara was his wife, and only a few hours remained until their marriage was over. She watched for a second or two longer, fantasizing that it was she being pleasured by her man, and then turned and walked away. As she made her way to the front door, she decided to sit in the car and pretend she'd just pulled up. But before reached the door, she heard someone say her name.

"Meagan?"

She turned, gazed in the direction of the entrance to the kitchen, and saw Clara, who was fully dressed. *If Clara is right here, who the fuck is that on William's desk?* she thought. Before she could make it back to the office to find out, a sloppily dressed William emerged, straightening his clothes, with Meagan's mama, Rita, right behind him.

"I tried to find a tire shop open, but there weren't any twenty-four-hour ones, like I told you," Clara said. "Come on, Rita. Let's go. We'll be back at eleven thirty for your bullshit business meeting, and if you haven't gotten your tire fixed, we'll take you then. Oh, and I need twenty dollars and a pack of cigarettes for waking up out of my sleep to bring you to work. Time is money, so pay up." Clara stuck her palm out, ready to have it greased.

William kept his eyes on Meagan, because he could see the flames glowing in her eyes as he handed his wife the money.

"See ya later, William," Rita said.

He didn't say it back, and he wouldn't, not with Meagan glancing from him to her mother with a murderous look on her face. Feeling fearful and defeated, he lowered his head in anticipation of the fight that was about to occur, and just then Rita leaned in to kiss her daughter on the cheek, but Meagan jumped away from her.

A puzzled look fell on Rita's face, and almost instantly, it was replaced by a smirk. She knew her daughter like the back of her hand. Plus, she spoke ho fluently. She could tell Meagan's anger wasn't related to the fact that she, Rita, had betrayed her best friend, Clara's trust, so that meant Meagan must have caught them fucking. Meagan was furious because she and Rita were once again sharing the same dick.

Part One

Disrespectfully Me

Chapter One

Only a few minutes had elapsed before Devin was in position for round two. He didn't have to verbalize it, because his actions spoke volumes. There he was, standing in front of a tired-out Meagan, with his swollen girth in hand, pointed in her direction. He hovered over her, deciding he would get the approval to go another round, just in case she found him rude for thinking he didn't need it.

"He really likes you, Tammy. Can I hit one more time before you bounce?"

Meagan's mind was consumed with the beating Devin had just placed on her, and she almost didn't respond when he called her by her alias.

"I really like him too, but maybe we should call it quits for the day. It's my birthday, and I'm supposed to hang out with my girls this morning, remember?"

Only half of her words were true. It was Meagan's fortieth birthday, but it wasn't her girls she had to rush off to. She needed to show her face soon before her husband, William, sent out a search party to find her. He had arranged for Meagan to have a day of pampering, and if she missed her brunch date with him, she would need a makeover to cover the evidence of his abuse.

"That's cool and all sexy, but we need our time with you," Devin said, making reference to his meat. "Every time we meet up, you got to bounce, and you leave me with a glass slipper to hunt your sexy ass down with. You stay doing me wrong, baby." He sat on the edge of the bed, and his meat deflated like a whoopie cushion losing air, but without the sound effect. "Is it my age? I told you that I turn twenty-five next month, and you act like because you're thirty-two, a nigga isn't worth your time. I can't even call you, because you keep your number a secret, and the only time I get to see you is when you come into the store, looking for me. What happens when my mixed tape drops and you can't find me? I'm not going to be a stocker at Walmart all my life. I got goals."

Meagan hated when Devin wore his immaturity on his sleeve, but the fact that he always did shouldn't have surprised her. She had known he had a lot of growing up to do since the day he helped carry her TV out to her car and handed her a demo of his latest underground club banger. But he was fine as hell with his coconut-shell complexion. Standing over her at six feet three, he had a rock-solid body and the beautiful features that only a 99.9 percent black man would have, with a wide nose as proof. There was no debating that he could kill a headboard and a box spring. Meagan was sure he could wear a suit better than his Walmart uniform, and if he acted right, she'd get him one to strut in for her.

His hygiene seemed to be on point. She couldn't smell anything foul coming from him, and his teeth were shoe-polish white, confirming he routinely brushed them. She could tell that he sat in a barber's chair frequently by the wave patterns in his hair, and she could also tell he fancied smoking tree by the darkening in his lips. Her only issue with Devin was his age, but the nine inches of Angus beef he carried in his pants was too addictive for her to cut his ass off for the error in the year he was born.

Her pursuit of Devin was supposed to be a walk on the wild side for her and also her taste of the cup of ice water that she used to be for the older men she screwed when she was a minor. She longed to sample the youth she had sacrificed for marriage, college, and her husband's business and had never written into her life's plan. Having a sexual relationship with a twenty-five-year-old who constantly drooled over her had made her feel young and desirable again. He wouldn't take no for an answer, and the way he begged to be in her presence made her feel important, which was what she had never seemed to be in the history of her marriage. She hadn't been on a hunt for him, and she'd tried to shoot Devin down when they first met in the mall's parking lot, but he had been persistent. She thought back on that time.

"Why do you keep saying no, beautiful? Your sexy ass must be scared of what my young ass can do to you, huh?"

"No," she said, giving him a partly suppressed laugh. "I'm scared of how you're going to act after you get a taste of me. That would be cruel of me to feed you this full-course meal and then send you back to those value meals you've been snacking on."

"Then be cruel, gorgeous. Man can't live on fast food alone. Too much MSG in it to get full. Let me taste that Sunday dinner."

"Taste? Boy, please. I don't give samples, and there's no kids' meals on this menu."

"Sounds like you spend more time on marketing and advertising these full-course meals than you do on touching the souls of real men. I'm trying to fuck you, so keep the commercials."

He took the time to boost her ego with flirts and compliments in such a manner that it made her long to play his game. So she lied about everything she could to leave him with no real lead to track her down. She lied about her name being Tammy, she supplied him with a fake age and job too, and told him to meet her in the lobby of the tallest hotel on Peachtree at 8:00 p.m. if he really wanted a shot. To her surprise, he was waiting on her at the bar when she walked into the hotel's lobby, with a look on his face that read he was there and ready to put in work.

"Reservation for M. Tolliver," Meagan whispered to the front-desk agent. She didn't want Devin to hear her government, nor did she want her name to sound familiar to those within earshot. She hadn't modeled in years, but her beauty wouldn't let her be forgotten.

"I'm sorry. Can you repeat that?" the agent said.

"I have a reservation."

"I heard that part," the stout front-desk agent said, rolling her eyes at the obvious. She wanted Meagan to repeat her name not because she hadn't heard it, but because she was tired of every black person with a little bit of change pretending to be somebody important. The trench coats, dark shades, and whispering had become an irritation for her, and it had become her new quest to expose all hidden identities. "What did you say your name is?"

"M. Tolliver."

"M. Tolliver? That's your name? I don't see an M. Tolliver in our system, ma'am. How are you spelling M.?"

"Tolliver is my last name. Can't you look me up by it?"

"Can I please have your identification? A driver's license, passport, or one of the items we accept, as listed above your head on the wall, will do," she said, ignoring Meagan's question.

"You should have said that from the beginning." After fumbling through her purse, she took her driver's license out of her wallet and slammed it on the counter in front of the young woman.

"And you could have just said that your name was Meagan Tolliver." The front-desk agent picked up her driver's license, and a wallet-size picture that had been stuck to the back of it flew off and landed on the counter.

It was a picture of Meagan and her husband. The agent picked it up. "Is this your husband, the funny guy from Georgia Peach's?"

In a panic, Meagan snatched the picture out of her chubby little hands and quickly turned to see if her play date had heard the question. Once she was sure he hadn't, she answered, "Yes, that's my husband and me. How do you know him?"

"I just told you how I know him. I eat there all the time," the woman replied.

"Then you should stop. It's starting to show."

The insult was for the treatment she had received thus far while checking in, but a part of her didn't believe the woman's response, because, sadly, she was familiar with William's side-piece standards. Chubby, big breasts, probably could cook, and a mouth that looked like it picked up the slack for all of her shortcomings by swallowing the head, shaft, and balls at the same time. Meagan was seconds away from welcoming a growing smirk when the agent gave her a sample of what her mouth could do.

"Don't worry. When I go get my blackberry cobbler when I get off in an hour, I won't tell Mr. William that you're in room twenty-two-oh-one with that youngster over there." Meagan's mouth dropped when the agent offered an explanation of how she knew this. "The baby boy has been here for about an hour, looking for you, Ms. Tammy. He described you and even asked me to check the check-in list again, in case I overlooked you, but I told him I needed a last name, which he didn't have. Here are your keys. Do you want me to grab you anything while I'm there?"

Meagan closed her mouth and dug through her purse again. This time she pulled out a gift card to her husband's restaurant.

"No. I'm about to get full up there. Here's fifty dollars' worth of cobbler on me. Are we good?"

"Of course we are, Ms. Tammy," she said, loud enough to get Devin's attention. Then she said, "We are real good. And let me get those keys back. I just realized we have a suite open on the forty-fifth floor, with a beautiful view of the city. Go get real full, girl. The way your husband flirts with everything that comes in there, you deserve some playtime."

"Thank you."

Meagan walked away from the desk, and Devin followed her. They didn't greet each other and rode the elevator to their hotel room like strangers heading in separate directions. Once they stepped off the elevator, Meagan continued to lead the way as a stone-faced Devin followed behind her slowly. When she went into the room, Devin continued past it and snatched up a few items from the maid's cart that sat at the end of the hallway. Then he doubled back and entered the room. After he closed the door behind him, he remained silent and went straight to work. He wet a towel and placed it along the bottom of the door frame. Next, he turned the hot water on in the shower and allowed the entire bathroom to fill with steam. Then he disappeared behind the closed bathroom door.

Meagan didn't know what the hell was going on, and she couldn't ask. She had requested the sneaky and silent behavior when she'd agreed to give Devin a shot. He was only doing what he was told, and she'd stand by her request. A few minutes later, the bathroom door opened. Devin stuck his arm out and motioned with his hand for her to come join him. After she walked into the steamy fortress, he closed the door behind her and did his signature move of placing a wet towel under the gap in the door.

The steam floated heavily in the air, causing Meagan to become slightly light-headed. Then he passed her a lit blunt. The two of them had passed the blunt only twice before beads of sweat formed across her forehead. That was Devin's cue to get the ball rolling. He undressed her as they shared the weed-filled cigar, and once he finished, he stared at her naked body like it was a buffet filled with of all his favorite foods. Then it was time to eat.

He sat on the floor, with his back against the toilet, extended his neck, and rested his head on the closed toilet seat. Without looking up, he grabbed her by the legs and forced her onto his face. At the touch of his tongue, Meagan was in heaven, but her mind wouldn't let her relax. She wasn't sure if he was being smothered by the combination of her juices, the weed smoke, and the steam, but eventually, his tongue licked away her thoughts and she let go. She didn't ride his face like most women in that position would have. Instead, she did squats on it, not by choice but by necessity, owing to the force of the tongue-lashing he was putting on her. With every sporadic move of his tongue, she jumped, relinquishing her bent-leg position over his mouth, only to bend down again.

When she exploded on his face for a second time, Devin scooted out from under her, slid on a condom, and then hoisted her in the air. Her feet off the floor, Meagan came to rest in an uncomfortable position on the toilet seat, and then he put in work. He made sure he left an impression on her that night by using every inch he had to please every inch of her. If she were a schoolteacher, she would have given him an A+ in all subjects, especially in foreign languages. The way he French-kissed her pearl tongue enabled him to pass French with flying colors. She couldn't fathom how a man so young could have already mastered what men twice his age still needed lessons on. It wasn't her intention to stay the night with him, but the dick wouldn't let her to go. After fucking William's geriatric dick for all those years, the young man's dick felt like her second opportunity at losing her virginity.

What Devin didn't know about that night was that he had busted Pandora's box wide open and released a cougar into Atlanta's youth-filled streets. If he could make her body feel like she'd taken a trip twenty years back in a time machine, she wanted to see if any other person or people could. It may have started with him, but she was now fucking two other men that were a few years older than Devin but more than ten years younger than her.

What Meagan didn't know was that she wasn't the first older woman Devin had played cougar and cub with. When he was in twelfth grade, he'd been invited to stay the night at one of his school friends' houses. He hadn't been able to sleep, and so he'd lain in bed in Jamal's room, staring into the dark for hours. He wanted to go home, but the power was out again, and there wasn't any food. With all his siblings staying at their grandmother's house until his mom could pay to get the electricity reconnected, he had accepted the sleepover invite like it was a free night at a bed-and-breakfast.

Devin, restless and uncomfortable, crept out of bed, found the door handle in the dark, opened the door slowly, and made his way out of the room. The rest of the house was as dark as the room he'd left, but then he noticed light coming from under the last door at the end of the hallway. Curious to see what the source of the light was, he began walking own the hallway. As he crept closer, he could hear the sound of soft moans, but he questioned their authenticity when he heard background music. Someone was watching a flick, but who? Judging by the setup of the house, the room had to be his friend's mother's bedroom.

He moved closer to the door to listen for sounds of the real thing happening at the same time, and just then the door opened.

"Baby, you scared me. I thought I heard someone coming down the hall, but no one ever knocked. Are you okay?"

"Yes. I was looking for an, um, TV to watch, because I can't sleep," he lied.

"There's one in here, but you don't want to watch what I'm watching," she said, with a laugh that caused her big breasts to shake under her robe. "But you can come in here with me, and I'll change the channel."

Ms. Betsy, as everyone called her, stepped to the side and let him into her bedroom, and then she simply muted the DVD she was watching. She took the time to lock the door, straighten up her bed, and clean up the clothes she had on the floor before she mentioned the TV again.

With the threesome in action on the screen, she asked, "Is there something in particular you wanted to watch? I can watch *this* all night."

She made a quick turn to face Devin, and her robe became untied, revealing her naked body. It wasn't by accident that it flew open, because shock was missing on her face and she took her time to close it up again.

With his dick on hard from the naked women on the TV, he said, "We can watch this. This is cool."

"Is it? How old are you, Devin? You said that like you've done what you see them doing on the TV."

"I have, and I'm seventeen, but I'll be eighteen soon."

"You're a baby." For the first time since he had entered the room, she finally looked shocked and slightly embarrassed. "I thought you were one of those older boys

Jamal hangs out with. I'm sorry, baby. Here's the remote. You can sit on the floor if it makes you more comfortable."

He didn't know what she meant by calling him a baby and offering him the floor instead of the spot on her bed she had cleared for him, but he didn't like it. Her words made him feel like he was young and inexperienced, and offering him the floor felt juvenile. He was down for proving her wrong.

"I'm good. I told you this is fine. That's like watching Saturday morning cartoons to me. Dude can't handle neither one of them, like that robe can't handle your big ass and those titties. No disrespect, Ms. Betsy, but I've been checking you out. You don't have to play with that pussy. I've been wanting to feel you on my dick. Even with clothes on, I could tell your body was going to be bad."

He rubbed his meat out of habit, and she caught the move.

"Boy, you are going to talk yourself into a world of trouble."

"Then fuck talking. You don't have to be shy about that pretty pussy throbbing. It's natural. I just don't see a need for you to use your fingers when you can get this dick. I'd love to satisfy your pretty ass."

"Thank you for the compliment, but I don't think you're up for the task of handling all this," she said, then gave a laugh.

"Yes you do. That's why you gave me a sneak peek at it. If you really want it, get on all fours and make her smile at me."

"And now what?" she questioned once she was in the requested position, tail up.

"Shit. What do you think happens next? You cum."

Devin beat her down until the credits played on the flick. He was fine while he was hitting her from the back, but when he flipped her over and dug her out while she lay on her back, her legs spread, he knew he fucked up. They began kissing like they meant something to one another, and when he needed to catch his breath, he sucked on the nipple nearest to his mouth.

From that night forward, his friend's mama was sneaking him in and out of her bedroom while her son slept down the hall, until she realized Devin had grown feelings for her. It was only a ride on a big dick that could last all night for her, but to Devin, he was damn near engaged. He started hustling and dropping money off on her bills and treating his boy Jamal like he was his son by making sure he kept money in his pocket. Ms. Betsy thought it was cute at first, and then she didn't.

"What's all that stuff?" she asked him one night.

"My clothes. I thought I should just leave some over here, since I'm here almost every night. I might as well keep a few things over here, so I don't have to leave in the middle of the night," he said as he continued to unpack his bags and fill an empty drawer he had found in her dresser.

"You can't leave stuff here. Jamal would have a fit if he knew what we had going on. That's why I tell you to leave after we're done. If you want to spend the night with me, we need to get a hotel room somewhere."

"Why pay for a hotel when I help pay bills here? And I was thinking maybe we should tell Jamal what's been going on between us. I've been keeping money in his pocket and making sure he's straight while we are at school. We should tell him that we are in love. I'm tired of hiding it."

"In love?" She laughed so hard after repeating the words that tears rolled out of her eyes. "Devin, I'm in love with your dick and head, baby, not you. We are just having fun. Don't mess that up with feelings. I don't want to have to call it off with you, because you can't handle our situation."

"Ain't no feelings involved. I was just making sure you didn't have them. I didn't want to seem fucked up because I didn't."

The lie didn't flow or sound like the truth, and it didn't matter, because after he fucked her good that night, he never called or came over again.

It must have been history repeating itself, with an added twist, because the time had come for Meagan, aka Tammy, to call it quits, too, with the aspiring rap artist because the sex was making her grow attached to him. Out of all three men she cheated on her husband with, Devin was the most skilled with his tool and had her hooked. When she found herself scribbling his name with hers in a heart, like a teenager in love, during an idle period at work, she realized it was time to grow back up. The only adult way to handle it that came to mind was for her to call it quits. She decided to give him one more taste of her goodies before she did.

"You got her sore again, little daddy. I need you to kiss her and apologize. Can you do that for me?" Meagan purred at him.

"Hell yeah, sexy. Your big daddy will do whatever you want," he said, correcting her reference to their age difference, seeing that he felt it would have been smarter for her to reference the size of his dick. "Make her smile at me."

Meagan turned on her stomach and got on her knees. Her ass sat high in the sky, like two mountain peaks unreachable by any mountain climber, but he rested a hand on each of her peaks, confident that his climb would be victorious. Placidly, Devin stood behind her, slow to attack the hurdle before him due to him seeing her mountains as nothing more than speed bumps. Meagan didn't know it, but he was in love with her and would do anything to get her to take the next step with him. He had picked up more hours at Walmart to buy extra studio time so he could record a track that would make enough noise to get him signed by one of Atlanta's many record labels. When that happened, not only did he have plans to give Meagan the world on a platinum platter, with a chain to match, but he'd also ask her to marry him and birth his child. He didn't know much about her, because the secrecy of their relationship turned her on, and he liked that it did, yet it didn't stop him from feeling like she was the one for him, and his dick agreed.

He attacked her face-first now, with the thought of their wedding night on his mind. *Tammy, you will be mine, no matter what I have to do*, he thought as his tongue went into overdrive.

The restaurant was packed with partygoers. The crowd ranged from Atlanta's big-name celebrities and athletes to Meagan's employees from her modeling agency and the restaurant's regulars. Georgia Peach's on Peachtree was always packed, due to the restaurant having the best food in the city and the hottest live entertainment around, but only once a year was it packed in honor of Meagan's birthday. She had made it to forty, and although she didn't look it, her private battle with rheumatoid arthritis made her feel every bit that age.

She had left Devin at the hotel early enough to make it on time to brunch and her hair and nail appointments, but she intentionally arrived late at her own party. It was not that she wanted to make an entrance; she stalled to ensure she that was the best dressed at the party. She had the limo driver park across the street, in one of the empty business offices' parking lots, so she could check out her guests, just in case one of them outshined her in her black, knee-length designer dress with the V cut to the belly button. On the limo's backseat, she had backup outfits that were just as fabulous, but as it turned out, they weren't needed, because no one she saw could hold a candle to her.

"Okay, Mr. Hurley. You can drop me off at the door now. And remember, if you leave, don't go far, and return quickly. When I'm ready to go, I don't want any delays, or your ass is fired, like the last three drivers. You understand me?"

"Yes, ma'am." The driver let the words drag off his tongue to give her more of his country accent, since she seemed to like to talk to him as if he were her slave.

"What have I told you about calling me ma'am? Either your ass is stupid or you're slow. Which is it?"

"Neither. And I apologize, but I never know when to call you Mrs. Tolliver, Ms. Meagan, or Ms. Tammy. No disrespect, but can you give me an update before each trip? Because it's hard to keep up with who you are for the day."

"Don't worry. You won't last long enough to get an update, Mr. Hurley. Now take me to my destination," she yelled.

"I have to call you by what you want to fucking go by on any given day, but you can't call me Angelo, like I asked," he mumbled, not caring if Meagan heard him or not. She threatened to fire him every time she opened her mouth. He wished she'd just get it over with at this point.

"Excuse me? This isn't a friendship, nor are we on a first-name basis, Mr. Hurley. You're the hired help. Know your place. I swear, if I had time to hire another driver, I'd fire your ass right now. I knew you wouldn't make it ninety days with that smart-ass mouth."

Angelo cranked up the limo and then stopped in front of the restaurant. He rushed to open her door. When she was about to step out, he said, "Enjoy your birthday, Ms. . . ." He paused, not knowing what to call her.

"Mrs. Tolliver, and I plan to." She exited the limo, took two steps toward the door, and stopped, in a panic. "Mr. Hurley, you haven't expressed concern to my husband in regards to my names, have you?"

His thick, beautiful lips, which Meagan hadn't noticed until that very moment, curved into a crooked smile that revealed a mouth full of white teeth and a slight overbite.

"Nah, I haven't mentioned it," he said as his dark brown eyes looked her up and down like she was nothing more than a skank and then fixed on her eyes. "I know what you got going on. Your secrets are safe with me. I'm just the hired help."

He didn't afford her the opportunity to respond. He shook his head at her, got back in the limo, and drove off.

His ass is fired, Meagan thought as her husband, William, planted a kiss on the back of her bare neck. He had snuck up on her.

"Happy birthday, beautiful."

Meagan scanned the area for onlookers before she spoke. "What did I tell you about putting your mouth on me, William? Only God knows where it's been this week."

"There you go with that shit again. Can we please enjoy your birthday without all the accusations? I fucked up in the past, I'll give you that, but you want to hold the shit against me for life."

"Don't make it sound like it was only once," Meagan retorted. "Your cheat list is twice the length of your dick. Just because old age has sunk in and you can't sling him around Atlanta like you used to, don't think for a second that I have forgotten."

William shook his head and wrapped his arms around his wife's waist. "I love you, baby, and I hope you enjoy everything I put together for you tonight."

Meagan tried to maintain her defensive attitude, but she knew William must have gone out of his way if he was saying that. She couldn't stand him for all the bullshit he had put her through over the past twenty-one years. If she wasn't in his ass about his other women, she was healing from the beatings he would give her. Their main issue was that William couldn't decide if he wanted to treat Meagan like his wife or his goddaughter. Since history provided the evidence that she held both titles in his life, William treated her both ways and beat her whenever he felt it was necessary.

Whenever she thought she could have a heated argument with him, like most married couples did, he reminded her in a heartbeat that he was the closest thing to a father in her life and disciplined her as his child. Sometimes he beat her with a belt across his lap to keep it authentic. However, the majority of his beatings were with his closed fist. Meagan had to admit that through her hate, he still had her heart, and after all the hell-filled years, when she had often had a sore bottom and needed to wear sunglasses to hide the bruises, she was still physically attracted to him.

Though he was sixty-one years old, William didn't look a day over forty. He kept his salt-and-pepper dreadlocks freshly manicured and tied in the back. His had perfectly trimmed sideburns, and although he was extremely hairy, William kept his face hairless and smoother than a newborn's booty. Only the rings encircling his light brown eyes marred his looks, giving him a slight raccoon look. Those circles were evidence of his ongoing battle with diabetes. Still, no one could say he wasn't handsome and well kept for an older man.

The way he sauntered in his shipshape attire, even if it was only his master chef uniform, was what had caught Meagan's attention so many years ago. He had a style all his own—one that didn't quite fit the country air of the little city of Albany, Georgia—and he had Meagan's nose wide open to it. William wasn't the first older man she had slept with, but he was the first one she had lusted for. She had slept with men who had twice the looks he possessed, but she had never drooled over them, because sex with them had been strictly business.

When Meagan was younger, her mother, Rita, had told her about a game she used to play with Clara. In reality, it was more of a hustle than a game, and the older men in Albany were the hustled. The way the game worked was they'd get the older, hopefully married men to do something inappropriate with them and then would blackmail them for money. It wasn't a new game. Women had been pulling "the cry wolf and beg for dollars as Kleenex" stunt for years, but for a woman to teach the game raw to her eight-year-old daughter was rare.

"When men look at us, do you know what they see?" Rita asked Meagan while the little girl sat Indian style on the carpeted floor of their home, brushing her doll's hair.

"Yes, ma'am. They see ass, tits, and two wet mouths."

"Good girl. They see fuck tools. Which is why we see what when we look at them?"

"Paydays and deposit slips for them depositing their dicks in us. No matter where they stick it in us, there's a price they got to pay for the poking."

"I know I taught you better than that. Put that damn doll down and pay attention." Rita snatched the doll out of Meagan's hand and tossed it over her shoulder like salt. "Now finish answering the question."

"We charge for the poking, but a real woman gets paid for her time, attention, conversation, and pretty face. The goal is to get the payday without the poke."

"Now, that's better. What type of men give the best paydays?"

Meagan folded her fingers into the palm of her hand and then stretched her arm out in front of her mother. As she named the types, she released her folded fingers one by one and counted.

"One, a married man. He has more to lose and will do anything to lose you first, so he won't lose his family. Always set your eyes on them first, but be careful of the lurking wife. If it's easy to get his attention, the wife might already know he isn't shi . . ."

"Go ahead. You can say it. I told you, say what you want when you want, baby. Just don't talk that shit to me. Finish it up. What might the wife already know?"

"That he isn't shit," Meagan replied, and her mother gave her an approving nod.

"Don't forget that every woman knows her man, even the bitch that likes to play dumb. Never drop your guard when chasing him down. And if you get caught, remember that no matter what that bitch says, she isn't your friend. You will learn that hoes like to team up against men. But you are your own army. Understand me?"

"Yes, ma'am, I understand."

"Now, who is number two?"

"Number two is any man over twenty-five with a job. It doesn't have to be the best paying. Money is money."

"And why is a man twenty-five and up with a job number two?" Rita quizzed.

"Because I'm not eighteen, and no man wants to go to jail for touching or fucking on a little girl."

"Okay, that's right. Keep going."

"Number three, a man with deep ties to the church, like a bishop, pastor, or deacon."

Rita laughed. "That's your godmama's favorite type. She gets them all the time because she knows that Bible forward and backward. She starts asking for help with saving her soul, and next thing you know, she's sucking their souls out of them and filling that pocketbook up. What's four and five?"

"Four is a man in a position of power, like a judge, senator, or mayor. And five is a man with long money."

"Good girl."

Meagan was sure that no other eight-year-old had ever been trained to be a ho by her mama during nightly bedtime stories. As a child, she was smart, and from spending nights over at her classmates' houses, she figured out that what her mother was teaching her was wrong. But the stories her mother told were more interesting than those lame-ass children's books that were stacked up next to her bedside. Listening to her mother's version of blowing hard things down kept her attention more than the big bad wolf's huffs and puffs. Thanks to those stories, by the age of twelve, Meagan knew how to fake pregnancy symptoms, the going rate for abortions, and how to smear lipstick on a man's collar to taunt his ever-so-faithful wife, but she refused to use those skills on her own.

Her first go at the game was by force. Bills were piling up, and her mother was dating a guy who could quickly catch them back up. Rita knew she couldn't boldly offer her daughter in exchange for his money to pay the bills and continue to enjoy his respect, so she back doored it. She forced her daughter to play the game and taught her how to dress to play the part. Meagan started slowly, with long drawn-out stares at the guy, and then progressed to walking through the house dressed inappropriately. By the time she offered to suck on Charles's meat, like she had done to her corn on the cob as he watched in awe, he was already debating about making the first move.

She soon began asking him for money, and the first time he said no and began to threaten that he would tell her mother about their three-minute fuck sessions. He came out of pocket for a while, but when he could no longer afford to, she told her mother he had sexually abused her. Since it was Rita's plan in the first place, she cut his ass off, pretending to be distraught. Meagan began to enjoy playing the game once she saw it was profitable, and this sent her right into the arms of William. Her plan was to cash in on him behind her mother's and godmother's backs, but it backfired, and after twenty-one years, she was still in love with him.

As Meagan made her entrance into the restaurant now, William at her side, she was greeted by the sound of "Happy Birthday" being sung to her by a female neo soul artist. The woman sat on a tall bar stool at the center of a stage. The overhead lights grew dimmer in the room with each step Meagan took, but the lights that surrounded her five-tier birthday cake got brighter. The cake caught her attention, but the gifts that adorned the tables took her breath away. She was impressed with the details her husband must have worked out when it came time to decorate the restaurant. Everything was about her. The front of the menu explained how the restaurant was named after the nickname William had given her, and the back of the menu displayed only the items that were Meagan's personal favorites. Pictures from her modeling days hung on the walls, and the biggest picture in the house was of her cutting the red ribbon at the grand opening of her modeling agency.

In her honor, every guest in attendance wore black or gold, which were Meagan's favorite colors. An oversize black-and-gold bejeweled throne had been built behind her cake and gift table for the queen of William's heart, and it was called just that. Meagan stood in front of her throne as the song came to an end, and like magic, a single candle was lit atop the smallest tier on her cake. She took a moment to make a wish and then blew it out. Simultaneously, confetti fell from the ceiling, and the crowd roared, "Happy birthday!" She was speechless and refused to take the microphone when her husband held it out to her. Instead, she mouthed a tear-filled thank-you and sat on her throne.

"I just want to take a second to thank all of you for coming out to help me celebrate the love of my life's birthday. Y'all have her speechless, which we all know is very hard to do." William laughed. "She's such a beautiful woman, isn't she?"

The crowd screamed and clapped in agreement.

"My life is nothing without her. Please believe me when I say that. Georgia Peach's would still be a dream in the back of my mind if it weren't for Meagan pushing me to bring it to life. We've gone from a small diner in Albany, Georgia, to five major city locations, and we've been voted number one in Atlanta again this year. It's all thanks to her. I know I'm talking y'all's ears off and you're ready to get back on the dance floor, but let me say one more thing, and I promise to let y'all go. When my first wife died in that car accident feet away from my diner, with Meagan's mother in the car, I died. And I'm sure Meagan did too. I thank the Lord every day for allowing us to re-suscitate one another in His love. Meagan, my beautiful Georgia Peach, can I please have this dance?"

William held out his hand, Meagan took it, and he led her to the dance floor. The piano started playing, and then the rest of the band joined in. In a voice not as powerful as Patti LaBelle's but just as beautiful, the singer began singing "If Only You Knew." Meagan placed her head on her husband's shoulder, and they danced alone for the first verse. Then William invited everyone to join them on the dance floor. He turned off his microphone, which gave Meagan the opening she was looking for.

With her lips pressed closely against her husband's ear, she said, "Muthafucka, this is my night. Don't you ever steal my joy again by shining light on your ex-wife's and your side bitch's deaths. You sounded sad about it, too, like if the bitch hadn't died, you weren't about to leave her for me. Those hoes' deaths prevented you from having to break their hearts. You should be glad that you were saved from the agony of doing it. I am."

"Watch your tongue, little girl. It takes only a side step to get you in my office to fix your mouth. Let me remind you of one thing. I wanted to divorce Clara. I didn't want her dead. I am still sad about it, and about the loss of your mother too."

"Fuck them both. May they rest in shit."

William shrugged so that Meagan's head would no longer rest on him; he needed to look in her eyes. Her eyes never lied, and the hate he saw in them now forced him to get the hell away from his wife quickly so as not to attract attention. He pecked her on the cheek and disappeared in the crowd, leaving her standing there with a painted-on smile. Before she could formulate a thought, men started approaching her and asking for a dance. She wanted to decline, but it was her party. Why should she let the senior citizen who was consumed by his feelings ruin it?

The live entertainment ended, and a DJ took over. He was killing the ones and twos. He mixed hip-hop with the oldies track the artist had sampled from, and R & B with the jumpy beats of reggae music, and the crowd loved it, but nobody more than Meagan. She was feeling it and danced herself right out of her heels, leaving them behind without a care that they might go missing. Meagan was in a zone, and the music had her lost in it. She didn't realize it, but she was now on the dance floor, dancing by herself.

"Y'all looking good out there tonight, Atlanta," the DJ said into his microphone. "Georgia Peach, I need you on your feet for this one. Where's the birthday girl at?"

Meagan threw her hands in the air and screamed out, "I'm right here."

"There she goes, looking all good and shit. Black don't crack, and that body ain't slacked," the DJ announced. "Happy birthday, Peach. This one is dedicated to you."

The DJ mixed two familiar tracks, and then a beat dropped that Meagan wasn't familiar with. A woman's voice came through the speakers, and instantly, Meagan was feeling the hook. The artist was signing about holding her man down while the checks piled up. She had never heard the song before, but the voice and the rhythm had her hooked. Meagan's body swayed to the beat, and she loved the feeling it gave her until she realized that the male voice that was now singing belonged to Devin. She stood frozen on the dance floor as she scanned the room for her lover, but to no avail. She raced to the DJ's booth as she listened to her and Devin's love story being told through his lyrics, and she damn near died when he ended the first verse with "I love you, Tammy. You're the one."

"Switch the track now," Meagan calmly told the DJ, somehow maintaining her composure, but he was conversing with someone and didn't stop to acknowledge her.

"It's some young cat named Devin, but he goes by Young Diablo," the DJ said to a guy who was wearing too much gold jewelry.

"If he isn't signed, tell him we want him. Here's my card. See that he gets it. And if you make it happen, I got a finder's fee of two racks for you." The record executive handed the DJ his card.

The DJ nodded. "I don't know the guy, but I'm on it. Somebody just handed me his CD and said it was for her."

"Who?" Meagan and the executive said in unison.

The DJ scanned the crowd and then pointed in the direction of the restaurant's entrance. "That's the cat who gave it to me right there."

Meagan turned her head and gazed in the direction in which he was pointing, and there was her limousine driver. He held up a glass of champagne in her direction before he took a sip from it.

Meagan stopped a waitress who was carrying a tray of champagne-filled glasses, snatched one up, and mirrored his toast. She killed the glass in a single swallow, never taking her eyes off him, and then mouthed, "You're dead."

He gave her a devilish smile and then mouthed, "I can't be dead. I'm just the help," before he walked back out the door.

Chapter Two

Meagan's night had been ruined, and she was ready to go, but she managed to mingle with her guests for an hour more as she looked for her husband. Once she realized he was gone, she asked a few of her employees from her agency to help her carry her gifts to the limo. Her car door had barely closed when she laid into her driver's ass.

"What in the fuck do you call yourself doing, Angelo?" she yelled.

He laughed. "Damn. We're on a first-name basis now?"

"We ain't on shit. Where did you get that CD from? And why did you feel the need to give it to the DJ and have him play it?"

"Aw, don't play stupid, Tammy." Angelo tried hard to get serious, but the shit was too funny, and his words came out in between his laughter. "Your little boyfriend, Devin, gave it to me and made me promise that I would play it for you once you got in the limo this morning, but it slipped my mind. Since you're firing my ass tonight, anyway, I thought I should make good on my promise to him and fuck with you a little bit."

Devin had decided to break their rules in honor of her birthday. He had promised never to give her a gift, and she had told him that they would never go out. They had a sexual relationship only, and even speaking about it was against the rules, but he was slowly getting her to break that one. He had invested long, expensive hours in the studio, putting the song together, to give it to her as a birthday gift. The hardest part of all had been figuring out a way to give it to her so that she couldn't reject it, and so he had asked her limousine driver for help. He had given him fifty dollars to play the song as he drove her around that morning and to tell her happy birthday for him once she caught on that it was him rapping. Devin was determined to melt the lock on her heart one way or another, and Angelo had used the token of Devin's love to get revenge for her acting like a bitch.

"Fuck you, him, and your promise. Do you know what you could have done to my marriage if my husband had been there?" she screeched.

"No disrespect, but I don't give a fuck about you or your marriage. You don't even give a fuck about your marriage, Tammy. Sorry to be blunt, but remember, I'm unemployed after this trip unless . . ."

"Unless what, muthafucka?" Meagan asked as she made her way to the seat next to the partition.

"Unless you're going to let me keep my job as your driver in exchange for me not telling your husband about all the places I've taken you, and the niggas you've fucked in the past two months in the backseat of this here limo. I mean, I do like my job, and since you're going to up my salary, too, to keep my mouth shut, I think it's a win-win situation. What about you?"

"You gutter rat. You think you can just blackmail me and I'll agree? Who's to say I care if you tell? I got dirt on my husband that will stop him from divorcing me, anyway. I'll pass on your deal. Take me to my house. You're fired."

Angelo stayed silent, but the smile on his face never moved. His mind was racing because his surefire way of keeping his job had just proved to be useless. He had dirt on both the Tollivers, but he liked Mr. Tolliver more. Besides the fact that he was beating his wife, Mr. Tolliver was more respectful and friendlier than his wife, and he tipped well. Angelo had one more shot at keeping his job, and if it didn't work, he'd say fuck it and call the company he worked for to get back on the driving schedule.

"You're right. I fucked up. I shouldn't have tried to blackmail you to keep my job. I should have tried the shit with your husband. He has way more to lose, if you knew the shit he did and said in the limo."

"Like what?" Meagan didn't mean to respond that fast, but her reflexes took over, as Angelo prayed they would.

"Never mind, Mrs. Tolliver. It doesn't matter. I'll get you home and be on my way. I apologize for the stunt I pulled at your party. Happy birthday."

"Hell no! You can't just say, 'Never mind,' after saying that shit. I need to know now."

Angelo continued to drive silently. He had already told himself to be patient with the information. If she wanted to know anything, she'd have to ask him three times, and even then, she'd have to let him keep his job before he'd feed her any information.

"Don't play deaf now, asshole. I'm waiting."

That's twice, he thought, still staying tight-lipped.

Meagan waited a minute and then said, "Fuck it. You're probably lying, anyway. You've already shown me that you can't be trusted. You just said some shit to try to save your job."

"You're right. I might be lying, but you're wrong about the trusting me part. Your husband asks me every time I pick you up and drop you off where you're going, and I feed him with whatever lie you've tried to feed me. Let's just drop it, because you're right. I am trying to keep my job. My pops gave me the limo and told me not to show my face until I can introduce him to the man version of myself. When I told him I was driving for a big-time model, he invited me home for dinner. Yeah, I definitely want to keep this job. Working for your reckless ass made my pops proud of me again."

Meagan rolled up the partition after Angelo's last words, and her mind went into overdrive with questions she wanted answers to. *Is William cheating on me again? If so, with whom this time? And is he fucking these bitches at the restaurant, in his office, like he used to do me?* she thought. She tried to get the bullshit off her mind, but her thoughts kept going right back to it. She was beyond tired of William's shit, and she wasn't getting any younger. It was bad enough that she'd spent the past twenty-one years getting her ass whupped, but to add the continuous cheating to it was too much for her to keep putting up with. If she found out William was back to his old tricks, she'd take half of everything he owned and start over at forty. She wanted kids, but they weren't in William's plans, and she'd sacrificed her wants for him. If he was still creeping, she was done making sacrifices. She rolled down the partition.

"Okay, Mr. Hurley, I mean, Angelo. That's a sad fucking story, and you're more pathetic than I originally thought. I know I'm going to regret it. Spill it. If you want to keep your job, you better produce enough information to get me every dime he has when I file for my divorce, and I'll type up something saying how great a driver you are so your pops will allow you to stay for dessert or whatever."

"I have enough dirt on him to get you every dime he has, *and* the quarters he's making on the side."

Angelo hit the gas and exited the interstate. He had decided he could show her better than he could tell her, but he wasn't stupid. He would play it like a hand of dominoes and allow her to think she was winning before he locked down the board.

"Where are we going?" Meagan asked, seeing that they were no longer headed in the direction of her home.

"I'm keeping my job. That's where we're going. Sit back and chill. We're almost there."

Twenty minutes later, Angelo pulled up at a new condo complex in Riverdale, right outside of Atlanta, and parked.

"Welcome to your husband's condos. I'm sure you didn't know he owned these, did you?" he said.

Meagan's heart skipped a beat. If Angelo was telling the truth, then he was right. She didn't know her husband owned the complex.

"Where's the proof that these are his? I'm not dumb, Angelo. You can't just pull up to a building and say he owns the condos inside and think I'll just believe you. You know, it's very hard to make big purchases like this when you're married. It's not like buying shoes. I need some proof."

Her heart was tearing away at her chest, and she could feel her throat getting that forced, dried feeling caused by unwanted tears released from the soul. William was always handling business, and she never inquired about that business, because it kept him out of her face, which meant it kept his hands off of her. *If he does own the complex, why wouldn't he tell me?* she thought.

Angelo paid her no attention. Instead, he pulled out his cell phone, dialed a number, and put the call on speakerphone.

"Sorry to interrupt, Mr. Tolliver, but you told me to call you when I dropped Mrs. Tolliver off."

"You're fine, Angelo, and thanks for calling. Where did you take her?" an out-of-breath William said into the phone.

"She asked if I could take her to the agency and pick her up in an hour. She was alone, and I circled the block twice to make sure no one pulled up. She didn't make any phone calls on the ride there, either, but she did ask me if I saw you."

"I wonder what that is about? Did she say why she was looking for me or what she needed to do at the agency?"

"No, sir, not really. She mentioned something about wanting to see if a fax came in for one of her models, but that was all. I'm downstairs at your condo now. Are you ready to go, or should I come back?"

"Go ahead and take her home first and then come back for me. I'm still tied up with this one. She's complaining about time again. You know how that goes." William laughed.

"Yes, sir, I do. You said she's been upset since you mentioned the party you were throwing for your wife."

"*Upset* is putting it lightly. If I hadn't come here when I did, she probably would have popped up at the restaurant, and then all hell would've broken loose."

"Ouch. I'm glad you made it back to her in time, then. Oh, and before I forget. How much are you selling your condos for? I know now isn't really a good time to be asking, but one of my driver buddies has been taking his employer condo hunting. He's a defense lawyer that just moved here from Los Angeles, so I'm sure he can afford whatever you're asking."

"Yeah, now really isn't a good time, but give your friend my number and have the guy give me a call tomorrow. I'll get him set up for a tour. Make sure that he calls me tomorrow, because I have only three units left, and they are selling fast."

"Yes, sir. I'll return in two hours."

"Thanks, Angelo. I appreciate you."

"No problem."

"If she makes any detours or calls on the ride to the house, make sure you let me know."

"Yes, sir. You know I'll let you know."

Angelo ended the call and looked in the rearview mirror at a pissed-off Meagan. He didn't say anything as he drove off.

"Stop this fucking car now. What unit is that bitch in? I'm going to fuck up him and his little bitch. I told him the next time I caught his ass cheating, I'd kill him. Where are they, Angelo?"

Angelo hit the locks on the doors to prevent Meagan from jumping out, and he continued to drive. "Hold your horses, killa. You can't go in there raising hell. There's still a lot you don't know. The only way all of this will work is if you calm your ass down, take notes and, once you have everything you need, move smart. I took you there to secure my job. Do we still have a deal, or are you going to snap off every time you find out how fucked up your husband really is?"

"He's in there playing house with another bitch, and you want me to be calm!"

"Don't point the finger without counting all them niggas you passing out pussy to. You got all these Similac-drinking niggas eating your pussy as I drive you around Atlanta, and only God knows whatever else you're doing with them. You can't play hurt that he's doing the same. You have to play smart."

"That ain't the same thing," Meagan yelled at him. "I don't have in-house dick nowhere else but with William. I get mine on the side because he's been doing it from the jump. Don't make it sound like what we're doing is one and the same, because it's not." She let the handle on the back door snap back into place and then crossed her arms in front of her as a defensive mechanism. Meagan had finally realized Angelo wasn't going to unlock the car door, and they were too far away from the condos for her to walk back in heels at that point.

"Question," Angelo said, breaking the silence. "If he has been cheating on you from the jump, why have you stayed with him this long? He's whupping your ass, and you haven't busted a move yet. What are you staying for?

I know you don't think after all these years, his old ass is going to up and change. Y'all hoes kill me with that shit. A man isn't going to change once you've shown him you will accept his shit. That's a freebie from the man code, so you're welcome."

"Take me to Waffle House and watch your mouth. I'm far from being a ho," Meagan barked, completely ignoring his question. She knew the answer to it but didn't feel like Angelo was worthy of knowing it. Truth was, she was scared to be left alone in the world. Her mother was dead, she didn't have any siblings to help her get over a breakup, and William was all she had ever known. He had made her into the successful woman she was.

Although William credited her with his success, it was his drive that had made him achieve his goals. He made the plans, and she was his cheerleader, water girl, and whatever else he needed as he struck out to see them through. He had made her major in business to use her as a tool for his success, but that wasn't her life's dream. The only dream Meagan had was to be William's wife. He had even forced upon her owning her own modeling agency. William had convinced her that if she lost her childhood weight, she would be pretty enough to model, and once she'd been on her way to the top, he had made her stop and turn to managing others. He dictated her life, and without his direction, Meagan knew she would be lost.

She dug in her purse, retrieved a joint out of her holder, and sparked it up as the limo came to a stop in the Waffle House's parking lot. She smoked the joint longer than usual and then offered it to Angelo.

"I'm straight. I smoke, but not when I have to drive for you," he told her, declining the offer.

"Well, shit has changed. The new rule is if I smoke, you smoke," she said, offering him the joint and pulling out another one. He took it this time and started smoking.

"Why are you helping me?" she asked. "Don't lie and say it's to keep the job with more pay. You don't like me, and you know how I feel about your smart ass. So why help me out?"

"Shit," he said before pulling on the joint until it went out. "I owe you for not jumping over the seat and beating his ass for putting his hands on you." He sparked the lighter, lit up the joint, and pulled on it softer. He released the weed smoke from his lungs as he said, "Y'all both ain't shit for the cheating, but he's a real bitch for putting his hands on you. That morning I had to pull over really fucked me up. I ain't never seen anything like that shit before."

Meagan knew the morning he was referencing. It was the morning she had decided to check her voicemail on speakerphone as she and William rode together in the limo. There had been nothing for her to hide, because the men she crept with didn't have her office phone number or know where she really worked. She had gone through four business messages and then had activated her speakerphone and placed her phone next to her on the seat in order to jot down notes and reminders from the calls. If she had known Jerell—yes, the world-famous underwear model—had finally got the balls to flirt back, she wouldn't have done it.

"Hey, Meagan. This is Jerell. I . . . Well, I wanted you to know that I've been enjoying working close to you these past few months, and it's starting to bother me that this will be our last week together. I know this might sound crazy, but there's a chemistry between—"

Meagan reached out to grab the phone and shut him up by ending the call, but William's open hand met her face before she could.

"Let the shit play, as a matter of fact. Start it over," he growled.

"Why? So you can beat me because another man de-cided to flirt with me? You might not find me attractive anymore, so you don't see it, but I get flirted with every day. I'm a model, for Christ's sake. Stop beating my ass off of what somebody else does. I can't control his feelings."

"You were a model. Now you're an agent. But I see you don't know the difference. You're at that job, doing more than agent work. Niggas don't leave messages like that because the bitch is cute. They leave them when they've been doing a lot of communicating and spending time. That's how you build chemistry, you lying-ass bitch."

"Yeah, I'm sure you would know."

William's arm shot up like dick to its first piece of pussy, and then his hand grabbed her neck. "There it goes, that smart, disrespectful little mouth of yours. Didn't I tell you to watch how you talk to me?" he said, shaking her while taking off his belt with his free hand. "I gave you the money to start that business, and you use it like a motel, with a bisexual nigga at that."

"No I don't. I don't have sex with my employees or cli-ents. Can you say the same?" she retorted while trying to wiggle her way out of his grip.

William had the belt folded tightly in his hand by the ends, ensuring the buckle was tucked into his palm. She had squirmed enough to get out of his reach. All she had to do now was dart out of the limo door, and she'd find safety in the oncoming traffic. Three of her fingers were wrapped around the door handle; however, freedom never came. William cocked the belt back home run style and swatted Meagan across the face with it.

"Hey, boss," Angelo mumbled.

"Hey, boss, nothing. Roll up the partition and drive us home."

"But, boss!"

"That's right. I'm your boss, and I hired you to do what?"

Angelo didn't answer. He didn't know if he should pull over and beat William's old ass or do as he was told. He searched Meagan's face for the answer, but it was emotionless. He reached for his seat belt, and Meagan reached for the button to roll the partition up herself.

William beat her with the belt as Meagan sang a heartbreaking song of pain through her yells and screams. He had beaten her with a belt plenty of times, but not like this. He had always used caution when it came to hitting her and leaving marks in visible places. His reputation was a concern, and he'd go the extra mile to keep it intact. That didn't mean there hadn't been a few "accidents" that left Meagan with a busted lip or a bruise or two on her face. However, today he overreacted due to his own bruised ego and guilt. He swung the belt, and wherever it landed was its unforeseen destiny, and that wasn't the worst part. The rush of power he felt from disciplining his wife recklessly turned him on. Not only did he make Meagan suck on him the rest of the ride home, but he also called Mr. Underwear model and left a message full of Meagan's fake moans as he rammed his fingers inside her. It was degrading more than embarrassing to Meagan, and since Angelo was a witness to the violence, the thought of using cabs from then on crossed her mind.

Yes, she knew the exact morning Angelo was talking about as the two of them smoked joints in the limo.

"Like I said, I ain't never seen no shit like that, and I feel like a ho for watching and not beating his ass, but that's what you wanted," he said. "You didn't have to roll the shit up, but you wanted to save him from getting the ass whipping you were getting. Real talk, I'd kill him, but I don't like you enough to go to jail for you."

"And you said all of that to say what?" she asked, rolling her eyes at him. "You don't owe me shit."

"You're right, I don't, but I feel like you deserve to get a check for all those beatdowns, though. Anybody who goes up against the boxing champion gets a check. Why not help you get yours? Shit, if you hit the lotto in divorce court, I don't want you to forget about me."

"Hmm . . . ," she hummed, taking in everything Angelo had said. She could see him helping for money, but when it came to everything else he had mentioned, he could have saved the words he invested. "You're real good with words. I'm impressed. Although I trust you to be exactly who you've shown me you are, which is a hustling, shit-talking piece of shit, I don't trust you. Make sure you don't forget that."

"Photographic memory. It's saved."

Though he kept it to himself, Angelo was just as stressed out over their arrangement as Meagan. She didn't know how treacherous her husband was, but he knew. If Angelo's partnership with Meagan failed, he would be signing his own death sentence.

Part Two

Disrespectfully Mine

Chapter Three

Eleven thirty wasn't coming fast enough. Meagan was becoming frustrated with each check of the clock. Her morning had been straight from hell, and the only thing that would make it better was the meeting with William, Clara, and her mother. She and William had had a nasty falling-out after his wife and the bitch that birthed her had left. She had confronted him about fucking her mother, and without hesitation, he had put Meagan in her place.

"Where my dick goes isn't any of your business until I'm married to you. I don't owe you shit. I didn't want you to find out that way, but I also gave you the day off. Your mother and I have been fucking around for years, and the meeting today isn't just for Clara. It's for her too. I'm done with both of their asses, because I chose you. Now, you can woman up and deal with the shit, or you can be a little girl about it and find yourself a new man. What's it going to be?"

"Who else are you fucking?" Meagan couldn't think of anything better to say.

"Again, that isn't any of your fucking business until you get my last name. All you need to know is, after today you are the only one who is getting this dick."

"What? It is my business. You sound dumb as fuck. Now, stop acting like a bitch and—"

William cocked his hand back and struck Meagan in the mouth with his closed fist. Instantly, her blood leaked onto her clothes as her lip swelled.

"I see we have a respect issue, little girl, but I know how to fix it," William shouted at her as he unbuckled his belt. With his free hand, he grabbed Meagan by the arm, spun her around, and started spanking her across her butt and legs with his belt.

She yelled out in horror, "Stop hitting me!"

The louder she screamed, the faster he swung his belt. He spanked her into silence as her cries got stuck in her throat. She attempted to run and almost got away, but William's reach was long, and he managed to grab the hair that dangled from her ponytail. After wrapping her locks around his hand, he pulled her back to him and continued striking her with his belt until he saw the puddle of urine she was standing in and the wet piss stain on her pants.

"Now get your ass in there and put on a clean uniform. You have five minutes to get that stove going and the coffee brewing. And while you're at it, ice that lip. I don't want to hear shit else about where my dick has been, you understand me?"

Meagan nodded her head yes as she suppressed her sniffles.

Hours after her birthday party, Meagan lay in bed, with tears keeping her company as she recollected when William's beatings had first begun. No matter how hard she wished she had ended it then, the reality of it was that she hadn't. Nowhere in the lessons she had received from her mother or godmother did it mention what to do about a man who couldn't keep his hands to himself. The ugly reality was, William had never hit Clara. Meagan hadn't been around them for every tick of the clock, but she knew Clara, and Clara wasn't going to take anyone's shit. The way she used to check William in front of anyone and everyone they were around had caused Meagan to feel sorry for him, because he had never defended himself. Clara had even gotten into the habit of throwing stuff at him, sometimes directly at his unprotected face. Meagan wasn't sure if it was fear or respect that had made William keep his hands off his late wife, but she wished whatever it was, she would have inherited it.

She hurriedly dried her tears on her sheets, because this was the life she had chosen, and her tears wouldn't wash it away or grant her a do-over. *It is time for a change*, she repeated in her head until she found comfort in those words and they put her to sleep.

"It's a boy," the doctor announced.

Meagan had no clue whom he was talking to. Only seconds ago, she had been crying into her pillow in bed, and now she was in a hospital room, with a doctor, two nurses, and someone in scrubs, whose back was turned. Oddly, there was a large picture window and people were packed together in front of it and were snapping pictures of everything in the room.

"Where am I, and why are they taking pictures?" she asked.

"You're in the hospital, sweetheart. You just gave birth to your son." one of the nurses replied, but her back was turned now, too, and Meagan couldn't see her face.

"I thought I couldn't get pregnant. Isn't that what the doctors told us, William?"

The man whose face she had yet to see was handed the crying newborn baby and was congratulated as the father.

"Thank you. I'm so glad my son is here. She's been holding him hostage for nine months. Ain't that right, little nigga?" The voice didn't sound familiar, and the size of this man's body was nothing like William's.

"I wouldn't call it holding him hostage. That's a little extreme, don't you think?" said the other nurse. This was the first time she had uttered a word, and when she turned around, Meagan saw that it was her mother.

"Yeah, let's say she was baking him for a long-ass time," *joked the first nurse, and then she laughed. Meagan* *knew that voice. It was Clara.*

"William, is that you?" Meagan said in a low voice.

"Baby, who are you talking about?" the man replied.

"You!" she yelled.

"I don't get the question, beautiful."

"Then turn around and look at me. Is that you, *William?" Meagan screamed.*

"Only you know if that's William," her mother said *quickly before bursting into flames. "Is that who you* *want him to be?"*

"I think she does, Rita. She wanted us out of the picture, *so she can have him to herself," Clara noted now. Then* *she chuckled as she, too, went up in flames. "Is that who* *you're pregnant by? Are you pregnant by the husband* *you stole from me?"*

Meagan wasn't happy to see her mother and her godmother, but she'd never know who the mystery man in her dream was, because she was awakened by the sensation of William sliding her panties off under her nightgown. She wanted to protest and then snap off on him, but she had promised Angelo she would play it cool and wouldn't change anything up.

"Happy birthday, beautiful," William said, the strong scent of liquor lacing his words.

She didn't respond. She just allowed him to do whatever it was he wanted to do, which was to feast between her legs. His head was garbage and always had been, but she had never realized how bad it was until she had been devoured by Devin. The entire time William's mouth was at work, she stared at the digital clock next to the bed. When he had been down there ten minutes, the urge to cum still had not seized her, so she decided to pretend.

"Oh, Daddy, I'm about to cum," she yelled out, hoping she sounded believable. Judging by William's reaction, she did.

"Cum on Daddy's tongue, baby. You know you can't fight it," William moaned.

"Oh, Daddy," she yelled, forcing her legs to shake and squeezing them tightly around his face. Still angry with him, she purposely kneed him in the side of his face, as if by accident, while she was fake cumming. He took the hit as a sign of a job well done and didn't stop, although the hit dazed him.

William licked faster, thinking he was really taking her there, as she yawned silently and shook her head to keep herself from falling asleep. When he removed his face, Meagan rolled over on her stomach and got on her knees. It was the routine in their bedroom, head followed by doggy style until he climaxed, but not that night.

"No, baby, Daddy's tired. I've been ripping and running all day to get your party together. I just wanted to make sure I gave you a birthday nut." He kissed her on her round butt. "Good night."

Meagan stayed in doggy-style position, not out of disappointment that he wasn't about to hit it—because she wasn't in the mood, anyway. She didn't move, because she was biting her tongue so that she didn't mention the real reason he was tired. She wanted to blurt out that he was tired because he had danced around in somebody else's pussy that night. Instead, she said, "It's okay, Daddy. I understand," as she made her way out of the bed to head to the shower. "And thank you for tonight. Everything was beautiful."

William was in bed snoring before she turned the water on in the shower to disinfect herself from his touch.

She grabbed her body wash and went to work, but when she finished, she could still feel his saliva on her body. So she stepped out of the shower and grabbed the hand sanitizer from the sink. Thirty-five minutes later, her body was hot pink from her scrubbing it with the antibacterial solution, alcohol, vinegar, and astringent she had under her sink, and she still felt filthy.

The workday on Monday was busier than usual. Meagan walked in to find an answering machine full of messages from clients demanding models for upcoming events and shoots. Normally, a busy Monday would put a smile on her face, because busy meant money, but not that day. All she wanted to do was go to the tax assessor's office and look up the information on the land parcel belonging to the condo building. She couldn't believe William had gotten away with buying property without her knowing. Perhaps it wasn't in his name, she decided, but he didn't have any living family members, so whom would she trust enough to put property in that person's name?

"Mrs. Tolliver, you have a call parked for you on line five," her secretary, Stacey, said over the intercom.

Meagan pushed the button on her phone to respond. "Stacey, take a detailed message and tell them I'll call them back as soon as possible please. Thank you."

"I tried to, Mrs. Tolliver, but the gentleman said it was urgent. Life-or-death urgent."

"Who is it?" Meagan asked nervously.

"He wouldn't say. I'm sorry."

"Stacey, can you help me out with something? Because I'm confused."

"Yes, Mrs. Tolliver?" she responded, knowing her boss was about to say something fucked up to her.

"Is answering phones and taking messages a part of your job description?"

"Yes, it is."

"Is it part of what I'm paying you for?"

"Yes, it is," she said, tight lipped.

"Remind me at your annual review of the tasks that are in your job description that you don't do, please. Thanks for nothing. I'll take it." Meagan hung up in Stacey's face and picked up line five. "This is Mrs. Tolliver. How may I help you?"

"Hi. Is this Meagan Tolliver, the modeling agent?" a man's voice yelled through the phone, music playing loudly in the background.

"Yes, it is. How may I help you?"

"I told you her name was Meagan. Hold on a second." Before Meagan could question the caller, another person was on the phone.

"Damn, you played the fuck out of me, Ma."

Meagan knew Devin's voice, but her stomach started bubbling, and she lost her own voice.

"You played me like a fool," Devin continued. "You lied about your name, your age, and your job. I thought you said you wasn't fucking with nobody, but yo' ass is married to an old-ass millionaire. That's all the way fucked up. I guess a nigga wasn't good enough for you, Miss Big-Time Modeling Agent. It's all good, though. I should have known a travel agent wouldn't be riding around in a limo and living in one expensive hotel after the next. Anyway, I just wanted to call and tell you thank you for playing my joint at your big-ass party I wasn't invited to. Johnni D. Manz just signed me. I ain't a broke-ass Walmart employee anymore. And guess what else?"

"What?" Meagan managed to ask.

"I'm not in love with your disrespectful ass anymore, either."

"Bye, little boy," Meagan said before she hung up the phone.

She fell out of her chair laughing at Devin's attempt to hurt her feelings; she thought it was cute. What they had was over Saturday morning, when she left him at the hotel room, and he was the only one involved that didn't know it at the time. Devin might have won the battle of the phone call, but she had definitely won the war. He hadn't realized it yet. He would always be indebted to her, whether he wanted to admit it or not. It was her that he was rapping about on a track that had been played at her birthday party, and that exposure was what had led to him getting signed. She was one up on him without even trying, and she was in the mood to celebrate Devin being the second man she had turned into a success by merely spreading her legs.

Hey, Eric. This is Tammy. You want to meet me at Treasure Island later tonight? she texted the twenty-eight-year-old manager at a large hardware store, one of the three younger men with whom she had been cheating on her husband.

After almost five minutes, he texted her back. Hell no, I'm straight on you. Lose my number.

She was shocked and thought there had to be some kind of confusion, so she called his number. She was met by a recording that said, "At the subscriber's request, solicitation calls will not be accepted at this time."

"No, this motherfucker didn't put me on the 'rejected calls' list," she said aloud.

What the fuck is going on? she thought. Before putting any energy into it, she dialed *67 and her other play toy, Keith's number. He was a little sexy thing who worked for a package delivery service, and he didn't mind breaking company rules and fucking her in his delivery truck from time to time. He picked up on the second ring.

"Hey, boo. It's me, Tammy. What are you doing tonight?"

"Nothing," the thirty-year-old responded.

"Can we meet at the bat cave at the same bat time?" she laughed.

"I've been waiting on you to call," Keith said, with no energy in his voice. "Give me a second. I'm right here waiting on a customer to sign for their package."

Meagan held on and rubbed the warmth in between her legs as she waited. No one treated her body as perfectly as Devin did, but Keith was definitely the runner-up. He needed a little work, and she didn't mind employing him if the other two men were off her list.

"You still there, Tammy?" Keith asked, returning to their call.

"Yes, boo, I'm here."

"Look, I've been thinking, and I can't keep doing this with you. I know I said it wouldn't be a problem to play by your rules, because I didn't think it would, but it is. We meet on your terms. I don't even have your number if I need to reach you. And as you said up front, we are only fuck friends, which was cool when that was all I wanted, but now I'm looking for more. I'm ready to get off work to a home-cooked meal and some good conversation, not just a pretty face and some pussy. If all I needed was some pussy, I can go fuck one of my baby mamas or one of their friends."

"So what are you saying, Keith?" Meagan asked, attitude present in her voice.

"I already said it, Tammy. We've been fucking around for almost three months, and you still ain't put your mouth on me—"

She cut him off. "If you wanted some head, all you had to do was say it."

"I shouldn't have to. Let's just keep this short and sweet. It was cool while it lasted, but I'm good. Plus, some nigga named Angelo called me, talking about he's your husband and dropping death threats. And, shit, you're not even worth me going back to jail over."

"He is not my husband," Meagan yelled into her cell.

"It doesn't matter if he is or not. If we're just fuck friends, no one should be calling me about you. That's a violation of the rules, right?"

Meagan didn't answer him. She was too pissed to form words.

He went on. "Anyway, I'm on the clock, but my answer is no. No hard feelings?"

Meagan hung up without answering. She had driven herself to work that day to dodge Angelo, because she hadn't recovered from their conversation, but it was evident it was time for another one. He had crossed the line. And better yet, where did he get Keith's contact information? Something about Angelo wasn't adding up, but she'd play his little game until she figured it out.

She walked out of her office at ten minutes to seven, and all she felt like doing was showering and getting in her bed, but not before she drove by her husband's condo building again. The tax assessor's office closed at 5:00 p.m., but the investigator in her was open 24/7. She pulled into the parking lot and sat there, debating her next move. A black sports car pulled up, and she jumped out of her vehicle before the owner could open his car door.

As soon as he had one foot on the pavement, she blurted, "Excuse me, sir. I've been trying to catch the business office while it's open for the past two weeks, but I can't seem to get here before they close. Would you happen to have the company's contact information by chance?"

The driver looked annoyed, and although Meagan was wearing a business suit, he looked at her as if she were panhandling. However, with a sigh, he dug in his pocket and retrieved his wallet.

"It's owned by Second Time Around. Here's their card, but I'll need it back."

He handed her the card, and she pulled out her BlackBerry to jot down the information. The card didn't list a corporate name or number; instead, it had her husband's name on it, with the title of property manager and leasing agent. There was a cell phone number listed for him, one that she wasn't familiar with. Once she had written all the information down, she returned the card to its owner and got back in her car.

She sat behind the wheel and didn't put the key in the ignition. "Property manager. Huh, muthafucka!" she yelled, feeling like she wanted to explode from the anger that was building. She looked down at her cell, locked her eyes on William's cell phone number in disgust, and initiated the Google Voice application on her phone.

"Second Time Around Realtors in Atlanta, Georgia," she told her phone.

After a few seconds her search results populated, and the first item shown was a Trulia link. She double-clicked on it, and five listings appeared. One condo, two apartment complexes, and two newly built homes. Scrolling down for more information, she learned that the company had been established five years prior and the name of the owner was listed as unknown. The only contact information she could find was the same name and number she had gotten off the business card.

She hit the BACK button and returned to the Google results screen and hit the images at the top. There were a few pictures of the homes, and then she came upon a picture of her husband looking completely like the male bitch that he was. He was wearing pink, which she knew wasn't a color he had selected himself. He was a manly man, and even if the color was in fashion at the time, at his age, there was no way in hell he would follow the trends.

"So the bitch dressed you for your photo shoot?" she asked her digital husband, as if expecting the picture to respond. "I give you my entire life, and this is how you repay me?"

Tears dropped onto her phone's screen, and she didn't even know she had been crying. If it wasn't for the horn blowing behind her, she would have had a nervous breakdown. Her eyes shot up to her rearview mirror, and she saw that an old-school royal-blue Chevy Impala sat behind her. She cranked the engine and threw her car in reverse to get out of the way of the owner of the parking spot. But as she exited the lot, so did the Chevy Impala. She turned right, and the Chevy followed her. She made a left without signaling, and so did the Chevy. She drove with the car tailing her all the way to a fire station. She didn't know who it could be behind the wheel of that car on her tail, but she wasn't going to try to find out without help nearby.

She parked in front of the SAFE PLACE sign at the fire station, and the Chevy Impala parked perpendicularly behind her, boxing her in. This was one of those times she wished she carried the gun she had gone through the trouble of getting a license for. Her heart raced as the driver's tinted window rolled down slowly. She still couldn't make out who was driving, because the sun was setting on that side of town. Instead of prolonging the outcome, she reached out to honk her horn to signal for help, but just then her cell phone rang. The number was unknown, but she answered the call, anyway.

"Leave your car right here and come take a ride with me," said a male voice.

"You fucking asshole! You scared the shit out of me," she yelled into the receiver.

All she heard was laughter in return.

After grabbing her purse, keys, and cells, she made her way to the passenger side of the Impala and tried to snatch the door off its hinges. Then she dropped into the seat.

"What's good with you, Ms. Meagan?" Angelo asked, enjoying the shattered look of fear and anger on her face.

"What is your problem? Why would you follow me and not announce yourself? You saw me trying to lose you in traffic."

"I'm in a race car, and you're driving that heavy-ass fake Bentley. You're crazy if you thought a Chrysler three hundred was going to shake me."

Once the fear subsided, she remembered why she needed to talk to him, and she grew even angrier.

"Why did you call one of my friends and tell him I was married? And how in the hell did you get his cell phone number?"

"Which one of those diaper under the boxers–wearing niggas told you that I called his cell phone number? Because he lied. I called their jobs. Don't make it sound like I had to do some major investigation to get to them. How many times have I taken you to their jobs so you could get fucked in my limo? All I was trying to do was to look out for you. You have too much going on right now to be playing hide and go get it with those little boys. Your focus should be on this shit with your husband."

"Who gave you the right to decide where I put my focus?" she screamed.

"You did when you made me your partner. And stop all that screaming. That shit won't make me change up my answers. You ain't my bitch for your tones to move me."

She rolled her eyes at him, got herself together, and then asked, "So I guess you called Devin too?"

"Nah. He called me to tell me how fucked up you did him. I guess the kid looks at me like his mentor or some shit, because I listened to him speak his dreams and shot some truth his way."

"Is that right?" she said, doubting anyone would look up to a limo driver. "And how did he get your number?"

"You ask a lot of dumbass questions, I see. You don't remember giving him my number so I could pick him up? You told him to call me when he was ready for me to scoop him up from his mama's house and bring him to you. That's the shit *you* started."

It had slipped her mind in her moment of anger, but that contact was something for which she had granted permission.

"Either way, you should have given me the opportunity to cut them off on my own terms. If you want this little arrangement we have to work, don't cross those lines again."

"Okay, you're right. I'm sorry."

Damn right, your ass is sorry, she thought.

"Anyways, I was following you because you need the protection. I found out that you're in more shit than you know. Buckle up, sexy. Let's ride."

Part Three

Disrespectfully His

Chapter Four

Meagan wasn't eating or sleeping, but every time she thought about Angelo's words, she managed to empty her bowels like she was on an all-you-can-eat chili diet. William was out to get her, and neither she nor Angelo knew the how, when, or why of it. While she'd ridden around in the limo with Angelo the other day, he had told her that he overheard a distraught William speaking to his lawyer on the phone. He didn't know how the conversation had started, but it had ended with William saying, "I have to get away from her, Tommy. The love of my life confessed to me that she's a murderer, and I think I might be next."

"That doesn't officially mean that he was talking about me. What if the other woman is the love his life, and he already confessed it to his lawyer? I haven't said anything to him for him to assume that we had a problem." she'd told Angelo.

"Yeah, I thought about that, too, so I asked. I was like, 'Is the side piece giving you the blues again, boss?' and he was like, 'Nah, man. The wife is, and please try hard not to listen to my conversations. I wouldn't want you to potentially get pulled into something you have no business being in.' I was like, 'Cool. I ain't heard shit.' Then he handed me this."

Angelo had held up a check that was written from a bank account in William's name from a bank Meagan didn't know her husband was a customer of. It was writ-

ten for ten thousand dollars, and in the memo portion, it
read "Bonus."

"Bonus? Bonus for what? What else did you do for him
to deserve a bonus?" she'd questioned.

"I don't deserve it, and I haven't done shit besides drive
my limo. He said it was a bonus for not hearing his conversation, if I was ever questioned about it." He looked at
her face and could see the skepticism on it and snapped,
"Hold the fuck up! Instead of trying to figure out if I'm
double-crossing you, don't you think you should be
jotting down the information off it before I deposit it into
my bank account?"

"Why would you accept a check for a job you didn't do?"

"Because that's what we broke niggas do. We don't turn
down money, and if we do, we cause suspicion. If his
bank notifies him that my limo-driving ass that's paid by
the hour didn't cash this check within forty-eight hours,
he's going to think something is up, and if he's plotting
to get you, I'm not trying to be next on the list. I run the
chance that I might be on the list as cleanup as it is. I'm
not trying to confirm my spot."

Two days had passed since that tense conversation
she'd had as she rode around the city with Angelo, and
his words had begun to make more sense. She hadn't
seen or heard from her husband since her birthday night.
She had tried calling him to feel him out, but her calls
had been forwarded to voicemail each time. Now she
was behind her wheel and headed to William's condo
building. She got within three miles of the building and
then parked and called a taxi to take her the rest of the
way. She wouldn't sit in the building's parking lot in her
own car to see if William pulled up. That was too much of
a risk. Instead, she'd use the cab. Once she was in the cab,
she gave the driver direct instructions.

When they reached William's building, she said, "Drive through the parking lot slowly and don't stop."

She didn't spot any of William's cars or his limo, so she had the cabdriver take her back to her car. Instead of heading home, lying around the house, and waiting for her husband's return, she thought she'd be safer if she got low until she heard from him. So that was what she did. As she drove, she decided she would go have a talk with Devin's agent. Fifteen minutes later, she pulled into the parking lot at Johnni D. Manz's office and headed inside through the double doors.

"May I help you?" the receptionist asked as Meagan approached her desk.

"Yes, I'm here to see Johnni D. Manz."

"Is he expecting you?"

"No, this is more of a pop-up visit, but if you tell him Meagan Tolliver is here, I'm sure he'd be happy to see me."

The receptionist rolled her eyes to the ceiling. She was fed up with groupies acting like they were VIP just because they might have been lucky enough to perform fellatio on the producer. In her years of working the front desk, she had witnessed a lot of desperate women coming in, in hopes of being Johnni D. Manz's fling of the week, but this old bitch took the cake.

"Look, ma'am, Mr. Manz doesn't accept walk-in visitors who have no appointment. If you wish to speak with him, I suggest adding him on Facebook or tweeting him and seeing if he tweets you back. I'm afraid I'm going to have to ask you to leave," she said, eyeing the security guard, who seemed to know the routine.

"Oh no, this isn't *that*," Meagan said, laughing at being accused of being a dollar-sign chaser. "He's a friend of my husband's. He came to my party last week, and I just wanted to follow up with a conversation we had. I promise you if you tell him Mrs. Tolliver of Georgia Peach's is here, he'll tell you he wants to see me."

"I bet. Mr. Douglas, please escort Mrs. Tolliver out the door and off the premises. If the old head gives you any trouble, call the police." With that, the receptionist went back to playing the game on her phone, as she had been doing before her concentration was broken.

The security guard grabbed Meagan by the arm and began escorting her out the door.

"Let me go, jerk! Don't touch me. I'm a friend of Mr. Manz," Meagan barked.

"Uh-huh, sure. Everyone is a friend of Mr. Manz," the guard said, now dragging her.

"Let me go!" Meagan was at the double doors now and was putting up a fight in order not to be tossed out.

"What's going on up in here?" a voice behind her asked.

"Another groupie, but this one looks kinda old," the guard responded to the group of men who stood right outside the double doors. They opened the door that Meagan was not blocking and walked right by her, laughing.

"Devin!" Meagan yelled. "Devin, please. I'm here to see you."

The group of men stopped in their tracks, and all eyes were on Devin.

"You know her, man?" someone in the group asked him.

"What the fuck you want with me, Tammy . . . I mean Meagan?"

The men started whispering among themselves.

"I came here to talk to you," she said.

"I'm not trying to listen. You fucked up your chance."

"I know I messed up, but I need you right now. Can you please come talk to me?"

"You don't need me. You got millions. I'm trying to get in this studio so I can get my paper up like you." Devin wanted to go with her, but after Johnni D. Manz had told everybody how he had been played by the bitch who got him on, he had his pride to shield. He tapped one of the guys closest to him and urged him to keep walking. "Let's go. I'm not trying to hear what that ho has to say," he said before turning his back and walking away.

"Devin, please!" Meagan called after him. "All I need is fifteen minutes. Don't forget who got your ass out of having to stock at Walmart." She regretted saying that as soon as the words rolled off her tongue.

"Bitch, that's not you on the track. That's Young Diablo," one of the guys yelled, and the entire group agreed.

Devin turned around and walked back toward Meagan. "Hey, man, watch your mouth. I didn't give you the okay to disrespect her," he said, ready to knock the fire out of his new record-label entourage. He caught Meagan's eye. "You have ten minutes," he added, then walked past her through the other door and out into the parking lot.

"Devin," she called as she ran behind him.

"You got nine minutes and some seconds left. What?"

"I need you right now," Meagan pleaded.

"You keep saying that, but that's all I'm hearing. If that's all you got to say, your time is up."

"I'm in some shit, and I need your help."

"What's going on?" The look on his face told on him. He still loved Meagan, and the thought of her being in trouble made him want to save the day. He couldn't conceal it.

"It's too much to say in nine minutes, and here isn't the place that we should be talking. Can we go get a room?"

Devin's look of worry transformed back into anger. "Aw, so there goes the truth. You need some dick. What's the matter? That old-ass nigga ain't fucking you right? Well, listen here. My dick is done with you too. Take your ass back home to your husband." He headed back toward the double doors.

"I don't want sex. I need you," she said, stopping him in his tracks as the tears came pouring from her eyes. "I haven't eaten or slept in days. I'm going crazy, and the only person who can help me get through this is you."

Unbeknownst to Devin, he was the closest friend she had. All the so-called friends she had were grandfathered to her from William, and she couldn't disclose his behavior to them without it getting back to him. Her creeping with Devin had started out with silent meetings in the beginning, but slowly, they had opened up to one another. Although the information she had fed him was mostly lies, she knew the stories he had shared with her were true. On one of their many escapades, Devin had been distraught about an issue one of his friends was going through. His mood had vibrated through their sex, and she'd decided to let him get it off his mind so he could better please her in bed. He had refused to go into the details, and the fact that he had dropped fill-in-the-blank clues had irritated her. With his frustrations rubbing off on her, she had decided to question him to get the details.

"I really can't say the real, beautiful. It's not my business to be sharing."

"I respect that, but it's not like I know the person, anyway. Tell me so I can help you figure it out, so we can get back to doing us," she'd said while rubbing on his meat, hoping it would get hard again.

"I know you don't, but I really can't. That's my nigga, and he told me what was popping off in confidence. There's loyalty there. You understand that, don't you?"

This same loyalty Devin had displayed for his friend was what she wanted now. She hadn't come to him to find a solution for her problems. She just wanted to talk to someone other than Angelo about what was going on with her, and if she had to get low, she didn't want to be alone. She knew he loved her by the song lyrics he had written, and although she didn't feel those exact feelings in return, she would be lying if she didn't admit that he had a small piece of her heart.

"But you haven't said shit yet," Devin snapped.

"I told you we can't talk here."

He shook his head. "That's not what I'm talking about. You haven't said it."

"Said what? That I need you?"

He shook his head again, and disappointment flashed across his face. "Look, I'm going back inside. When you are ready to say what you need to say to me, I'll come running. My number is still the same."

He left her standing there, drowning in her own tears. She didn't know what he had expected of her. She dialed his number when she pulled herself together, but he wouldn't answer. A call came in before she could crank up her car. It was William.

"Hey, baby." He sounded exhausted.

"Don't 'Hey, baby' me. What the hell is going on? Why haven't I heard from you? Where are you?"

"I'm sorry, baby. The restaurant in Florida got shut down temporarily due to an outbreak of food poisoning, and I had to rush down here." He didn't sound believable at all.

"Uh-huh . . ."

"Why don't you ever believe me? Look the shit up. It's public information and has been in the news. When have you known me to just disappear on you without a reason? You said you forgave me, but I'm still being punished for the past. Damn, Meagan. Let the shit go. I'm not cheating on you."

She literally had to put her hand over her mouth to stop herself from blurting out the little information she had received from Angelo.

He went on. "I'll be here for about week, and then I'll be back to loving on you. I gotta go, but I just wanted to check in and make sure that you were okay."

"Why wouldn't I be okay?" she countered.

"Because Daddy isn't there to protect you. I know you can handle yourself, but it's the other people I'm worried about."

"Like who?"

"Like . . . Wait, what's up with all the questions? You sound guilty. I hope you're not in Atlanta, doing shit you're not supposed to. I'd hate to come home and have to punish you."

"So you're not going to apologize for shitting on me?" Devin asked. He was standing in front of her rolled-up driver's-side window, with his arms crossed thug style.

"Of course I'm not guilty," she said to William, holding her finger up at the agitated man in front of her. "I'll see you when you get back. Be safe." She ended the call with her husband and got out of the car to speak to Devin. "I'm sorry I lied and played games with you. I didn't think we'd last this long, and when we did, I couldn't build up the courage to tell you the truth. I didn't want you to—"

Her words were stolen from her when Devin's tongue took their place in her mouth. They had never displayed public affection, and now wasn't the time for her to protest about it. She needed him, his company, and his show of affection right now. Not even the immature grip he had on her butt would make her stop him. His touch had actually turned her on and made her feel safe. She'd apologize another hundred times if she could keep permanently the feelings he was causing her to have. If it wasn't real, it sure felt like it was.

"Real talk, though. I have to get in this studio for a couple of hours before we can talk. But if you're not doing shit, come up here and watch me lay this track. I'm going to be featured on another artist's album he's getting ready to release before he puts me out solo."

"No, you're at work. Just call me when you're done." She pulled out her phone and texted him, revealing her number for the first time in months. "Call me and I'll give you directions to my house."

"To your house?"

"Yes, I'm inviting you to my house." With her husband having contacted her, she no longer needed to hide out. And the fact that he was out of town gave Meagan the opportunity to relax with Devin in the comfort of her home.

"Invitation accepted, baby." He kissed her again, repeated the ass grab, and then walked back in the direction from which he had come.

Something was definitely going on with William, but she wouldn't look upon Angelo's words as a prayer book, either. All she could do was sit back and wait for the future to unfold.

"That's it right there," Johnni D. Manz said into the intercom. "You killed that verse, Young Diablo. You're done for the day."

"Cool," Devin replied. He had the headset off in a flash and almost ran out of the booth to ask his boy for a ride over to Meagan's house before he called it a night.

"To whose house? I know you didn't say that bitch Tammy. Isn't she married?" J. Seed said, and his words snatched Johnni D. Manz's full attention. Devin kept his eyes on his boss, because he wasn't sure how close the man was to Meagan and her husband, given that he had been invited to her fortieth birthday party.

Manz must have felt Devin's eyes on him and read his mind. "You don't have to worry about me going back and saying shit. The nigga ain't my friend, and I know him only because of the black business owner organization I'm in. You know, the rich meet up with the rich and talk about how to stay rich and get richer. Truthfully, I don't even like the nigga. And if he keeps putting his hand on his wife, I'd take her from him, but you look like you got that on lock, Diablo."

"I'm trying to, but the bitch plays a lot of games and got secrets. I didn't know that she was married or that she was getting her ass beat. Everything that I've learned about her that's real, I got from you," Devin confessed.

Manz was shaking his head in disagreement before Devin even finished talking. "She has to. Her husband is rich and powerful. And until yo' music is playing all over the world, you don't compete with what she already has. Play the game with her if she's worth it, but don't get your feelings all tied up in it until you know what's really going."

"I feel you. Good looking out."

"I haven't looked out on shit, and I haven't told you shit. Keep me and my business out of your business with her. Make sure she doesn't come back up here, looking for you, like she did today too. She doesn't let you walk into that restaurant or her modeling agency, so don't let her come up in here. If I had known you were fucking her when I heard your track play at the party, I would have passed you by. It ain't her you have to worry about. It's her husband. He has a lot of underhanded shit going on, which he brags about his wife not being a part of. I don't trust him." Manz walked off like he had never been involved in the conversation.

"Did you hear him, Diablo?" J. Seed said. "That means you don't need to go to that bitch's house. Make her meet you at a room or something, like y'all always do."

"I heard him, and I feel both of y'all, but this is my shit, and I'm going to deal with it accordingly. I haven't even decided if I'm keeping her around or going back with my ex when I get this money. I need to see if this bitch can be real with me. Can you please drop me off?"

J. Seed looked into his boy's eyes and saw in them the love he had for the bitch. He was crazy about the older woman he had been creeping with for months. J. Seed didn't know what she had done to his boy, but he knew Devin was too in love with her to think clearly when it came to anything involving her.

"I can do you one better, since you like to learn everything the hard way," was all he said.

Meagan instantly regretted inviting Devin to her house when she opened the door at one in the morning and saw he had his entourage with him.

"So this is where you lay your head?" he asked, looking past the foyer into the enormous living room. From the outside, the house looked like the ones he had seen on *MTV Cribs*, but the inside screamed black history museum. Where he'd expect a television to sit, there was a life-size elephant, tusks up, surrounded by smaller animal statues, potted safari-looking plants, and oil paintings of black matriarchs. There was an ivory sectional in the African-atmosphere room, but it looked as if it had never been sat on.

Devin had been in this subdivision once to see his cousin off for prom. He had dreamed of living here, but the fact that he had been raised in College Park had made his dream feel more unrealistic than his mind would let on.

"Yes, this is my home. Can I speak to you in private for a second?"

"Anything you have to say to him, you can say in front of us," said the tallest guy in the group. He was clearly unmoved by her success.

"This is my right-hand man, J. Seed," Devin said, introducing the young man. He actually looked older than the rest, but it wasn't uncommon to see a grown-ass man hanging with those that needed direction.

"Hello, J. Seed. It's a pleasure to meet you." She held her robe closed to conceal the nighty she had put on for Devin. When she extended her hand to shake, he didn't take it. He gave her a nod and continued eyeing his surroundings, like he was expecting an ambush.

"I just thought you'd be alone. I didn't expect to have a house full of guests at this hour," she told Devin.

Devin shook his head. "Shit, you're married. I wasn't going to come way out here by myself. If it's a problem, we can bounce."

"Let's bounce, Diablo. This shit don't feel kosher," J. Seed said, revealing the gun in his waistband.

"No, it's not a problem," she lied. "Come on in."

She led the six men to her entertainment room and handed J. Seed the television remote. He turned the television on, sat on the couch, and crossed his ankles on the coffee table.

"Where's your husband?" he asked, eyes locked on the big screen.

"He's in Florida for a week," she answered.

"Damn, you ain't shit. So when your man is away, your ass gets ready to play, huh? Hey, real talk, my nigga ain't no toy. If you're not going to be straight up with him, leave him the fuck alone."

"I got this, J. Seed. Y'all just chill in here, and I'm going to see what shorty is talking about," Devin said, finally speaking up in her defense.

"We good. Go do you," J. Seed told him.

Once he received the okay from his boy, Devin followed Meagan upstairs to her bedroom.

"Let me see what you got up under that robe, Tammy," he said once they were behind closed doors.

"Meagan, my name is Meagan Tolliver. I am an ex-fashion model turned modeling agent with my own million-dollar agency. He's a multimillionaire, but I have my own," she said, addressing the concerns he had voiced during his call.

"Oh yeah. Well, Meagan, show me what you working with, Miss Independent."

She untied her robe and let it fall off her shoulders, and lust filled the room. Without saying another word, she fell on her knees and crawled to him. When she made it to him, she reached up and unbuttoned his jeans.

"You know what you're doing down there?" he said in a low voice.

She didn't answer as she pulled his boxers down and gripped his semihard meat. She'd wanted to pleasure him with her mouth for months, but that was a pleasure she had reserved for William alone. Now that she had him in her mouth, with her tongue sliding along his shaft, she could kick her own ass for putting it off for so long.

"Oh shit, baby. That mouth is atrocious," he said, curling his hand around the back of her head. She quickly removed his hand, then pulled her head back, causing him to come out of her mouth. Her lips closed back together with a smack.

"I don't need your help. I got this," she told him.

"I didn't know. Tammy didn't suck dick."

"That's why I'm introducing you to Meagan."

She held his meat up diagonally and began licking his sack before humming and sucking on it at the same time.

"Hell yeah, suck on Daddy's day care. My unborn kids need attention too."

Now she remembered why she preferred quiet encounters with him. He was twenty-five, and he talked like a twenty-five-year-old. She forced herself into a zone so she could block him out and continued bobbing and weaving like boxing greats. She was winning the fight with her defensive moves alone, and Devin didn't mind losing. Excess saliva dripped from his steel now, and she wiped her crotch with it as if it were a tissue, then walked to the chaise in front of her bed and got down on all fours.

"Why did you invite me to your house and not tell me to meet you on Gilligan's Island?"

She almost laughed in his face when he mentioned her nickname for the hotel. She called the W Hotel Treasure's Island, the Hilton her bat cave, and the Marriott Gilligan's Island.

"We'll talk about it later. You're going to make her dry up with all this talking."

"I know how to get her wet again," he shot back, feeling immortal.

Meagan wasn't in the mood to talk, but her real reason for not getting off the chaise to face him was that her arthritis had flared up, and it would take her a minute to get out of her current position. Surrendering at his words, she fell over and rested her head on the bed.

"I didn't meet you at the Marriott, because I wanted you to see the real me. I've lied and played games with you for months, and you trusted me. I want that trust back. I want us back. I'm married, but I'm unhappy. And the only time I feel good is when I'm with you, lying in your arms. Does that answer your question?"

"Hell yeah," he said, nodding his head. "Now make her smile at me."

Chapter Five

"Hey, baby, go downstairs and tell my boys I said to bounce. I'll get your limo driver to drop me off."

Devin was sitting on the chaise, breaking his weed down on a dollar folded lengthwise. Meagan had heard him, but sex with him always left her in a state of needing recovery and outpatient rehabilitation.

"Angelo's off tonight," she said as she lay facedown on her animal-print throw rug on the floor.

"Nah, he was out there in the limo when we pulled up. He shook my hand and everything." He was trying to seal his blunt with his saliva, but his cotton mouth was interfering. "Bring me back something to drink too."

With strength that had to come from God, Meagan leapt to her feet, threw on her robe, and went downstairs. She couldn't hear the high volume on the television from her bedroom, but as she headed down the stairs, she was sure they were putting her surround sound to full use. Will Smith's loud voice from a rerun episode of *The Fresh Prince of Bel-Air* gave her the feeling that it was being filmed live in her house.

As she approached the entertainment room, she called, "Hey, fellas, can you turn it down a notch? Devin told me—"

"I been put them studio gangstas out." Angelo was smoking a blunt on the couch, with his feet up on the coffee table, exactly like J. Seed had done. "Why did you let them College Park niggas in your spot? You—"

She cut him off as she stood in the doorway. "What in the fuck are you doing in my house?" Meagan scanned him from head to toe with death in her eyes.

"I'm here to make sure you don't let the young man spend the night at your house." He hit the blunt again and then put it out on the base of the pot holding her plastic flowers.

"Who I let spend the night ain't none of your mother-fucking concern. Get the fuck out." She walked over to him, knocked his ankles off her coffee table, and wiped the ash stain off her pot with her hand.

"So now we're touching each other?" He jumped to his feet and locked his blunt-free hand around her jaw, forcing her to pucker her lips. "You don't want us to start touching each other. You're scared to get fucked by a real man. That's why you married that old-ass dick and are getting wiener from the Boys and Girls Club of America. You know you can't handle dick your age."

She grabbed his surprisingly hard dick and squeezed as hard as she could, but he seemed to enjoy it. Honestly, she enjoyed it too. She had always had a thing for fore-play but had never encountered a man willing to play the "get rough and then get fucked" game. After letting his army base go before his soldiers came marching out, she dug her nails into the wrist of the hand holding her face.

"You're right. I have never been able to handle dick my age. It's never enough," she confessed.

He released her and took a step back so she could see him smiling at her. She was beautiful, but so were all the distractions in life that could send you to hell, he thought. He knew better than to tempt fate.

"I wouldn't fuck you if I could. I'm in your house, waiting to talk to you. I didn't want to interrupt what you had going on but . . ." He shrugged his shoulders. "I had to come by and tell you that I was in the car when you talked to William earlier. He came back from Florida today, and you know where he's at and with whom."

"I don't know *with whom* he is. Who is she?"

"That's thing," he said, sitting back down on the couch. "I've never met her or seen her. He won't even say her name around me, and he got her, her own driver. When they go out, he doesn't use me." That was partly a lie. He knew exactly who this woman was, well, sort of, but he had never driven her around by his own choice. William had asked him if he had an issue driving for his mistress too, and he had said yes, so William had left it at that.

Meagan joined him on the couch. "Why didn't you just call and tell me?"

"Shit, I was with him at the strip club until a little after midnight. I came by here to see if the lights were still on. I didn't expect to see the fake Wu-Tang Clan pull in behind me."

"So y'all hang out now?" *The strip club* were the only words of his she'd heard.

"He has been asking me to go with him for a while now, and since I'm working with you, I took it as an opportunity to get more information out of him. What I really want to know, though, is how did William's first wife die?"

Meagan's mind took her back to the meeting that was supposed to happen so many years ago.

The clock read twelve o'clock, and William had failed to make it back. He'd said he was just taking Clara's car to put gas in it after he'd used her car to get his tire fixed, but that was forty-five minutes ago. Meagan was getting antsy, and so was Rita.

"Clara, if he doesn't come back by twelve thirty, let's take his car and leave. I'm not about to keep wasting my time waiting on him," Rita said, rolling her eyes up to the ceiling.

"Girl, we can go now. He knows I don't wait."

"No!" Meagan yelled, joining the ladies by standing up. "It's really important that y'all stay for the news."

"Well, if you know what the news is, Georgia Peach, you can tell us, so we can go," Clara countered.

"I . . . I would prefer that he told y'all. It's his surprise. I'll be right back."

She ran to the restroom and stood before the mirror, smiling from ear to ear. So what if her face and ass still hurt from his discipline? And who cared about him fucking his past one last time? In minutes, he would be all hers. She used the restroom, washed her hands, and began brushing her hair back in place with the palm of her hand. Just then the restroom door opened, and her mother walked in.

"So, what's this bullshit about? I know you know, because you changed clothes for it. What do you have going on?" Rita asked, eyeing her daughter like she was in a face-to-face conference with the other woman.

"You'll find out when he gets back. If you were important to him, you'd already know, but you're not, so you'll find out when she does."

Meagan nodded her head at the back of the restroom door and then continued to look at herself in the mirror. A smile formed as she vainly compared herself to the two older women. She was sure she had them trumped in bed too, because William had no problem telling her that she was the best at everything he asked her to do. In minutes, he would share the news with all of them as he announced their engagement.

Rita stepped behind her daughter in the mirror and played in her own curls as she said, "You're so beautiful, baby, but don't forget you're my copy. Not a carbon copy. That's too close to the original. You're more like that third copy that doesn't get printed clearly."

"Mama, your jealousy is showing again. We do look alike on the surface, but the original is played out and overused. From what I can see, your old ass can't even hold your legs up anymore."

"So, you were watching us this morning. I hope you were taking notes. You know, William has a very big dick, and it would take a bitch to have no walls to allow him to dig deeper by keeping her legs up. I think you've played the game for too long if you can take my dick with your knees on your shoulders."

"Your dick? Bitch, please. I was in good spirits this morning and felt like giving to the less fortunate. That was called goodbye dick. This little meeting my man called was to give Clara her divorce papers and to tell you that he no longer needs your rent-a-ho services. You're being dump, Mommy. Your garbage-ass pussy didn't make the cut."

Rita stared into her daughter's eyes through the mirror, and she saw the truth in her evil look. Her daughter wasn't lying, and she knew it. All those years of holding on to William in the hopes he'd leave his wife for her had been a waste. He'd fuck her and make promises that he was going to leave Clara soon, and that was the truth. The lie was that he planned on leaving Clara for her. Not knowing what to say back to her daughter in her own defense, Rita ran out of the restroom. Meagan took her exit as her first victory of the day.

She was feeling good about breaking the news to her mother and was sure that her mother wouldn't share the news with Clara before William did. It would incriminate her to tell Clara his plan to leave her, because Clara would want to know what had made her privy to his plan. As she folded a piece of gum in her mouth to freshen it for their first kiss once they announce their engagement, the restroom door opened and, simultaneously, the entire restaurant shook.

"What was that?" her older coworker asked with one foot in the restroom and the other in the hallway.

"I don't know," Meagan replied, ready to find out.

When she made it to the front of the diner, half of its customers were outside, staring at the side of the building, while the others, their mouths open, were glued to the windows. She couldn't get a clear view of the outside, but she made out enough of the scene to cause her to run out the door. William's car was in a ball of flames, its front end inside the brick barbershop next door. The men from the diner had formed a ring and were urging the onlookers to move back. There was another loud bang as the hood of the car flew up, and that demolished brick wall became her mother and her godmother's burying place.

"So are you going to tell me or what?" Angelo asked, snapping her out of her recollection.

"They died in a car accident. Faulty brakes, clogged gasoline line, or something. I don't remember what the investigators called it."

"Who are *they*? There was somebody besides his wife in the car?"

"Yes, my mother was in the car with her. They were always together."

Angelo looked puzzled, but then the information he had been collecting started to make sense. He had the what, when, where, and how. Now he needed to find out who and why.

"Well, I told you what I came to tell you," he said. "Are you done entertaining the child, so I can drop him off?"

"He's staying with me until it's time for me to go to work. And you never told me what you found out."

He stood up and rubbed his head, which she recognized as the gesture he made when he was becoming frustrated. "Let me dig a little more and make sure I know what I'm talking about first."

"You don't sound as confident as you were before. Is he out to get me or not?"

He walked to the front door and looked back at her. "Cloudy thoughts can show only blurred visions of the truth. Let the weather change, baby," he said, quoting Devin's lyrics from the song he had written about Meagan.

She didn't have a clue whom he was quoting, and so she just shrugged.

Angelo walked out the door and hit the interstate to take a two-hour drive to clear his mind and retrace his steps. He hadn't thought his plans through and didn't have a clue about what he was getting himself into. He had heard rumors about the deadly crash back in Albany, but he didn't remember hearing talk of there being someone in the passenger seat with William's first wife. Instead of questioning Meagan on a subject he could tell she knew nothing about, and not wanting to look suspicious to William, he decided right then that his best bet was to go back to the crime scene.

It was early, and the residents of Albany were just beginning to get out and start their day. Instead of wasting time waiting for the barbershop to open, he drove straight to the mortuary. It was seven o'clock in the morning; he knew someone would be there. An older man in a Sunday school shirt with a bow tie and overalls met him in the parking lot.

"That's a company car, not your own private property to do as you wish with. And where have you been? You know your mama will be back from her treatments soon."

"I know, Pops, but I told you I picked up a side job driving your limo. I can't eat off your plate forever."

"You sho' know what to say. But I stopped feeding you. Yes, this here is my mortuary, but you are an hourly employee. You make your checks and eat thanks to them and him." His father pointed his index finger at the sky. "And why haven't you made it to church?"

Angelo couldn't help but to laugh. "Pops, why are you nagging like a little old lady? I see all those years playing both parents have caught up to you."

"Watch your mouth, Junior." He chuckled. "I never played Mama to you. You got everything you needed from me and God."

Every time he brought her up, Angelo Sr. could still see traces of hurt in his son's eyes from being abandoned by his mother. Her return gave him no comfort because he knew she had come back only because she was dying of cancer.

"Whatever you say, Pops." He laughed. "Look, do you remember when that car exploded at the barbershop on Oglethorpe Boulevard when I first started college?"

"I remember when you dropped out of college to work on the production line at the candy factory. All those years of praying you through high school, only to watch you throw away your chance at furthering your education to pack chocolates. Pop the hood so I can check the oil. I'm sure you haven't been checking it."

Angelo popped the hood like his father had requested of him. "I'm serious, Pops. Do you remember that car explosion?"

"Yes, I remember. How could I forget? That was the biggest thing to happen in the city since Ray Charles. Why?" he said, shaking his head at the dipstick, which showed that the limo was low on oil.

"How many people were in the car?"

"One. It was a member of our church. Mr. Tolliver's wife. They owned the building where Auto World is at now. It used to be a diner. Good food. Lousy customer service."

"Are you sure there was only one person in the car, Pops? I heard it was two."

"It could have been seven people in that car, son, and we wouldn't have known. The car blew up, and the body or bodies blew up with it." Angelo Sr. silently prayed for forgiveness. He didn't like the feeling of lying to his son or the feeling of knowing he was lying under God's listening ears. He quickly changed the subject. "Go look in the back of my pickup truck and grab four bottles of oil and the funnel before the engine locks on you. If you blow a head on my limo, I'm taking it out of your check."

"What check?" Angelo mumbled.

"The check you haven't been earning that I still deposit into your account each month. That check."

"Ah, you're talking about my allowance." He chuckled.

"At forty-three years old, you should be ashamed of yourself for still needing an allowance. I don't know where I went wrong with you, boy."

Angelo walked to the truck to dodge listening to his father voice his disappointments. Now wasn't the time for him to hear how he had turned into nothing and wasted his life. It wasn't in the blueprints he had made for himself to purposely fail, but truth be told, he had. After high school his dad had given him the option to go college, pursue a trade, or join the service. He had chosen school and then had dropped out before he'd been given his first test. Not because it had been hard. He had dropped out because getting educated didn't put and keep money in household pockets like a full-time job did. He had understood that you get the knowledge to make the money, but bills hadn't seemed to comprehend that process. He had wanted to have his own place, but if he'd stayed in school, he'd have to continue to live with his father, and live by his father's rules. That meant God was first, next was God, and finally, he'd have to structure his life around God. Angelo Jr. loved the Lord, just not as much as his father did.

While his father had drilled marriage before sex, everything and everyone who was Angelo Jr.'s age had believed in sex, no marriage. Sex had been one of the issues, but it hadn't been the biggest. His true reason for wanting to fly as far away as he could from the nest had been that he didn't want to be expected to be the next pastor in the family. It wasn't his calling. After many years of going back and forth with his father, someway, his dad had still won, as Angelo Jr. was known for driving funeral cars and driving a limousine for those with money. Doing funerals by day and being a hired driver by night seemed to please both him and his father, but there had to be more for him, and he was going to get it. If everything worked out the way he had planned, his father wouldn't need the building fund he collected every Sunday to expand the church and the mortuary. Angelo Jr. pay for the upgrades himself.

His father was old, and death had been following him of late. It wasn't a secret. Knowing that everything his father owned would one day be his, Angelo Jr. looked at the upgrades as an investment in the future he had left. He wouldn't take on being a pastor or a funeral home director, but renting the place out to someone who could take on both titles would be profitable.

"Why all the questions about something that doesn't concern you?" his father asked, taking the items from his son.

"I was just curious, that's all. How long is that going to take, Pops? I gotta get back to work."

"As long as it takes. I hope you don't plan to leave without seeing your mother when she gets home. She's been asking about you. You got to let go of all the anger you have toward her, or you're not getting through those pearly gates. She's repented for what she did to both of us. It's time to let it go, son."

"You let it go. *I* don't have to. She owes me more than her dying days. I guess that's enough for you." Angelo waited until his father had poured the last bottle of oil in, and then he cranked up the limo. "Call me when she gets back, and I'll show my face. Is that what you want?"

"What I want is for you to grow up and act like a man. That's what I want. As a matter of fact, keep the limo, make your own money, and live out of it if you have to. I refuse to keep taking care of a disrespectful grown child." Angelo Sr. slammed the hood of the car down. "Make sure you see your mother when she gets back, but I don't want to see you again until you can approach me as a man."

"So what do you expect me to do for money?"

"You said you're working a side job. Like the Bible says, if a man doesn't work, he doesn't eat. It's up to you if you go hungry or not. I'm done letting you eat of the plate the Lord has given me." He walked back into the mortuary, never looking back.

"You say the same shit every time I pull up to this bitch. I love you too, Pops."

Chapter Six

Devin was up with the rise of the sun and decided to cook his queen breakfast, but he couldn't find any breakfast meat to prepare. He didn't know his way around the kitchen, but after all the mouth Meagan had given him the night before, he wanted to show his gratitude. He threw two eggs in a pot of boiling water and preheated the oven to five hundred degrees. He couldn't find a baking sheet, so he lined a cast-iron skillet with aluminum foil, drizzled vegetable oil on top of it, put three pieces of bread in it, and threw it the oven.

After that, he went into the entertainment room to watch the latest music videos he had missed from not having cable back at his mama's house. Before the rapper in the video made it to the hook, the fire alarm was blaring through the house and the phone began ringing off the hook. Meagan was making her way down the stairs, with the cordless phone glued to her face.

"Thank you for calling, but everything here is fine," after she went into the kitchen and sized up the situation. "The smoke from the oven triggered the alarm," she said, waving the smoke out of her face as she opened the oven door and reached for the cast-iron skillet with her bare hands.

"Fuck." She dropped the phone at the feel of the heat against her index finger.

Devin rushed into the kitchen. "I'm sorry, baby. I was trying to bring you breakfast in bed. I left the kitchen for only a second."

"Sorry won't cure the throbbing in my finger. What the fuck were you thinking when you put bread in a cast-iron skillet? And look at those eggs." The eggs had broken open when they were immersed in the boiling water, but he hadn't paid them any attention. His thoughts had been on the conversation they had about her husband's sneaky moves and him wanting to replace her pain with a smile. "If your young ass doesn't know what you're doing in the kitchen, stay the fuck out of it. Now move." She turned the fire off beneath the burner and retrieved the butter from the refrigerator.

"Don't put butter on it, baby. Let it soak in some cold water for a while."

She gave him the look of death as she massaged the butter on the palm of her hand. She had worked with William in the kitchen all her life. If he used butter, so would she.

"My husband always uses butter."

"Fuck your husband. I'll kill him."

"What?" Meagan said, with attitude still present. He had gone from one extreme to the next, and with the uncomfortable burning sensation in her finger, she wasn't in the mood for his temper tantrum.

"I'll kill him, and if your driver is on some slick shit, I'll kill him too."

"Because your ass almost burnt my kitchen down, now you want to kill people? Don't talk like that," she said at the speed of light.

"Why not? How am I supposed to show you that I'm the man you need, and that I have your back, if I sit back and let these old heads fuck you over? You're my woman, Tammy . . . I mean, Meagan, and can't no nigga on this earth fuck you over while I'm still breathing."

"Shut up. You sound stupid. Nobody is getting killed."

"I sound stupid because I'm in love with you or because you think I'm too young to make that kind of decision? Which is it?"

"Neither," she said, wrapping a dish towel around her finger. "You sound stupid because you're ready to take a life or lives before you know what's going on. Are you willing to do life in prison and not know what you're there for?"

"You get life only if you get caught, and love is a good enough reason to me."

"Love ain't shit. I told you what the driver told me and what I found out on my own. Divorcing him gives me half of all of this to go with what I already got. If—"

"But if I kill him, you get all of this, plus what you already got," he said, cutting her off. "And if you love me like you said you did on this dick, take that *young* word out of your vocabulary and see me as the man that I am."

She was at a loss for words, and the conversation had kept heading south. "Change the subject, Young Diablo. My finger is in need of your lips."

He walked over to her and unwrapped the towel, revealing the greasy redness of her finger. Softly, he planted kisses all over her hand, making his way up to her wrist. From there the kisses moved up her arm to her shoulder blade, her neck, and finally her lips. He was so smooth with his movements that she didn't realize at first that he had picked her up and sat her on the island in her kitchen.

"What am I doing up here?" She giggled like a teenage girl with a crush on her favorite teacher.

"Feeding me breakfast, since I can't cook to feed you. Now open up."

She spread her legs, giving his eyes a view of the pearl in her oyster, and he wanted to suck it out of its shell. She lay back, missing the condiments on the counter by an inch, and closed her eyes. The conversation about murder was no longer on her mind as he penetrated her over and over again with his tongue.

William walked into the foyer just then and was met by smoke. "Baby, I'm home. What the hell is burning?"

Meagan jumped off the counter and didn't know which way to turn. There wasn't a way for her to get Devin out the kitchen without him passing William, and he was dressed too hip-hop to say he was a fire marshal. She scanned the area, and there were only two choices. She could stuff Devin's ass in the oven or the pantry. With about three seconds to go before her husband was in her face, she grabbed Devin and pushed him into her pantry.

"When we go upstairs, leave," she whispered. She closed the pantry door a half second before her husband walked into the kitchen.

"What the hell happened in here?"

"I put breakfast on and went back upstairs to get ready for work, but my RA flared up, and I couldn't get off the bed. You're back early." She walked over to William and kissed him on his cheek.

"Why did you try to fry bread in the oven?" he said, looking into the skillet. "You must have been smoking again."

"No. Just wanted to try something new. Everything must be back to normal in Florida?"

"No. I was missing you, baby, so I took the red-eye back. I got something for you," he said, putting his bags down and unzipping his pants. Meagan placed her hands over his, preventing him from pulling his pants all the way down. Curious about the gift William was about to give his wife, Devin cracked the pantry door just enough to see.

"I missed you too, and I want that gift, but let's take it upstairs. The smell is starting to bother me."

"Then hold your nose." He grabbed her arms and forced them behind her, as if he was going to apply hand-cuffs. "Because I want my fat cat now." With vigor, he bent her over onto the island.

"You can have it, but let's take this up—" He words were silenced by the palm of his hand.

"I'll take one of my pills when we get upstairs, and I'll give you some up there too. This hard dick is all natural right now. Let's not fuck that up." He slid his fingers under her robe and was met by hot fluid.

"Damn. You want Daddy bad, huh? You're soaking wet."

Devin wanted to bust through the door and yell, "I got her like that, nigga." But this was his chance to prove to Meagan that he had her back, so he bit his tongue and continued to watch.

"I do want it bad, but in our bed."

Deaf ears heard her words as he slid his meat inside her and began pumping. The geriatric porno Devin watched made him feel sick more than it pissed him off to watch his woman being penetrated raw by another man. There was a huge age difference visible between the two, and being a witness to molestation wasn't his thing, although he was watching his and Meagan's situation in reverse. When his eyes had seen enough, he grabbed the open bag of potato chips off the shelf in front of him and had himself a snack.

He's old as fuck. They'll be done soon, so I can bounce, he thought.

"It's about that time, baby. Where you want it? Fuck it. I ain't getting no younger. Let's work on this baby."

Before he could let the built-up pressure out, she yelled, "I want it in my mouth." She pulled him out of her and turned around to face him, but it was too late. Her face got painted, from her false eyelashes down. Devin dropped the bag of chips at her words but never thought the sound would be so loud.

"Did you hear that?" William asked, pulling his pants up from his ankles, eager to check the pantry.

"No, I didn't. I'm kinda blind over here. Can you get me a washcloth out of the linen closet please?"

"Yeah, after I see what that sound was."

Meagan's heart stopped beating. She hoped she'd die before William had the chance to kill her. She watched her husband grab the door handle and push the pantry door open.

"The chips fell off the shelf. I'm going upstairs to get ready for round two. Make sure you clean this shit up before you come up." He closed the pantry door.

"What happened to getting me a washcloth?" she asked, and her voice cracked with each word.

"Use the dish towel next to you. I'm tired."

"Typical," she said, not wanting to roll her eyes lest his semen get in them.

"If it's typical of me, then it shouldn't come as a surprise to you."

She washed her face with warm water in the kitchen sink and waited for her husband to reach the top of the stairs before she went into the pantry. Chips were everywhere, but there was no sign of Devin. There wasn't a way out besides through the kitchen, and she was sure he didn't know magic, which meant he had squeezed his little ass into the broom closet. He stepped out and handed her the broom and dustpan before she could open the door.

"You gotta go now," she whispered.

"I know." He went to give her a kiss but remembered what had made him drop the chips in the first place. Not wanting to be in the vicinity of her mouth, he kissed the tip of her nose and made his way out of the kitchen and out of the house.

William was in the shower when she made it to their bedroom.

"Georgia Peach, come here for a second. I need to talk to you."

"What?"

"Why are you standing in the doorway? Come get in the shower with me."

"I don't want to get in the shower with you."

"I don't recall asking you what you wanted, little girl."

The age shit was getting on her nerves, and she swore if she ever considered giving Devin a real shot, she'd drop the words *young, little,* and *boy,* like he had asked.

After she got in the shower, William said, "I need you to take the day off. We got some business to handle at the lawyer's office today." He handed her the washcloth. "Get my back for me."

"And what business is this?"

"I want to make sure if anything happens to me or you, we are both straight and everything is situated. I'm talking insurance policies, our businesses, grave plots, and all. We've been putting it off long enough, don't you think?"

"I told you that a long time ago. Why the change of heart now?" she asked, scrubbing his back harder than she had done before.

"Because I run this show, and now I feel like it's time we get it done."

She smacked her lips, and he smacked her across her face. For the first time in years, she was ready to fight back. She dropped the soap and the washcloth and then dug her nails into his neck. William was getting old, so his reflexes weren't as fast as they had been in the past, nor did he expect retaliation. It wasn't until he felt the sting of his open flesh meeting the warm water that he quickly grabbed her by the neck and flung her through the shower curtain. She fell face-first over the rim of the connecting tub and onto the marble floor.

"I'm sorry, William. Please don't." Her hands were the white flags as she curled her body up into a ball and waved them desperately in front of her face, but William didn't attack.

"I don't have time for this shit right now. We have business to handle. Take yourself down the hallway and get ready. You better be ready before I am too. Don't think I'm going to forget about my neck."

Meagan was showered, dressed, and ready before William had applied lotion to his body. He was on the phone when she walked back into their bedroom.

"I don't have an hour to wait on you to get here, Angelo. Next time you decide to do a drop off in Chattanooga, make sure you call and let me know first. Now I have to use Mr. Perkins's slow ass. Meet me at the lawyer's office when you get back." There was a silence. "Everything is okay. I got Mrs. Tolliver with me. Yep . . . nope. Uh-huh . . . hell naw." And then he laughed. "See you when you get back."

"So I take it that you and the new driver have become friends?" She couldn't help but ask as the smile lingered on his face from his phone conversation.

"He's an all right young man. I think he's about your age. He has a lot of growing up to do, but hell, at forty years old, you do too. I shouldn't have to keep disciplining you to get you to do right. I don't understand why you need to learn everything the hard way."

Meagan was going to attempt to answer his question, but the folded dollar bill and the empty condom wrapper on William's nightstand required her immediate attention. She scooped the items up, and before she could put them in her bra, she noticed multiple puncture holes in the condom's wrapper. She wasn't sure if they had been there before they used the condom, and now wasn't the time to try to figure it out. She stored the traces of another man being there in her bra and then grabbed the lotion to rub on his back.

"I'm sorry, my love. I'll do better," she said with a smile on her face.

Part Four

Disrespectfully Dead

Chapter Seven

The meeting at the lawyer's office was awkward, to say the least. Tommy Hunt couldn't concentrate on the documents he had been working on, as he was staring at the scratches on his client's neck and the swelling of his client's wife's jaw and eye.

"I'm sorry, but before you sign your will making your wife the executor of your estate, Mr. Tolliver, I have to ask . . . Are you being forced to do so? I mean, your neck is scratched up, and look at her jaw. And that other swelling has almost closed her eye. Maybe we should be discussing the parameters of your assets if the two of you decide to divorce."

"We're fine, Tommy. Meagan slipped on the bathroom floor and tried to grab me to stop the fall. Instead, I got scratched up, and she hit the marble floor."

"Save the crap, William. I'm a family lawyer, too, and I see domestic violence cases on a regular basis. They mostly involve divorce. Y'all are killing each other, and after that phone call . . ." Tommy closed his mouth before he destroyed his client's confidence. He was William's lawyer, and he refused to let himself get caught up in his emotions and forget that fact.

"What phone call?" Meagan asked, looking into her husband's eyes.

"He's talking about the call I made to him about the food poisoning," William lied. "The boxes of dressing that made everyone who ate it sick were shipped to

Florida as overstock from Atlanta. It looked as if they were shipped there on purpose, and since either you or I had to sign off on it, it made it look suspicious."

"Suspicious? How?" she questioned.

"The dates had been changed on each container. The salad dressing had been expired for almost a year when it arrived, and you were the one who signed off on it. That's it."

"I always check the dates."

"As I know you do. That's why I didn't bring it to your attention, Georgia Peach. But I had to call my lawyer about the whole thing because they had me on the news and portrayed me in a not so good light. Now, Tommy, can we get through these signatures? I have the limo driver waiting." He read the text Angelo had sent him announcing his arrival.

"Sure. Mrs. Tolliver, your paperwork is done. If you don't mind, can you take it down the hall and have Katrina stamp the pages for me, please? My pad seems to be out of ink."

She hesitated and then snatched the folder out of his hand. She walked out the door a few steps and then eased back toward it to listen.

"It would have been nice if you had told me which love of your life wanted to kill you. I was almost certain you were talking about your wife," Tommy said, with his fingers speeding over the computer's keys as he composed an instant message to send to Katrina.

"I'm sorry. I assumed you knew which one I was talking about."

"So how is she doing?" Tommy asked, without a care in his voice, as Meagan prayed that one of them would slip up and eventually say her name.

"Besides crazy and wanting all my time, she's fine. She's been trying to get me to buy a cabin to rent out in

Gatlinburg, Tennessee, since we're doing well with the other real estate. But I'll get with you on that another time."

"I noticed you kept that real estate out of your will," Tommy said, giving William his full attention.

"That's hers. You know that, Tommy. Whatever she decides to do with it is no business of mine. My only goal is to keep it lucrative while I'm living, and judging by the numbers, I'm doing a damn good job at it."

"And if she dies, what happens to it then?"

"Then it goes to whomever she leaves it too. As a matter of fact, I've been meaning to have her meet with you to get her affairs in order. If she lists names in her will, I'll pay you more to find out their relationship to her. She claims to be visiting her younger sister in Savannah when she leaves Atlanta, but I don't believe it."

"Hire a detective, then. If she becomes my client, there's no dollar amount that will allow me to break her trust."

William eyed Tommy in disgust but respected his words. "Your loyalty is why I hired you. I understand."

"Mrs. Tolliver, are you ready to have me stamp your documents?"

Meagan hadn't heard Katrina approach her and didn't know how much of her eavesdropping she had seen.

"Oh yes, I'm ready. I thought I heard my husband call my name . . . but I guess not." She shrugged.

"I'm sure you did. This way please," Katrina said, then led the way down the hallway, not believing a word Meagan had said.

Trapped in his thoughts, Angelo was waiting for the couple to exit the building. There had to have been two people in the car that exploded at the barbershop on Oglethorpe Boulevard that day, but who was the other dead body? Pops had said it was Mrs. Tolliver from church, and William had confirmed that his first wife died in that car. Meagan had said her mother was in the car, too, but Mama had mentioned there being only one person in the car, and that was her best friend. Could her best friend be William's wife, and could she not have known that Meagan's mother was in the car too? he thought.

During one of his mother's dementia moments, she had assumed she was at the pearly gates and was holding a conversation with God. From what he had gathered, she was appealing her sentence to spend eternal life in hell for killing her best friend. He had walked in at the tail end of her episode, but he had heard her say it was an accident, and she wished she had never thrown her cigarette. Angelo had been too young when his mother had walked out on him to remember who her friends were, but his father would have told him it was his mother's best friend in that car, instead of saying, "Mrs. Tolliver from church." Which left Meagan's mother as her best friend, or there was a third person that no one really knew.

Not that Angelo remembered who Mrs. Tolliver was, since he had never heard her name mentioned. His mother had said that Mr. William Tolliver, being her lifelong friend, had volunteered to pay for her medical treatments. Why hadn't she said she was best friends with his deceased wife, and that was why he was being so kind and generous? At first glance, he thought it was generous for a friend to step up and help out, because his father couldn't afford to, but after securing a spot on William's payroll, Angelo had realized William wasn't doing it for free. He was taking sexual advantage of the old cancer patient with dementia.

If it wasn't for the hatred Angelo had for his mother, his fist would have met William's face when he first realized what was going on. The reality was that Angelo enjoyed knowing that she had to sell pussy for medical treatments. To him, it was part of her punishment for walking out on her family, and he wouldn't dare step in the way of what she had coming to her. Sad but true. Angelo had ill feelings for William only because he beat his wife. He couldn't care less about the way William treated his mother. Angelo was on a mission to find his truths and to learn more about the moves his mother had made during her disappearance. Everyone else's problems didn't belong to him, although it was becoming evident that they all somehow tied in to one another. He decided to let it go as he watched Meagan walk toward him.

"Angelo, I really need to find out who this bitch is he's shacking up with. Do you know he's scared of this ho? It almost sounds like she's controlling him. Apparently, she is the same bitch that threatened to kill him, and he was never talking about me. I heard it while eavesdropping on his conversation with the lawyer. That little agreement we made is void, but I'm going to let you keep your job. Because once I get all the information, I need to take half of everything I helped him get, and I'm going to need a limo driver I can trust. Are you up for the job?"

He couldn't answer her, because she had just given information he hadn't known anything about. When he'd overheard William saying he had been threatened by the love of his life, Angelo had been sure he was lying to plot against Meagan. Now he knew differently. His mother had some kind of power over William, and Angelo was sure it had something to do with the time she'd been absent from his and his father's life, but what? And why had she returned? Everything about her was becoming more suspicious by the day.

"Angelo, are you listening? I just offered you a job."

Snapping out of his thoughts, he opened his mouth to answer, but the purplish-black bruise on her jaw and lower cheek wouldn't allow him to focus on the job offer. "Man, that nigga is living a double life, and you keep letting him put his hands on you. I'm tired of the shit. I don't understand how you're not."

"He didn't hit me this time . . . He threw me out of the shower, and I hit the floor."

"So that makes it okay? What's the deal? You got Daddy issues?"

"Daddy issues?"

"Yeah, Daddy issues. I mean, you married a cat old enough to be your pops, and you allow him to fuck you up whenever he wants. Sounds like you were really looking for a daddy to me."

"So now you think you're Dr. Phil? No, Angelo, I don't have Daddy issues. But what's the real with you? You don't wear a wedding band, and I've never heard you mention a woman in your life. If I was to play Dr. Phil, you're either gay or have Mama issues. Better yet, you might be a mama's boy, too in love with your mama to date because you're scared to put somebody in front of her."

"Is that what you think?" Angelo was agitated by her words but held his composure. "I'm not married by choice. I haven't met anyone worthy of having my last name or carrying my child. I'm in and out of guts too often to be gay, by the way."

"Up the ass is the fastest way to get into the guts."

They both laughed as William walked hurriedly out the building. As Angelo stepped out of the limo to open the door for his boss, shots were fired in their direction. William fell to the ground. Angelo crouched down and then crawled army style over to him.

"Where are you hit?"

"I'm not hit, Angelo. But I've seen enough movies to know to play dead." William laughed as Angelo scanned the area for the shooter but came up empty. There wasn't a car speeding off nearby, nor were people fleeing the scene to get away from the shooter. Once he felt sure it was safe for them to move, he got up and helped William into the limo.

"Are you okay?" Meagan asked hysterically. She was on the floor of the car and refused to sit upright until they were away from the area.

"I'm fine, baby. You know I learned how to drop and roll when we opened up Georgia Peach's in Chicago." William laughed.

"How do you find this shit funny?" she retorted. "You could have been killed. It's obvious they were shooting at you."

"Who are *they*? I didn't see anyone. Angelo, did you?"

"No, sir," Angelo said, speeding away.

"The shooting didn't start until you came walking out." She retrieved a joint from her purse, and with shaky hands, she stroked her lighter until it was lit. She didn't know if it was smart to mention that she knew his life had been threatened, so she smoked instead.

William shrugged. "That's called a coincidence. You're all shook up now. Let's call it a day. Angelo?"

"Yes, sir?"

"Let's drop Meagan off at a spa to relax her nerves. We can go to the mortuary without her."

"I'm not going to the spa. I'm staying with you."

"Take her to that new one in Atlantic Station," William instructed. "I hear all the big names go there."

"Did you fucking hear me? I said—" Her words were cut off by his hand wrapping around her neck.

"I didn't forget about this morning," William growled. "If I were you, I would go to the spa and relax. Understood?"

With tears dropping from her eyes, she nodded her head yes, while Angelo pretended not to see what was going on behind him.

When they made it to the spa, William handed her his credit card and told her to get a top-of-the-line treatment. Once she was out of the limo, Angelo pulled off.

"Do you have any clue about who was shooting at you, boss?" Angelo asked as they watched Meagan disappear through the spa doors.

"I don't know who pulled the trigger, but I have an idea about who hired them." William dialed a number and waited for the party to answer. "Hey, baby. Did you make it to Savannah yet?" he asked.

"Almost. You hired the slowest driver in the world to take me. I should have top-of-the-line everything. This is bullshit," a weak robotic voice said into the phone. It was hard for William not to get squeamish when listening to her talk with her electrolarynx.

"I'll get you a new driver ASAP, but I thought you said if I did everything you asked of me, we wouldn't have any problems?"

"If I have a slower-ass driver that's getting me to my destinations late, you're not doing everything I asked, dumbass."

"I said I'd fix it. Can you at least call off your goons?"

"Call off my goons? What are you rambling about? Are you having problems?" The electrolarynx didn't properly display the emotion in her voice, but he was sure that she was laughing.

"I told you last night that I wasn't going to leave my wife. You wake up this morning to put me out and then you send your goons to come shoot at me? What happened to our arrangement, Clara?" William had decided to accuse her of sending someone to kill him and then see where the call went from there.

Angelo's ears perked up like nipples in the winter. Their arrangement was information he needed to complete his puzzle. It was immature of him to expend this much energy on filling in the blanks of his mother's past, but he knew he couldn't move forward in his life without knowing who she really was.

"William Edward Tolliver III, after all these years, you sound like you don't know me. You should know that if I had sent shooters, they wouldn't have missed. Killing you is my second option. It comes right behind what I'm doing to you now. As long as you continue to do as I ask, you don't have to worry about me sending shooters. Now that we got that out of the way, do you think your beautiful young wife might have sent them?"

Clara had lied to William about not making it to Savannah. The limousine driver had dropped her off at the emergency room a little over an hour ago. She would wait there for the three and a half hours it would take Angelo Sr. to get to her. That way, the lie she had fed him about getting free treatment in Savannah could stay in place and her trips to doctors in Atlanta, courtesy of William's pockets, could remain a secret. She had confessed only to her son that William had been paying for her treatments in Atlanta. She knew that Angelo could smell her bullshit, so she had decided she'd tell him the truth during fake dementia acts.

"Best friend, is that you?" she said.

Scared to make a move, let alone breathe, Angelo remained silent as his mother talked to the person only she could see.

"I've waited all day for you to come visit me so I can tell you what happened at the doctor's office. Well, I'm still making progress on my journey to be with you, but all the money William is paying has bought me a little more time. You said he'd never be a good friend to us, because he was born with a dick and balls. Do you remember when you said that?" she said. She started laughing and then tried to catch her breath from the laughing she was doing, but it quickly turned into a smoker's cough.

She inhaled deeply into her oxygen mask for help. Once she regained her breath, she continued by saying, "You said that his dick would keep him from loving us the way we loved each other and that his set of balls would keep him from being loyal to us, but you were wrong. I wish you were in the flesh to see how good of a friend his sorry ass has been to me in my time of need, but you're not. Lord knows I miss you."

It was not the entire truth but enough of to keep his curiosity at bay, or so she hoped. Clara's days in the flesh were numbered, and even forcing William to pay for the expensive treatments wouldn't keep her alive. She had been given six months to live seven months earlier, and she knew she was now living on borrowed time. Every night she prayed that she wouldn't wake up and that she would die peacefully in her sleep, but her book of life wasn't written that way. She would die painfully, she predicted, for all the hell she had raised in her younger days.

From the age of fifteen, Clara and her now deceased best friend, Rita, had made sleeping with grown men their job. They would get the men to have sex with them and then would blackmail them for whatever they could get. They had lived in the South, which was known as the most religious and family-oriented region of the United States. Unlike the rest of the country, it wasn't uncommon for a grown man to jump the broom with a teenage girl. The laws of the land came second to the laws of the Bible, which wasn't a problem for the girls. They just made sure to go after only the faithful men of God who attended their church. There had been a couple of single men in the congregation that Clara brought hell to, as well, but almost all of them had been married.

Threatening to tell their wives that she had been molested by their husbands, which had caused her to be forced to break the seventh commandment by committing adultery, had been something the men took seriously. They would pay whatever price Clara had requested to keep her quiet. Playing the underage dash, as they'd liked to call it, until they came of age had been the pact she and Rita made. Clara had broken that pact when she tried to play the game with the wrong person.

"Will you help me get closer to God? I need some saving," she begged.

"Everybody needs some saving and to get closer to God. You have to be ready to fight whatever it is that's standing in the way of that," Angelo told her.

Angelo Sr. was the pastor's son in training and was slated to take over his father's position. Besides preaching on youth Sunday, he was the church's full-time choir director and the youth Sunday school teacher. At the age of twenty-five, he wasn't married, but his single marital status was what made him Clara's number one choice. She knew if the pastor and congregation got wind of him having sex before marriage, and with a minor, his world would crumble, so she set her sights on him. It took much persuasion to get him to break his beliefs, and the fact that he was a virgin made it harder.

"Lust is standing in the way of it. How do I beat that? I pray for a renewed mind, cleansed of the perverted spirit that takes over me but that makes me lust more. Do you understand what I mean?" she said.

"No, I reckon I don't."

"You don't know what it's like to see something so beautiful in front of you, something that's so perfect that you know the Lord had to have made it, and you want to touch it, kiss it and make love to it? You want to bring it so much pleasure that it moans your name until the words get lost in its throat and you're left with reading its lips to try to make out the letters that its losing?"

Angelo Sr. Placed his index finger under his collar right above his tie and pulled it to the left to let out the built-up heat. Her words were hot and sinful, causing him to sweat, but he knew better than to get worked up over sinning.

"No, I don't, and when I'm married, I pray I do." He chuckled. "You're having premarital sex, Clara? That isn't good."

"You think I don't know that?" she snapped. "I came to you because I know you can help fix me. Not the pastor, you."

"What do you think I can do that my daddy can't?"

"That's easy. You can be the first and only man to love me. Love conquers all, right?"

After making him believe she loved him and begging him to marry her once she turned eighteen, he gave in. Their one-on-one Bible study meetings turned into kissing sessions, until he confessed to her that his soul was weak. He tried to end it after praying on it, but instead he ended up in between Clara's legs, pleasurably sinning on one of the church's pews.

She enjoyed taking his virginity and decided to put the blackmailing on hold so she could see how many of his other firsts he'd surrender to her. He began spoiling her, and blackmailing him was no longer necessary. He worked in the fields when he wasn't helping run the church, and since he wasn't obligated to pay bills while he was living with his parents, his income became Clara's. When she was only a few months away from turning eighteen, she became intrigued by the thought of being married to him.

The couple started secretly house hunting, with Clara conducting her escape from living with her father. She despised her always drunk and verbally abusive father, not because he drank moonshine by the gallon, but because she didn't see him as a real man. He didn't work and lived off the money his deceased wife had left him. He'd go days without bathing and always left a piss puddle on the bathroom floor for Clara to almost slip in. He was a slouch, to put it nicely, but if it weren't for him, Clara's unknown pregnancy would have taken her life.

She had been running a fever the entire day and having painful cramps along her lower stomach. When the pain became too much for her to bear, she blacked out, and when she woke up, she was recovering from surgery. She had given birth by C-section at thirty weeks pregnant, and as a result, she had to get an emergency hysterectomy a few weeks shy of turning eighteen. Her midwife told her the chance of her son living at his premature age was slim due to his underdevelopment. To her surprise, her father stood by her side through it all, even when her lover of the past two years stood before her and said he refused to take on the role of the child's father. Angelo Sr. told her some bullshit line about breaking his mother's heart and being disowned by his father.

"You're worried about hurting your parents because there's a baby involved? I thought the sin was in the sex, not the baby, pastor's son? What did you think would happen if you never pulled out?"

"I thought you might be on the pill or something. You never tried to stop me from . . . well, you know," a shaky-voiced Angelo yelled back at her.

"I don't know shit. What I do know is that you're older than me and you know how babies are made. You were talking about marrying me, and that's the only reason why I let you nut in me—"

"Language, Clara," he said, cutting her off, but it only fueled her rage.

"Fuck my language! That's what it's called when a grown man fucks some pussy and let's go inside of it, and that's what you did. You nutted in me and never tried to pull out, not once. You can use that birth-control shit, but tell me what book of the Bible you found it in, nigga?"

He hated when she used her words as swords. God didn't like it, and it wasn't ladylike, but if it made her feel better to do it, he'd give it a try.

"You were a ho. I assumed one of your ho duties was to shield and protect yourself from pregnancy. I don't want to tell my parents I sinned and got a sleazy girl pregnant when I knew I should have protected myself from all the shit you possibly have."

Clara's mouth fell open from shock. She had never heard him cuss, and in spite of the fact that his foul speech was watered down compared to what she could do, it hurt more than anything she'd ever experienced to be disrespected by him.

"Fuck you, Angelo."

"Isn't that why we are here? I already did that, and now you're trying to force me to take care of child I don't want."

Although he instantly became sleaze to her, she understood, because she had already decided she wouldn't be taking on the role of the child's mother.

"Well, you better want him, because I can't take care of him. Remember, I'm a ho."

"I know you are, but you pushed him out, so he's really yours. The Lord made Abraham get rid of the child he had before Sarah got pregnant. Abraham packed her up and sent her away. I'm his descendant, and I know the Lord would want me to give you money to go as far away from me as you can and never come back."

Having listened to the arguing fools go back and forth about whose life the child would ruin the most, Clara's father stepped up and took custody of his grandson and banished both of them from the child. It took Angelo Sr. three years and a lot of prayer to man up to his parents, get his own place, and get custody of his son, while Clara moved on with her life. She began dating William, a man closer to her own age, and he was also a member of the same church. He sang in the choir with Rita. and she enjoyed the fact that dating him was breaking Angelo Sr.'s heart. Thanks to the love she received from William, the life she walked away from became a grayed memory.

She hadn't disclosed to William that she had a child, and when he asked her to bear his, she lied about having tumors in her uterus at a young age, the only treatment for which was a hysterectomy. Life with him made her feel like she had walked into a fairy tale, as he accepted the fact that they would never have children. She had been the queen of his heart until Angelo Sr. decided to reveal to their son once he came of age that she was his mother.

"Angelo, do you notice anything familiar about this woman here?" Senior asked his son as he continued to block the car with his limo and prevent it from backing out of the packing space.

It was the first time the men had gone grocery shopping as roommates and not as father and son. Junior had finally made it to eighteen, had graduated from high school, and was a month shy of his first day of college. His dad had given him copies of keys to everything he owned and permission to use it all whenever he pleased. He had rent to pay, but his good grades and the work he put in at the church and mortuary would cover it. His monthly allowance was now his weekly pay minus his cost of living. The only reason why he didn't feel completely grown was that his father didn't allow his input on the rules that governed the house, and so he couldn't share the power that came with home ownership.

The men left the store, comfortable with the day's take, and drove off. Junior didn't see the look in his father's eyes as he passed the Toyota Corolla that was turning in as they turned out. If he had, he would have watched the pain in them turn into anger. That transition was what caused Senior to make four right turns out of the parking lot and drive back into it.

"Did we forget something?" Junior asked, pulling out the list they had composed together.

His father didn't answer. He needed to get a lot off his chest, and today was the day that he would. He boxed the car in and urged his son to climb out and follow him to the car's driver's-side window. He asked his son twice if the driver looked familiar.

"No, Daddy, but I think I might have seen the car before."

"You can't see yourself in her face," he stated, then addressed the driver. "Clara, roll down your window and meet your son. He's grown now and deserves to meet you at least once."

Junior didn't see their likeness at first sight, but with both of their jaws dropped at his father's revelation, he realized they were identical after taking into account the obvious gender differences.

"What are you doing, Angelo? We talked about this. This isn't right, nor is this the time or the place," Clara exclaimed as the shock of this moment settled deeper into her expression. She felt like a deer stuck in head-lights.

"When is the time? He's eighteen and about to start college at Albany State. Soon he'll be hunting down a wife and looking to have his own kids. Would you prefer to meet your son and grandchildren at the same time?" he yelled.

"It's okay, Dad. She doesn't ever have to meet me. Let's go."

His father was reluctant to leave, but after staring his first and only love in the face until he broke his own heart, he followed his son back to the limo.

"Angelo Jr.," a weak voice yelled. "Come here, son." Clara made her way out of the car and stood next to Senior, with her arms open wide, yet Junior didn't make a move. "I do want to meet you. I always have. I don't know what your father has told you, but I do love you and have thought about you every day since you were born. I've prayed for the strength to get my shit together so I could meet you. God must have felt that it was time. Please, son, please come here."

Without being asked again, he ran to her and wrap-ped his arms around her. He hugged his mother tightly and then lifted her off the ground to show her just how happy he was. He forgave her in that moment, but she was hoping that he didn't. Like any child, Angelo Jr. wanted to build a bond with his mother, but it had never been a desire of hers.

After Clara met her son, her half-a-pack-a-day ciga-rette addiction turned into a two- packs-a-day one. His father never told him that his mother had remarried, and Angelo had expected her to, but when Angelo Sr. learned she hadn't, he left it alone. Clara searched for a way to get her son to leave her alone, and when she tossed her lit cigarette at the puddle, which she assumed was water, she found one. As the car exploded and went up in flames before her best friend could get out of it, Clara realized that faking her own death was the best way to deal with William wanting to break her heart and to hide again from the son she had never wanted.

She knew William had filed for divorce, because she had made it her duty to go through all the drawers he'd declared off limits to her. There had to be another woman—this she was sure of—but she wouldn't learn until years later that the woman was her goddaughter, Meagan. She hid behind the barbershop as the first explosion sent the car across the diner's parking lot into the brick wall, and when the gas tank exploded, turning the car into nothing more than bent metal and melted rubber, she took off running, with the aim to hide in Savannah with her younger sister.

Once she learned that Clara Tolliver had been pronounced dead with Rita Glover, Clara Jones was born. She wrote her son a letter telling him she still wasn't ready to be a mother but promising she'd return when she was ready to be, and when that time came, she'd never leave his side. The letter devastated him, but the one she wrote to his father broke Angelo Sr.'s heart.

Angelo,
I couldn't keep living that lie with William when you are the only man I've ever loved, so I died. I died with Rita in that accident at the diner so that one day I can live, and when I do, I want it to be with you. I told our son I wasn't ready to be a

*mother just yet, to buy myself some time with this
death stuff, but I promise I'm coming back when it
has blown over. Don't tell Junior anything about
my life with William, and keep him as far away
from that stuff at the diner as possible. Seeing you
made me realize what I've been missing out on, and
I want my family. I'll be back, and I don't want my
past with William messing up our future. I'm tired
of missing you.*
    Clara

The letter was another lie, and she was becoming one
of the best at making up truths. She wanted a new life,
and that was exactly what Ms. Jones received. She never
dated a soul, and if any of the men she slept with got too
clingy, she got rid of them. Her years spent in Savannah
were peaceful and drama free, but they were coming to
an end. Reinventing herself as a new person meant she
could take only work that paid under the table and didn't
provide health insurance. When she was diagnosed with
lung cancer, the treatments took all the money she had
made and then demanded more. As she struggled to pay
for the treatments for her lung cancer, she learned that it
had spread to the lymph nodes in her neck and she would
have to undergo surgery.

With nowhere to turn and William being remarried
and rich, she went back to the family she had never
wanted. Angelo Sr. took responsibility for the way her
life had turned out, and vowed to take care of her. With
her poor health consuming her beauty, they were married under God at his church, and no one knew who she
was or had been. The congregation loved their first lady
and felt obligated to help her fight her battle with cancer,
but even with the collections they took up for her treatments, there wasn't enough money to help her battle the

disease. It was back to playing the underage dash, and her victim this time around was William. Her plan was to threaten him that she would tell the police he had murdered Rita and had attempted to kill her, so she had fled to Savannah to stay alive. However, when she learned he had married Meagan, it dawned on her that threatening to add her to the murder plot would yield a bigger payout, and it did. After pointing out to William how he and Meagan had both had a motive to kill her and her best friend, as it would enable them to be together freely, William vowed to do anything to keep his Georgia Peach out of jail, and it made Clara want to kill him instead.

Meagan was their goddaughter, for crying out loud, and the only child the two had between them. He needed to have his dick removed and stuck up his ass for abusing the child's trust. If Clara hadn't received her boarding pass to leave the flesh, she'd kill him on morals alone, but she needed his money to prolong her life and to make things right with her son. In her mind, making things right with him was the only chance she had left to get into heaven. Her shenanigans had ruined his life. If she couldn't give him back the time she had taken from him and impart the lessons she had neglected to give him, she'd fix her wrongdoing by letting him spend the rest of his life filthy rich.

The properties William had bought for her were all Angelo Jr.'s when her number was up, as was all the money she had saved in the bank. She just prayed that his constant show of disrespect and his double-crossing her by getting a job working for William wouldn't force her to leave it all to a charity for cancer patients. Angelo Jr. didn't know that his mother knew of his employment. This she was sure of. They had never crossed paths in Atlanta, so she'd go along with his game to keep it that way. She didn't know what he had up his sleeve, but she knew whatever his reasons were for going behind her back and getting a job with William would lead him to the truth.

After unlocking her wheelchair, Clara rolled herself to the restroom. She was supposed to be under hospice care or, at the very least, to have a live-in nurse, but she had refused them both. If she had pain and suffering, she accepted it as a part of her punishment. Her feeble sixty-year-old hands barely mustered the strength to turn the wheels a full turn, but she made it to her destination without help. She was now in diapers and didn't use the toilet, but that wasn't her reason for entering the restroom. The mirror was.

She looked in the mirror and didn't recognize her own reflection. She had turned into a raisin perched on a wheelchair, with two large oxygen tanks supplying air to her lungs through her neck.

"I'm a fucking neck breather," she said aloud after placing the handheld voice-amplification device under her jawbone.

She tried hard to see the pretty pie-faced girl with dimples who used to look back at her when she looked in the mirror. It had been years since she'd seen that face, as it had been erased gradually with each puff of the cigarettes. Now it was memory mist due to the morphine that kept her pain at bay, and all she saw looking back at her was a blur.

"Excuse me, ma'am. Are you Mrs. Hurley?" asked a manly-looking woman dressed in dark gray, with a hoodie over her head. Clara hadn't heard the young lady enter the restroom. It was like she materialized out of nowhere.

"Why? Who in the fuck wants to know?" she said, looking the twentysomething-year-old up and down. It was hot as hell outside, yet she was dressed in a sweat suit and had gloves on. Clara was sure that the young bitch was housed upstairs, in the psych ward.

"I do, ma'am. I have an important message for you."

"Stop all that 'ma'am' bullshit, psycho, and spill it. I don't have all day."

"You're right. You don't."

The woman snatched the tubing out of Clara's neck that allowed the oxygen to flow into her lungs. Moving quickly before someone entered the restroom, she pushed Clara's wheelchair into the handicap stall. Clara stuck out her arms in an attempt to grab whatever she could around her, but the loss of oxygen was making her weak. With the strength of two men, the hooded women flipped the chair over, causing Clara's head to hit the toilet. Clara was knocked out cold on impact. Her electro-larynx rolled on the floor and came to rest next to the attacker's foot, and she kicked it into the next stall. She knew Clara was knocked out and her lungs were in the process of collapsing, but she wanted to make sure she wouldn't be able to call for help, anyway.

After staging the scene to look like it was an accident caused by Clara trying to use the restroom without assistance, the manly woman locked the stall's door. She had to admit that this was the easiest hit she had been paid to do. So far the plan had flowed exactly according to the script she had been given. She had thought it would be hard to kill someone who was already dying, but that was what had made the deed easier. Plus, the old bitch had a smart mouth . . . well, neck.

"Oh, before I forget," the woman said as she got on her knees right next to where Clara lay. "The message is, 'Rest in peace, again.'" She shrugged, not understanding the meaning of the message, then crawled under the locked stall door and fled the scene.

Chapter Eight

Back in Atlanta, Meagan couldn't wait to disappear through the spa doors and head into the restroom. She had to make a phone call that she couldn't afford to put off.

"Didn't I tell your young, stupid ass no?" Meagan yelled into her phone once she was inside the spa's restroom.

"What are you talking about, baby? You need to calm down and watch what you say." Devin didn't have a clue why Meagan was so upset, but she had deposited too many checks with the word *young* into his bank. There wasn't many more he would be willing to take before he'd bounce.

"My husband was shot at today, Devin," she whispered into the phone, because she realized in her haste that she hadn't checked the restroom for occupants when she first walked in. She was already paranoid about having the conversation by phone. "And I was with him. I told you not to."

"If your husband got shot at, Meagan, that doesn't have shit to do with me. Didn't you say he's fucking with some other bitch too? Maybe she got him popped at."

The lie flowed off Devin's lips with ease because a part of it was the truth. He had confided in J. Seed the conversation he had had with Meagan that morning. Jason Seed was his boy, his partner in crime, and the only man he called big brother, so he wasn't surprised when J. Seed had volunteered to give him an easy fix to his problem.

"Off that nigga . . . If he's standing in your way and plotting against yo' bitch, hit his ass with the nine. Fuck it. I'll even do the shit for you," he'd said.

"Since when do you sign up to take on other people's troubles? I thought you said you weren't feeling Meagan for me?"

"I'm not," J. Seed had countered. "But that bitch would be caked up from the bake up if that nigga died. All you have to do is keep tapping it until she falls in love, and then we'll rob her ass."

Devin had been feeling the plan until J. Seed mentioned double-crossing Meagan. It must have shown on his face.

"I know you not feeling this old bitch after she lied to you?" J. Seed asked, staring intently at Devin's face. "She already showed you she can't be trusted."

Devin didn't see it that way. He looked at it from a business standpoint, after seeing the lifestyle she was living. He felt she lied to him about who she was only to keep him from fucking up what she already had going. After spending the night with her in her bed, Devin knew the love in their relationship wasn't one sided, but he had to play the role for his boy's sake.

"Naw, hell naw. I'll work on finding out where the money is stashed, and then we'll hit that bitch. I'll keep fucking her afterward, so she won't ever suspect it was us," Devin assured him.

"That's what I'm talking about, my nigga," J. Seed said, pulling him in for a handshake combined with a shoulder-to-shoulder dap. "Let's get this cheese . . . cheddar and mozzarella." He laughed.

They hadn't come up with a plan right then, but that didn't mean Devin's boy hadn't devised one and put it into motion. Devin knew he needed to get off the phone with Meagan right now so he could slow J. Seed down and figure out a way to renege on his agreement to rob her before his boy made a move on that too.

A week had passed since the shooting outside the lawyer's office, and William was still battling the same thought. *Would Meagan put out a hit on me?* The thought wouldn't free itself from his mind, and the liquor wasn't helping. He didn't know anyone as conniving and evil as his first wife. If she pointed the finger at Meagan, he'd take heed. But why now? He wasn't cheating, and he had made it his business to keep his hands to himself more. It wasn't only for Meagan's sake; the truth was he was getting too old for the shit. Whupping her left him feeling wiped out for days afterward. His battle with diabetes was getting worse, as he had advanced to the use of insulin by injection, and he felt like the only way he would beat the karma that was after him was by doing right by her.

William had worked in a kitchen all his life. It was ironic that his lifelong love for food would be the reason his life was shortened. He looked at it as his punishment for the treatment he had given the women that crossed his path. Although diabetes wasn't a laughing matter, he thanked the Lord that his infidelity had never given him more than VD, and that was almost forty years earlier. He had made it through a lot of incurable sexually transmitted disease epidemics, so he accepted his diabetes as a blessing.

The idea that Meagan wanting him dead, knowing his health was on a downward slope and she'd get everything he owned, didn't make sense to him. *Why would she rush the inevitable? She can't be that fed up with my shit?* he thought, but he had also thought before that he'd left his past behind him. Yet Clara was back and was blackmailing him for everything he had. He'd never forget the day of her return.

"I love you. And don't forget to call me as soon as the pilot gives the okay to turn on your phone," William said, his arms wrapped around his wife's waist. Their new Georgia Peach chain in Hollywood wasn't producing the numbers they had planned for it, and since Meagan was the one with the degree in business, they both had agreed it was best for her to go there for a week to see firsthand what issues the restaurant was having.

"You know I will," she said and then gave him a final kiss before she boarded her flight.

He didn't like sending her to the West Coast by herself, but it came along with the dream. He rode home in silence, hoping and praying that the issue wasn't the location. He had found the Gower Street location on the internet and, after visiting it a couple of times, had decided he would go forward with the location. The area was heavily populated, which meant lots of foot traffic, so he had thought he was making the right decision, but he had failed to calculate his competition. That street belonged to a Chicken and Waffles place; this he knew. Georgia Peach's was an upscale soul-food restaurant, which had led him to think he wouldn't face any problems, but at the same time, May & May Soul Food had recently opened their Crenshaw and King Boulevard location. The restaurant was miles from his, but with mass radio promotion and word of mouth from celebrity patrons, the restaurant had a buzz, and Georgia Peach's didn't.

After arriving at his house, William decided he'd take a nap until Meagan confirmed her safe arrival. He was two hours into his nap when his house phone rang. He picked up.

"Hello. This is Grady Memorial Hospital. May I speak with Mr. William Tolliver please?"

The word *hospital* sent his legs out of the bed and woke him all the way up. "This is him. How may I help you?"

"Your wife came into our emergency department, and she asked that we call you to inform—"

"Is she okay? What happened?" he asked, cutting the caller off. "I don't want her there. Send her to Emory."

"Your wife hasn't signed a release that allows me to provide information by phone regarding her care. I'm not at liberty—"

William slammed the phone down on its cradle, ran out of his house, and hop in his car. He was sure he made it to the hospital in record time. He asked several nurses for his wife's emergency-room number, and each one said the hospital had not admitted a Meagan Tolliver. Just when he decided he'd go from room to room, checking on his own, he heard a familiar voice talking down the hallway. He followed the sound, and it took him to a nurses' station and the nurse who had just called him.

When she stopped talking, he addressed her. "Excuse me, miss. My name is William Tolliver. I believe you are the one who called to notify me that my wife is here."

"Oh yes. You're Mr. Send Her to Emory. That's her room right there." She pointed. "Your wife was wondering if you'd show up or not, since you hung up on—"

William darted in the direction of the room before the nurse could finish talking. He ran through the door, and there was Clara, in a seated position on the bed, with a gun pointing at him. She had tubes supplying her oxygen through her nose

"Do you remember taking me to the shooting range on our honeymoon?" she asked. "I told you I didn't want to go. Hell, I even begged you when we arrived to change the plans, and you told me no. I'm glad you didn't agree, because after I pulled the trigger for the first time, I was addicted. You know, like I know, that I'm damn good with a three-eighty-five revolver. And at this distance even if I wasn't a good shot, you'd be dead if I pulled the trigger, so have a seat."

William had heard her words, but he was in shock. He shook his head erratically, because he was sure he was still asleep. For years, he had dreamed of Clara, but in his dreams, she'd been wearing angel wings and confessing her love for him. But the look on her face now showed anything but love.

"I said, have a seat." Clara cocked the hammer back to let him know she meant business.

Slowly, with his eyes moving from her frail face to the revolver, he took a seat. A million questions flowed through his mind, but only the most important came out of his mouth. "How are you still alive?"

When Clara had popped up six years ago, he'd been taken by surprise, since he'd believed she died in the car with Meagan's mom. Six years ago, he had felt that he had to agree to her terms. Especially after she'd told him that she knew he married their goddaughter and she was ready to get payback for it. She had threatened to lie and say that William had covered his car in gasoline and set fire to it as he forced her and Rita at gunpoint to stay in the burning car. She had even perfected her lie about how she made it out of the car alive and why she had to fake her death. She was going to be the key witness in the criminal case against him for murdering Rita and attempting to kill her. Just for kicks, she would also make Meagan an accessory to her mother's murder and her attempted murder. If money was what Clara had wanted back then to keep her mouth shut—and thus ensure that he and the true love of his life remained free, he'd give Clara every dime he had as payment for her pain and suffering.

Giving her money had been easy. It was her forcing him to have sex with her while she was close to death that had been the hard part. He had sworn after getting caught creeping with a customer seven years earlier that he'd never cheat on Meagan again, and he'd meant it. He had learned to tame his lust, but he had had to break his promise to dick down the almost corpse. Sex with her had been horrible before the cancer spread, but now that she was in the last stages of the disease, on oxygen full time, and in a makeshift hospital room that he created, it was gruesome.

"What's wrong with your dick now?" Clara grunted after finally getting her body temperature to rise a few degrees so William could stop complaining that he was fucking a corpse.

"That sound, it's distracting me."

"What sound?"

"I don't know what it's called, but the sound that comes out of the hole in your neck when you breathe in. That rattling, it's creepy," he explained.

"You're pathetic. Did you know that? And don't bother answering the question. The fact that you used that childish word *creepy* says enough. Creepy or not, I want some dick. If the medicine didn't fuck with my blood flow and make me numb down there, I'd have you to lick it instead."

"See? That's what the fuck I'm talking about," William said, climbing off her. "I know I told you that I don't like you talking like that through that thing in your throat. My dick doesn't like it."

"That's foreplay." She giggled. "You don't want me to talk about you licking my pussy through my voice box, Daddy?"

William fled the living room naked.

*****

If Clara could come back after fifteen years and put him through all this, he wouldn't sleep after the twenty-one years of hell that he had put Meagan through. He needed to hire someone to get close to Meagan and find out what she had going on. He prayed the meeting with Angelo would provide him with just that.

"What's up, boss? These condos are nice," Angelo commented as he stood in the hallway outside William's condo in his own building.

"Thanks. Come in and have a seat. You want your Hennessy on ice?"

"Come on now, boss. Only weaklings need the rocks. I'll have it straight." He laughed.

Angelo had never been past the entrance to the building, and he had gone that far only when William needed help with bags. He stepped into the foyer and proceeded into the living room. He immediately gained a newfound respect for his boss, as he saw that the entire living room had been turned into a hospital room. There were machines hooked up everywhere to monitor his mother during her stay. There were clean gowns and diapers stacked halfway to the ceiling. He had gone the extra mile to bring her comfort, and Angelo realized that was her reason for declining a nurse.

"Well, I called you here to talk business. Like your drink, I treat life straight, so let me get straight to the point. I want to hire you to keep tabs on my wife," William said, handing him his drink and placing the bottle on the coffee table.

"I already do. That's what I thought all those extra tips were about."

"They are, but I need you to turn it up a few notches. I'll give you twenty thousand dollars to become her best friend and report what you find out back to me."

"And how am I supposed to do that?" Angelo said before killing his drink.

"By fucking her," William said, refilling his glass and placing the bottle back on the coffee table. "She's lonely, and Viagra no longer works for me. My diabetes medicines don't mix with it. She needs some dick, and if you're giving it to her the way she needs it, that satisfaction will make her talk."

"You had me interested until you said that shit. Ain't no way in hell I'm fucking your wife, boss. You need to go back to the drawing board with that shit." Angelo had already killed his glass again and was extending his arm for round three.

"I know my wife, and that's the only way she'll trust you enough to tell on herself. I know I'm asking for a lot, so let's make that fifty thousand."

"How about hell no? This ain't a soap opera, where you can just do whatever you want. Who wakes up, pisses, and says, 'Today I'll just pay my limo driver to fuck my wife to find out what she's up to'? If you think the shit works like that, next, you'll think you can die and come back every other season because you're good at faking your death. You can't pay me to befriend your wife, and yo' ass can't come back from the dead. Shit just don't happen like that."

"If you only knew," William mumbled. "I'm not asking you to kill anyone. All I'm asking is for you to get closer to my wife for information. Why are you making a big deal out of it?"

"Because I'm black. Niggas don't just say, 'Hey, man, I have a job opportunity for you. It pays fifty thousand a year, and all you have to do is fuck my wife and keep me updated on how she feels about me.' Come on, boss. Listen to yourself. I know juggling to crazy bitches is hard, but why not pick one and throw the other away?"

Angelo tried not to look too interested in William's answer, but he knew his answer would resolve a lot of his questions.

"It's not that easy. Trust me when I say, if I could, I would. And, honestly, I'm not sure about what I want to do anymore."

That wasn't the answer Angelo wanted.

"How about we make it a hundred thousand and an extra fifty thousand dollars for me not to tell your wife about your plan? If we gone let this shit ride out like a daytime series, I'm signing up to be one of the evil villains."

William stared at the floor, then lifted his gaze. "You want me to pay you *not* to double-cross me and double to let you fuck my wife, when I know she's going to get your weak-minded ass sprung?"

"If the pussy is that good, and I'm going to have to walk away one day, then make it two hundred thousand. I mean, let's be real, boss. You just asked me to ho for you. History states that the pimp always comes out on top, so the only way you're going to get me to do this is to make it worth it for me to."

William wasn't in a position to agree to one hundred fifty thousand dollars or to two hundred thousand, not with him being blackmailed by Clara, but he knew Angelo wasn't up for negotiations.

"Get the fuck out of my building, and take that envelope on your way out. There's twenty thousand dollars in there. I'll pay you as you bring the information in. If you give me enough to dish out a hundred fifty thousand, then that's what you'll be paid. You can use that active imagination of yours to pretend that it's two hundred thousand. And, Angelo, you're officially on duty as of now. Pick her up for lunch, and then take her to get a manicure and a pedicure. Meagan will like that."

Angelo grabbed the overstuffed envelope on the coffee table and put his empty glass in its place. "If I spend my own money to wine and dine her, I need to be reimbursed. Don't worry. I'll keep the receipts."

"You're a cocky little fucker," William said before turning up his drink.

Angelo snatched the bottle of Hennessy and headed to the front door. He paused right in front of it and turned his head. "If that's the nickname you're giving me to ho with, you need to change that to cocky *big* fucker. Your wife will agree," he said, then grabbed his dick and walked out.

Angelo had done as William had told him to do, and with some convincing, he had got Meagan to take the rest of the day off and have lunch with him. Then he drove her to the nail salon without letting her know that was where they were headed.

"So, what is this all about? Lunch and now this? What have I done besides let you keep your job to deserve all this?" she asked when he parked in front of the salon.

"You keep taking his fist. It ain't my place to keep throwing the shit in your face, so I thought I would show you how he should be treating you."

"I don't need your sympathy," she snapped as they headed inside.

"Good, because I'm not giving it to you. I don't feel sorry for you allowing the shit. I'm sorry for throwing it in your face like I do."

They fell silent as two Vietnamese workers ushered her to a chair and held a conversation in their native tongue. One of them went right to work on her pedicure.

"Do you know what they're saying?" Angelo asked, attempting to change the mood.

"No, I don't have a clue," she said, with laughter in her words.

"The lady doing your toes told the man next to her that your feet smell like they've been soaked in old cooking oil. She said they are making her want to fry some egg rolls or something." He laughed.

"Oh, is that what she said?" Meagan chuckled.

"Yep. Said she's charging your ass more for putting up with it."

Meagan held in her laugh until the woman working on her feet put on a face mask.

"You see? I told you she said your shit stink."

They laughed until Meagan cut it short with her question. William had mentioned they were around the same age, but Angelo was so immature, she had to know if this was true. "How old are you, anyway, Mr. Hurley?"

"Aw shit. Here you go with that 'Mr. Hurley' shit. I just made forty-three the day I took this job. Is that all right with you?"

"You're older than me. Where are you from? And don't say Atlanta. You have a southwest Georgia accent."

"What do you know about southwest Georgia?" he asked, buying himself some time. He couldn't tell her they were from the same place.

"I'm a southwest Georgia, girl. I was born and raised in Albany."

"Not too far from me. I'm from Blakely." Blakely was almost an hour away from Albany, but it was still considered southwest Georgia. She couldn't dispute that.

"Okay, you're near my neck of the woods. So what brought you to Atlanta?"

"Work and opportunities. On a school trip in high school, we came to Atlanta. From then on, I knew I would be living here."

"Understandable. So . . . are you dating anyone?" She regretted getting more personal when the words left her mouth, but she was curious.

"No, haven't met anyone I'm ready to get a headache over besides one woman."

"And what's the problem there?"

"Well, she's unhappily married and getting her ass whupped. I'm just waiting for that to be over, so I can give her better." He walked out of the nail salon, as if he hadn't said a word. Meagan ran after him.

"Look, Angelo," Meagan said, walking by him and getting in the limo with paper slippers on her feet and what looked like a sponge wedged between her bright pink toes. "I'm flattered that you would be interested in me, but it would never work."

"You don't know if it would work or not," he said as he stood by her door. "You're shooting me down because you think you know my net worth. This 'driving you around' shit has you thinking that way. I don't blame you. But don't size up my pockets. You don't know why I'm driving this limo."

"I don't know why, but what I do know is that you were willing to cross my husband to keep this job. If it's not for income, why do you need it so badly?"

Angelo closed the limo door once she was settled in the backseat. "How do I get closer to you without it?" he said once he was behind the wheel.

Meagan cracked a smile as Angelo pulled into traffic, and he fought back the urge to throw up. He was laying the shit on so heavy that it had turned his stomach. He wanted to fuck her, especially after learning he would be paid to, but that "sweet nothings" shit was more than he could swallow. He had watched his father wither away to nothing from being weak over a woman, and he had vowed never to do the same. Although he was doing it only as part of his plan to get the green from William, the fact that it was a reality to her made him sick over it.

"I get it now . . . You want to fuck me, don't you? You've seen me get down with those younger men in the back-seat, and you see how much older William is than me, so you want a shot to show me what I've been missing."

"No, sweetheart. It's way more than that," he said, pulling over on the busy street. "But if that's where you want this to start, I can come join you in the backseat."

Meagan dug in her purse and retrieved a joint. She lit it and then hit it a few times to slow down the thoughts zooming through her mind. Then she passed it up to him. After he took a few puffs, she asked, "You want to get a hotel room?"

"Hell nah. I'm no better than the rest of those thirsty-ass niggas. You can give me the hotel money. I want you back there." He passed her back the joint and then stepped out of the limo to get in the backseat.

"If we do this, you have to stay silent," she said while inhaling her smoke version of Viagra. It gave her the "Fuck it" attitude she needed to fuck him, and anyone else, for that matter. She'd give him what he wanted so she could get the information she wanted from him.

"That silent shit worked on those little boys. You're dealing with a grown-ass man."

He sat on the seat across from her and rested his head on the opened partition. He pulled out his meat and held it while looking at her. She tried to play it cool as she passed him back the joint, but the mouth portion of the Zig-Zag wrap was wet, letting him know her mouth wanted to taste him. He hit it and then put the roach in the built-in ashtray.

"How long are you going to sit over there and stare at it? You don't have to play the good girl role with me. You know exactly what to do with this dick."

Like a vulture, she soared down to his lap and put her mouth to work. He couldn't believe how talented she was, even with all the practice he knew she was getting. Her mouth felt like virgin pussy, but the wetness of it felt like a pro's. From the day he first saw her, he had wanted to rub on her round brown ass, and now that he could, he wouldn't let her slacks stop him from doing it.

"Take them pants off."

She attempted to do what he had asked while keeping him in her mouth, but she couldn't maneuver like she used to. She fell back into her seat and slid off the slacks. Angelo made his way to her. He slid his hands under her butt and spread her bottom lips with his thumbs.

"You got a pretty pussy, Ms. Meagan," he said before planting a kiss on her opening.

"Thank you," she moaned.

"Nah, bitch. Thank you."

He spanked her hardened clit with his tongue and softly pulled on it with his full lips. Pussy had been his favorite meal from the time he had had his first taste, and he knew exactly what to do to keep the stream of cum flowing. Hands down, Meagan was getting the best head she'd experienced in her life. Although Devin could make her cum quickly, Angelo sent her into a full orgasm in less than two minutes. Unlike Devin's long, drawn-out head, Angelo had gotten up after giving her only one explosion. He turned her body around by the grasp he had on her until she was lined up lengthwise with the seat. He kicked off his shoes and pulled his pants to his ankles.

"I have a condom in my purse," she told him.

"Fuck that condom. I ain't had no pussy in over two years. I'm clean, and you stay at the clinic, getting that pussy checked out. We're going to enjoying this shit," he said. When he got no objection from her, his three-pound meat entered her womb. On impact, she creamed on him, and once he saw the milky substance covering his shaft, he had to look away to keep himself from ending this session prematurely.

"God damn, Angelo."

"You got me feeling the same way, beautiful." He tried to keep himself from drooling on her, but a small amount of his saliva hit her shoulder. "You got me drooling and shit."

"I'm cumming already . . . ," she yelled just as someone knocked on the front passenger window.

They were behind limo tint, so they could see the young black policeman flashing his light into the limo to try to see in, but he couldn't see them. They could dress and cover up their act, but what about the weed scent? He pulled his pants up and then reached through the partition, grabbed the air freshener, sprayed it for what seemed like an entire minute. Once they were both dressed, Angelo opened the back door.

"How can we help you, Officer?"

Chapter Nine

It took Devin a week to catch up with J. Seed for a face-to-face. He was on his way to College Park from downtown to meet him, but the police had a limo pulled over and were blocking traffic.

"Just stay there. I'm on my way," he said into his cell phone.

"I'm not going anywhere. What's up, though, Diablo?" J. Seed replied.

"I'll tell you when I pull up. Are you at your baby mama's spot?"

"Nah, I'm, um . . . I had to make a quick stop, but I'm on my way there now."

"Okay . . . What the fuck? Let me hit you right back." Devin hung up the phone as he watched Meagan and her limousine driver exit the back of the limo. He was a little over three hundred feet away from them, with traffic preventing him from moving closer, so he pulled into a gas station, parked, and ran across the street to them.

"What's going on, Meagan?" Devin asked. With daggers in his eyes, he glanced over at Angelo.

"Sir, I need you to stand over there," the officer said, pointing at a tree nearby.

"I'm not going anywhere until I know my girl is straight," Devin insisted.

Meagan shot her eyes up at the officer, because less than a minute ago, she had said she was on her way to pick up her husband, and Angelo chuckled.

"What the fuck are you laughing at, bitch?" Devin barked at Angelo.

"You clown," Angelo muttered.

"I'll show your ass a clown, faggot," Devin said as he charged at Angelo, but the officer intervened.

"Here are your driver's licenses back. Next time you decide to have a business pow-wow, make sure you pull over and park first. Y'all are free to go."

"Yes, sir," Angelo said, smiling, with his eyes still locked on Devin. "Let's go, Mrs. Tolliver—"

"Nah, playboy. I'm taking her home," Devin interrupted.

Angelo eyed him. "Oh, so you're taking her home? That's fine with me, but I don't think her husband would appreciate her getting out of a bucket with a no-name-having rap artist."

"Fuck you and her husband." Devin charged toward Angelo again, but this time Meagan stepped in between them.

"Angelo, I'm riding with Devin. I'm sure you have other business you could be handling, like finding out who's living in that condo. Let's go."

"Yeah, go run those errands, errand boy," Devin taunted childishly, but after getting a sample of Meagan's goodness, Angelo felt like the victor, so he let Devin enjoy the moment.

"I'll get up with you later, Meagan, so we can finish that conversation we started." Angelo gave Meagan a wink, jumped in the limo, and drove off so the police officer could do the same.

Mad didn't describe the way Devin felt. He was young, but he knew shade when it was being thrown at him. He didn't confront Meagan about it until they were in his mother's car on the interstate.

"What was that wink about?"

"What wink?" Meagan asked.

"Don't play stupid. You saw that nigga wink at you. What business were y'all in the backseat discussing in the middle of traffic, anyway?" His hands were locked at ten and two on the steering wheel, like he was taking the driver's exam.

"Just stuff about my husband."

"He can't drive and talk at the same time?"

"He could have, but I asked him to stop. And tell me, Is that a problem?"

"Hell yeah, that's a problem when you don't know if that nigga can be trusted. After listening to his ass try to stunt like he was the man, I got a bad vibe about the nigga. You can't fire him without your husband's permission?"

"If I wanted to, I could," Meagan said, slightly irritated.

"Then you need to fire little buddy."

"Why? Because you lost the word fight you started by jumping into business that didn't concern you? What were you doing? Following me?" She was trying to flip it on Devin, but it didn't work.

"However you want to put it, Ma, but that nigga needs to stay from around you. Next time I catch him smiling and grinning in your face, I'm shipping him back to Dougherty County, DOA."

"Dougherty County? What does Dougherty County have to do with anything?"

"Isn't that where the nigga's limousine company is at? That's what the license plate says."

Meagan had never walked behind the limousine and noticed what the plate said. She knew Angelo was from Blakely, Georgia, which was in Early County, because she had asked that earlier. His limousine being registered in Dougherty County, which was where Albany was, didn't mean a thing. She had rented cars in New York that had

California plates, and when they'd moved to Atlanta from Albany, the U-Haul they'd rented had Arizona plates. Devin didn't have a clue about what he was talking about, but that was a rare coincidence, she had to admit.

Rush hour made the normal ride from downtown feel like they were doing a round trip, and the silence made it feel even longer.

"I have to go to the studio after I drop you off, but when I'm done, can I come get in bed with you tonight?" he asked, preparing himself for rejection.

"That was a once-in-a-lifetime opportunity."

"So, because I told you I don't want you around that ho-ass nigga, I'm not welcome back at your house?"

"Oh my God!" she screamed out in frustration. "He doesn't have shit to do with you staying the night. I'm married. Did you forget that?"

Devin had temporarily forgotten that she was married. They were spending more time together than they had previously done, and the all-day phone calls and texting had him spoiled.

"Well, when do I get to wake up with you again?" he asked, turning up the road that led to her subdivision.

"I don't know, but I'll let you know when you can."

"I get my signing bonus tonight. You think you can take me car shopping tomorrow? And I've been thinking of getting my own spot. Now that I got my own money, my mama's house feels overcrowded to me."

As they turned left onto her street, a car went speeding past them through the stop sign, almost colliding into them. Devin hit the brakes and then his horn.

"That was a stop sign, ho," he yelled as the driver of the newer-model Nissan swerved and drove past them. "These people who live out here think rules don't apply to them."

"Is that what you think about me too?"

"Nah. You make the rules, baby."

He turned into her driveway, and they both instantly noticed that the glass window on the right side of her front door had been busted out and her door was wide open. Devin parked and pulled his gun from under his seat.

"Wait right here while I go check it out. Keep the car running," he ordered before he got out of the car.

Meagan didn't argue with him, because she was too scared to. The house alarm hadn't gone off, or the security alarm company would have called her by now. Her heart raced as she watched him enter the house slowly. He walked back into the doorway three minutes later and waved for her to come in.

"I don't know what's missing, but that office down the hallway is fucked up," he reported when she reached the front door.

Meagan went there first, and the room was in disarray. The computer had been knocked onto the floor, and all the drawers of the computer desk were lying upside down on the floor. The pictures William had hung up of all his restaurant locations had the glass busted out of them, and his bookshelves had been broken in multiple pieces, which were now resting on top of the books they had previously housed. She pulled out her phone and called the police. Next, she called William, who promised to get there as soon as the car allowed him to. Then, disgusted, she turned to face Devin.

"We've never been robbed—until I let you and those hoodlums from College Park into my house. Get the fuck out!"

"Hold on, Ma. You can't put this on my boys."

"Oh, I can't? Then stay here until the police come, and let's see who *they* put it on."

"You're tripping. How about checking to see what's missing first? Because right now it looks like vandalism to me."

"And who would vandalize my house?"

"I don't know, but it wasn't my people."

"On the morning of my birthday, I told myself I was done playing these high school games with you. First, you shoot at my husband, and now this."

Police sirens blared in the distance.

"I told you I didn't have shit to do with your husband getting shot at. I—"

"Like hell you didn't, little boy," she said, cutting him off. The sirens were louder now.

Devin had never seen this side of Meagan, and he didn't know what to expect. With the police probably less than a minute away, he felt that it was best that he left while he still had his freedom. "Let the police do their investigation. I'll be waiting on my apology when you find out the truth."

He kissed her on her cheek before she could dodge his lips and then ran out the door. J. Seed didn't know it, but the friendly conversation Devin had planned to have with him had just escalated to a "no conversation necessary" brawl. This robbery with unnecessary vandalism had J. Seed's signature written all over it. He wished he had stayed around to find out what was taken, but it wouldn't matter, anyway. If he knew his boy like he was sure he did, the stolen items were long gone and replaced with cash by now.

Twenty minutes later Devin pulled up at J. Seed's baby mama's house. There was a rental car parked in the yard, with bags from brand-name stores covering the backseat. Walking along the side of the house to enter through the back door, he passed an empty sixty-two-inch television box. It was sitting next to a trash can that couldn't close, because of the Blu-ray DVD player box that was perched on top of the trash bags. When he turned the corner, he could smell the high-grade weed seeping from the house and see his nephews riding on new bikes around the backyard.

"Jason Jr., is your daddy in there?" Devin called.

J. Seed's oldest son peddled faster to reach his uncle Devin, but he didn't know how to brake yet on his bike. The boy would have run Devin over if he hadn't grabbed the handlebars to stop the boy.

"Yes, he's in there, Uncle Devin. Look, we got new bikes and new shoes," the eight-year-old old boy said, showing off his retro Jordans. "Daddy said Christmas came early this year."

"I bet it did," was all he managed to say without taking his anger out on the child. He walked through the back door, which led into the kitchen. Pizza boxes covered the countertops, as if they were having a party. The television had been mounted to the wall in the living room and connected to a stereo system. The exact same stereo system Meagan had in her entertainment room. Devin hadn't fully checked her house to see what was missing, and since there weren't any boxes by the trash that he could tell the system had been removed from, he was sure it had belonged to Meagan.

He eyed the living room again, checking for familiar items from Meagan's house, but the music playing in the back bedroom had snatched his attention. It was his voice coming through the speakers. It was his love ballad playing, the one he had written for Meagan. Anger allowed him to float down the hallway and turn the knob, but the bedroom door that protected J. Seed from Devin's rage was locked. He retraced his steps to the kitchen, grabbed a butter knife, and popped the cheap lock on the bedroom door. The sun hadn't set yet, but candles were lit all over the room, and the lack of windows made the candlelight bounce off the blackened walls. He couldn't make out his boy's body clearly, because his baby mama was sitting on his face, with another woman straddling his lap.

For the first time since he had sped off from the crime scene back at Meagan's house, he had a change of heart. Until he saw J. Seed's Jordans next to the bed. They matched the ones his son was wearing. With fury blazing through him, Devin snatched the cowgirl off her mount, slung her to the floor, and then grabbed J. Seed by his ankles and pulled until his feet met the floor. Before he could open his mouth to ask Devin what was going on, Devin cocked back and hit him. Reacting purely from reflex, J. Seed gave him a three-hit combo with an uppercut Devin fell on his ass just a few inches shy of having his homeboy's birth-given bat and balls in his face. Devin could smell the fresh cum on him from the cowgirl he had thrown off him.

"What the fuck is wrong with you, nigga? You broke into my shit and snatched me out of my bed. You're lucky I saw your face, or I would have popped your bitch ass."

"Fuck you, nigga." The combination Devin had received must have knocked some sense into him, because his reason for being angry changed into something else. "You robbed my bitch and didn't offer me shit. I'm the nigga that plugged you."

"I didn't rob your bitch." He leaped in Devin's direction, and he scooted back, ready to go another round. Devin knew he wasn't any match for J. Seed, but he lacked fear. He'd die trying to whup his boy's ass before he'd run away from the fight.

"Then what's up with all this shit, nigga? Her stereo system is in your living room."

"That's *my* stereo system. If you had pulled up like you said you were going to, you'd already know what's up.

Johnni D. Manz hired me to be your bodyguard for one year. Did you forget it was payday?"

The frog that was in his throat had expanded its lungs, and Devin couldn't say another word. He instantly felt like shit.

"Yeah, you forgot, and I know why. That bitch has you tripping, straight up." J. Seed found his boxers rolled up on the floor like a pretzel and put them on. "Let me holler at you for a second," he said, storming out of his bedroom.

Devin followed slowly behind him, not knowing if his boy was moving their fight out of the sight of the women. He was about to punk out, but he knew he owed J. Seed an apology and should deliver it quickly.

"My bad, J. Meagan called me last week, saying her husband had been shot at, and then today her house got broken into. I know we had planned some shit, but—" Devin's words were knocked into the wall with his body.

"How long have we been boys?"

It was a rhetorical question, so Devin didn't answer, knowing that J. Seed wasn't done talking.

"Do you remember who robbed the fish market so you and all those damn kids your mama pushed out could eat? I'm the same nigga that stole the car to take your young ass to Walmart for your interview so you could help keep a roof over y'all's head. I've never looked out for me without making sure you were straight. That ho in there you snatched up off me, she was for you. I was picking her up when you called me as a surprise. You know why, little Devin?"

"Because you stay looking out for me, big bruh."

J. Seed continued to talk as Devin silently cursed himself out for being stupid. Meagan was fogging up his thoughts, and he had put her in front of his brother. Once

J. Seed took his arm off Devin's chest, Devin made his way to the back door.

"I fucked up, big bruh, but I promise I'm going to make this shit right," he called over his shoulder.

"Hold up," J. Seed said, stopping him in his tracks. He grabbed the rental-car keys off the counter and threw them at him. "I had Mimi pick you out some shit at the mall. Get them bags off the backseat of that rental. And, Devin . . . that old bitch means you no good, but I'm going to let you figure that shit out on your own."

Devin didn't have a response.

Part Five

Disrespectfully Hers

Chapter Ten

Meagan sat at the bottom of her staircase, feeling like shit, as the detectives took pictures throughout the house. Devin had been honest about his boy's involvement in the break-in, because there wasn't anything she knew of that was missing. She had wanted to call him and apologize the second she found out, but William was home.

"Mr. Tolliver, if you happen to realize anything else is missing besides your file cabinet and its documents, please give me a call," the older female detective said, handing him a card. "We got a good fingerprint off the inside door handle, but like I said before, it could belong to you or your wife. I will be in contact with you." She extended her hand, and he shook it.

"The file cabinet in your office is missing? What was in it, honey?" Meagan asked, concerned, but William didn't answer her. There were still a few lingering cops in their house, and he didn't want them to hear the answer he would give her, because it was different than the truth, which he had given them. Once the last thirsty cop, who had the gall to ask for a beverage, got in his squad car and left, he snatched Meagan off the stairs by her blouse.

"Did you have something to do with this?" He shook her back and forth.

"What . . . ? Why would you think I did? No, William! Why would I need to go through all of this just to get a locked file cabinet of yours?"

She was right. It would be extreme for her to stage a break-in just to search the office, which he had deemed off limits to her, and the contents of the cabinet would benefit her only if she had something up her sleeve. The file cabinet housed Clara's medical bills, receipts for the treatments he had already paid for, and the deed to the property he had bought in her sister's name to generate the extra income needed to keep Clara alive. No one would need that information, not even Clara, because she had copies of it all. However, if Meagan wanted a way out of their marriage without having him murdered, that file cabinet would provide it.

He ignored her questions as he slowly released her. "My office is off limits to you, understand?"

"Understood."

"Hey, boss. I got here as quick as I could." From the front door, which the cops had left open, Angelo had observed the hold William had on his wife. If he struck her, Angelo was ready to intervene.

"Hey, Angelo, come look at this shit. Whoever broke in had a good time rearranging my office." William escorted Angelo down the hallway, and Meagan tried to join in. "Go pack your bags. I'm sending you to a hotel for a few days," William said, looking back at her.

"But . . . why do I have to leave my house?"

"*Our* house," William snapped, correcting her. "Because it isn't safe for you to be here right now. I need to get the glass fixed on the door and get the security company out here to figure out why the alarm didn't sound. I have to get the security beefed up before I'm comfortable with you sleeping here. Now let the men talk and go do as you were told."

She looked to Angelo for help, but to her surprise, he agreed with William. "He's right, Mrs. Tolliver. Pack your bags, and I'll take you to get a hotel room for a few days.

Who's to say the burglars were finished? They might come back."

After turning on her heels, Meagan disappeared up the stairs.

"What's missing?" Angelo asked William once she was gone.

"Nothing but the file cabinet, with all the other one's shit in it. It was nothing but bills and receipts, but I have a funny feeling Meagan had something to do with it. Did you do what I asked of you?"

"Yeah, boss, I took her to Ray's on Peachtree for lunch and then to the nail shop."

"You get anything out of her?"

Angelo felt cheated by the cop's interruption of his first taste of Meagan, so he had decided not to disclose that part of their day. He needed the money to invest in his father's church, so he gave William enough information to get another payout. He looked out the door before speaking, then said, "She mentioned at the nail shop that she overheard you and your lawyer talking, but that was it."

"What did she hear?" William asked as he tried to think back to the day, but the only thing that came to mind about the meeting was the shooting after it.

"Something about finding out that some woman had threatened to kill you and that you already knew that you were the target of the shooting, but that was it. She was trying to figure out how to find out more information on who the woman is."

"That's it?"

"Yes, that's all," Angelo lied.

"She hasn't questioned me about it yet."

"I don't think she will, boss."

"Why do you think that?" William asked, with a puzzled look on his face.

"Because she asked me if I knew anything about another woman and if I could help her find out about her."

"And what did you say?"

"What do you think I said? I told her I was y'all's limo driver and I'd rather not get involved in your personal matters."

"Good job," William said as he picked up the computer screen off the floor.

"How long do you want her to get the room for? I'm sure you need to head back to the condo to take care of the other one."

"That's the strange part about it. I haven't heard from the other one since she went back to Savannah. She missed her doctor's appointment yesterday, which isn't like her."

Worried looks fell on both men's faces, and something was pulling at Angelo's heartstrings. For the first time since his mother had returned, he was hurt that she might be dead. His father was mad at him, but Angelo was sure that if she had passed away, his father would at least pick up the phone to tell him. He made a mental note to call his father to check on her once he got Meagan squared away.

"Anyway, to be safe, get the room for about a week. That will give me time to try to track down the other one."

"I gotcha, boss." Angelo stood there, waiting patiently.

William wanted to know for what. "You can go handle that now," he prompted.

"I will, once you pay me for the information I gave you."

William looked at Angelo like he was a piece of shit clogging his toilet. He was dealing with a lot at the moment and couldn't believe that the only thing on Angelo's mind was money. "Are you serious? My house was just broken into, and my plate is full, and you expect me to come out of the pockets right now?"

"I do," Angelo said earnestly. "I empathize, but your problems have nothing to do with our business arrangement."

Hesitantly, William pulled out his checkbook and wrote a check for five thousand dollars. Angelo felt like the information he had given his boss was worth more, but he let it go, not wanting to kick a wounded dog while it was down.

"I'll take a check this time because of what's going on, but let's keep this a cash only arrangement from now on," Angelo said, then exited the room before William decided to pick up the paperweight on the floor and throw it at him.

Meagan had had Angelo drop her off at the Renaissance Hotel. He'd offered to come up and keep her company, but his wasn't the company she wanted. She didn't like how chummy he had been with William that night, and she had some apologizing she needed to do. After receiving a text back from Devin in which he said he'd be there in two hours, she set to work waxing the hair off her body from her neck down. Her plan was to apologize to him both verbally and physically.

After she finished waxing, she emptied her suitcase. Normally, her rheumatoid arthritis attacked only her legs, but as she unpacked, her hands locked on her. She had medicine she could take for it, but she wanted a night filled with strawberries and champagne and knew it was best not to drink while on medication. When Devin knocked on the door, she had the lights dimmed and the love songs playlist that was saved on her phone on repeat. She hurried to the door and opened it.

"Hey, Dev . . ." Her words got lost when she found a man she'd never met before standing in front of her. It was Devin, but she hadn't met the version of him that stood before her. Every time they met up, he would be wearing his Walmart uniform or jeans and a white T-shirt, but that evening he was dressed to impress.

The parts of his outfit that stole her attention the most were his bright red sports jacket, his white dress shirt, and his thin black tie. She always knew he could hang a suit, but damn, he looked good in the closest thing to one she'd probably get to see him in. He was wearing loose-fitting designer jeans and retro red, black, and white Jordans. At first, she didn't know how she felt about the matching red golfer's hat he was wearing, but the longer she stared at him, the more it grew on her.

He leaned down, kissed her on her cheek, and handed her two large bags. "Get dressed, so we can go."

"Go where?" she asked, peeking into the bags, but everything in them was professionally wrapped.

"To get an understanding."

"We can do that here." She rubbed on the zipper of his pants, and he took a step back.

"No we can't. You fucked up with me this time. I'm going to need more than an apology and some pussy if you want to make shit right with me."

Meagan debated about agreeing to his terms or not. She had wrongly accused his friends of the break-in and had said a few hurtful words in the process, but that didn't grant him the right to decide the grounds of her apology. If she refused to go wherever he had planned for them to go, it might mean what they had was over. She went back and forth in the her mind, weighing the pros and cons of continuing the relationship, and she decided that the pros won. He loved her, he cared about her, and his newly found money did look good on him. She wouldn't agree to marriage or allow the relationship to get that serious, but having him as a boyfriend during her divorce process would make the hell she would go through a lot easier.

"Give me a few minutes to get myself together. Where are we going, anyway?"

"You'll see once we get there," was all Devin would say before a small smile spread across his lips. "Open your gifts first."

Like Christmas morning, she ran over to the bed and emptied the bags of gifts on it. She started with the smallest box. Inside were some cheap, fake gold accessories that she would have never picked out for herself. The bamboo earrings, the ten gold bangle bracelets, and the gold rope chain gave the impression that he had shopped at a store owned by a 1990s New York women's rap group and had hit the clearance rack.

"You do realize I'm forty years old, don't you?" she asked, holding the items up in the air.

"And you do realize that you don't look forty, don't you?" he countered.

"Yes, but . . . never mind. Thank you."

"That's my girl. You're welcome. Now open the rest."

The next to the smallest package housed soap on a rope and a bottle of mouthwash. She held them up. "What's this for?" she asked, confused.

"It's for you to wash the words *young* and *little boy* out your mouth for good."

"You can't be serious." She laughed as she tossed the items on the bed.

"I'm dead serious. As a matter of fact . . . " He retrieved the items. "You need to go handle that now. I need you to get a bad taste in your mouth every time you think of saying them."

"You're crazy. Ain't no way in hell that I'm washing my mouth out with soap. I apologize for continuing to make a reference to your age. I'll stop."

"I know you will, especially after you wash your mouth out with soap and get that burning sensation on your tongue from the mouthwash."

He headed to the bathroom, and she followed behind him, making promise after promise not to mention his age, but he needed her to pass this test. If she did it, he would take it as evidence that she really cared about him and that what they had meant something to her. If she didn't, he'd snatch up the rest of his gifts and find someone that was worthy to step out with him, like his ex-girlfriend Tesha. He had broken up with her once he realized her ghetto class had nothing on Meagan's. She had been blowing up his cell phone for months even before he had got signed, promising to make whatever adjustments she needed so that they could be together, and her immaturity had shown in her voice messages. Devin had decided that having to chase a woman, instead of having a woman chase him, was what he wanted the most. Meagan's confidence was sexy, and Tesha couldn't hold a candle to it.

"Here you go," he said, turning on the water in the sink.

"Don't make me do this. I love you, and if you feel like I'm disrespecting you, I'll stop."

"If you love me, prove it."

Meagan took a deep breath. She did love him, but she wasn't in love with him. At this point in her life, she wasn't in love with anyone. The reality of knowing she wasn't in love with William anymore was what made her lather up the bar of soap. *If I'm not in love with William anymore, why not show my love for Devin?* she thought. After sticking her tongue out, with her eyes on Devin, she rubbed the bar of soap over her tongue and gagged. She hurriedly rinsed her mouth.

"Are you happy now?" she asked.

"Almost," he said, pouring some mouthwash into the bottle's top and handing it to her. "Rinse your mouth with this for thirty seconds, and I'll be happier."

She swished the mouthwash around in her mouth, and it instantly burned her tongue. When she bent over to spit it out, Devin blocked the sink.

"Twenty-five more seconds," he urged.

He counted it down, and at twenty-nine seconds, she spit out the mouthwash and ducked her head under the sink to fill her mouth with water. The burning sensation from the combination wouldn't leave her mouth, so she continued to rinse it with water. With her face in the sink, Devin dropped his pants to his ankles, lifted her nightie, and forced himself into her dryness.

In a matter of seconds, she was wet and the burning in her mouth had disappeared. He was hitting her soft spot as hard as he could out of excitement that she did indeed love him.

"I told you I loved you," she said as her body bounced to the beat of his strokes.

"You did, but now you're showing it. Cut that water off and bend down farther in the sink."

His pace slowed down more as he went deeper. He wanted to find that spot inside her he had heard niggas talking about. There was a spot women held deep within that was only reachable by the right man. Dick length or width didn't matter; it could be found only by the right stroke. The man who found that spot would inherit a partner in love who was so loyal that nothing could separate them but death. If he could hit that one spot, Meagan would become his, with or without the paper-work that said it. He had to find, hit, and then kill that spot, because he was certain no other man had, or she wouldn't have bent over in the sink, professing love for him, but it wasn't enough. Love professed wasn't enough, because it came from her thoughts to her mouth. If he was lucky, the words would travel from her heart to her brain and then out her mouth, which was slightly better. But if he maintained the perfect pace and found that one spot missing from the map of a woman's body, love would come from her soul. It would bring loyalty, respect, submission, and faithfulness with it, and that was what Devin wanted. He wanted his wife.

"I'm about to gush," she screamed out, and he knew in that moment he had failed to reach that hidden spot in that sex position. Instead of missing the fireworks show Meagan was about to display, he fucked her faster, and they exploded together. He made sure to shoot some in her before he pulled out and spray-painted her ass with it as a throw off. Meagan was so lost in her eruption that his throw-off paint job wasn't needed, because she didn't feel him shoot inside her. When they were done, she got in the shower, and he stepped out of the bathroom to get the shower caddie she requested. On his return, he told her he had opened the rest of her gifts and they were waiting for her on the bed. Then he bathed his meat and balls in the sink.

He had bought her a black Victoria's Secret strapless bra and lace boy shorts set; a medium, formfitting black tube top that would reveal her belly button; a stone-washed, high-waisted, ankle-length jean skirt; and a pair of Jordans that matched his. She shook her head at the outfit as she applied lotion to her body, but then she put it on, anyway. After putting on the jewelry, she looked at herself in the mirror and had to admit he had done a good job of putting the outfit together.

"How did you know my sizes?" she asked with a smile.

"From handing you your clothes off the floor for the past eight months. But I also had help from the lady at the clothing store to get the look I wanted you to have."

She straightened her hair, brushed it into a diva-style ponytail, and made baby hair before they walked out the door. Devin sent the valet to get his rental car, which was a new-model all-black Benz.

"This is what I'm buying for myself tomorrow," he said when the valet drove up. He motioned to the valet to hold the door open for her.

"I guess rappers do make a lot of money," she mused.

"Naw. This is just chump change compared to what I'll be getting once I blow all the way up. If you act right, we will have his and her Benzs on my next payday."

She blushed and never once questioned where they were going until they had arrived. "This is the ghettoest strip club in Atlanta. You don't really expect me to go in there, do you? I'm not trying to get shot," she told him.

Devin didn't say anything. He parked and opened the car door for her.

"Welcome to Wild Donkey's. Ladies are free until midnight, and I need thirty dollars from you, pimp," said the man guarding the door. When he looked up and saw Meagan, he switched his tune. "That's you, playboy?" he asked, eyeing Meagan's curves.

"Yeah, that's all me, boss."

"Shit, you can get in free too. Shorty's bad," the man said, stepping to the side to permit them entrance.

"I appreciate that," Devin said before escorting Meagan into the building. They bypassed the floor and went to a table where two people were already seated.

"Damn, nigga. What took y'all so long?" J. Seed asked, with his arm around his baby mama.

"You know I had to tighten her up before we came out," Devin responded. He and J. Seed shook hands and went into formal introductions.

"Meagan, you remember my big bruh J., and this is his wifey, Mimi."

Mimi extended her hand and gave Meagan a goofy-looking smile. "You're wearing the fuck out of that skirt, girl. Yo' ass on fat." Mimi smiled, looking down at Meagan's shoes. "I see we all team Jordan tonight," she said, flashing her shoes.

"I guess so," Meagan said, providing her with a fake smile.

The almost naked waitress came to the table and asked if they were ready to order.

"Yeah," J. Seed said, speaking up. "Let us get a twenty-piece half and half. Make our ten lemon pepper. What flavor do y'all want, Young Diablo?"

"Let us have the Hennessy wings and—"

The waitress squinted at Devin as she interrupted him. "Hold up. You're the real Young Diablo? The nigga on the 'Thug Lovin'" track with Ice Man?"

Devin laughed. "Yeah that's me."

The waitress took off running through a door that read EMPLOYEES ONLY . When she walked back through the door, she had two suited men with her, and one was holding a camera.

"Welcome to Wild Donkey's, Young Diablo. I'm Mike, the owner of the club. Is it okay if we move y'all over to VIP and send you a bottle of whatever it is y'all are drinking on?"

"Hell yeah," J. Seed said, answering for his boy.

"Y'all don't mind if I get a picture with y'all, do you?" Mike asked, definitely starstruck.

"Naw, go ahead," Devin said, bringing Meagan to her feet. All six of them, including the waitress, smiled for the camera, and then they were moved to the VIP section.

They walked past the bar, and William ducked his head so his wife wouldn't see him drowning his sorrows in his drink. At first, he wasn't sure if it was Meagan or not, but when he got a whiff of the Versace perfume that he had bought her as she walked past, he was sure it was her. He wanted to snatch her up and cause a scene, but he decided to play it cool and keep a watchful eye.

Once they were settled in the VIP booth, their table was rushed by stripper after stripper, all of them wanting a private dance with Devin, which he declined. He was in at least twenty usies with the dancers, and his fame was leaving Meagan no choice but to up his value. As he wrapped his arms around one pretty girl after the next, she realized that she needed to lock him down. If he was going to be tied to anyone, it would be her.

The food arrived, delivered personally by the owner, and he cleared his employees away to allow the guests to eat in peace.

"Before we all throw down, Meagan has something she needs to say to you, big bruh." Meagan, looking shocked, didn't have a clue what Devin was talking about, and he didn't have a problem with putting her on the spot to remind her. "She wrongly accused you of something earlier, and now that it's official that she's my woman, she needs to make it right by you before I take our shit to the next level, right, baby?"

"Right," she replied quickly. "I apologize for falsely accusing you of—"

"Cut that shit short, Ma," J. Seed interrupted. "We good. As long as you're doing right by my little brother, I don't give a fuck about how you feel about me. Now let's eat, before our food gets cold."

William's eyes weren't the only ones locked on the VIP booth. Word of Young Diablo being in the building had spread to Tesha, and she couldn't believe he would disrespect her by bringing his new bitch to where he knew she worked. She wanted to beat down the bitch he had with him and worry if she still had a job later.

The table ate, and everyone enjoyed their wings and fries over laughter and random white Hennessy shots, until Tesha saw Devin and his new bitch tongue tied. William stood to his feet, ready for a confrontation, but Tesha beat him there.

"What's up, Devin? Who is this bitch?" Tesha asked loudly over the music.

"Go on somewhere, Tesha. My nigga don't fuck with you anymore. Skedaddle, ho. Kick rocks," J. Seed barked, dismissing her.

"Fuck you, J. Let the boy be a man and say it out of his own mouth, or let his bitch tell me," Tesha snapped.

Meagan's eyes were on Devin as Tesha stepped up and clocked her with her closed fist. She tried to reach for Meagan's ponytail, but Devin and J. Seed were already pulling her away from Meagan.

"Yeah, bitch, he's mine. Now run up!" Tesha said, kicking off her heels.

Meagan had never been in a fight in her forty years on Earth, besides the one time she had tried to fight William back. The feeling of fear was new to her, but her adrenaline sent her to her feet, and she slapped fire to Tesha's face. Tesha tried to break free from Devin's hold, but management saw the altercation and the bouncer took over restraining her. Mike shouted apology after apology as the bouncer carried Tesha back into the dressing room. He asked Devin to follow him to his office to find out what exactly had happened, and Mimi took Meagan to the restroom to fix her face.

"You should have beat that bitch's ass when she first walked up, talking shit," Mimi said, making a cold compress out of tissues and the ice from Meagan's drink, which was still in her hand.

"Who was she?" Meagan asked, looking in the mirror at the knot that was forming on her forehead.

"Tesha, the bitch he was fucking with before you. She's just mad that he left her for you and told that ho she needed to step her game up, that's all."

Devin's past relationships had never been a thought of hers, and he had never mentioned being in anything serious when they met, but Mimi was pouring the tea, and Meagan had her glass ready to drink it up.

Mimi went on. "Yeah, girl, they were each other's first, and that bitch don't know when to let go. They had been together since they were fourteen, I think. Anyway, he dumped her ass like a pile of trash when he met you, and ole girl is still in her feelings about it. Now that Devin is on the radio and shit, of course she wants his ass back. He's not broke anymore." She laughed and then continued. "The bitch came by my house last week, asking a million and one questions about him, but I didn't tell her bourgeois ass shit."

"How can she be bourgeois stripping?"

"Because she's stripping only to get through college. I think she's trying to be a social worker or something. She's from College Park too, but her mama and daddy kept that ass in the house, because they thought they were better than everybody in our neighborhood. They had jobs where they clocked in and shit, while everybody from around our way had a street hustle."

"Did Devin know that she worked here?"

"He sure did. That's why he wanted us to come here tonight, so he could show you off and piss her off. You know, since he upgraded and all." Mimi kept talking, but Meagan's anger was back. She felt like he had purposely put her in the way of danger, and that, she wouldn't allow. She stormed out the bathroom, leaving Mimi alone at her tea party, and headed to the owner's office.

"I'm ready to go now," she said, interrupting the conversation J. Seed and Devin were having over a blunt with Mike.

"Okay, baby, we'll leave as soon as the blunt is gone," Devin told her. "You want to hit it?"

She was sure Devin had lost all the common sense he had left. "Fuck it. I'll jump in a cab." She turned back in the direction she had come from, and Devin went to follow her.

"Let her go, bruh," J. Seed said, stopping Devin's pursuit. "Give her time to cool off. That shit was fucked up, and she has a might not on her head."

"A *might not?*" Mike questioned, not understanding what he meant.

"Yeah, that knot on her head might go away, but then again, it might not."

Both J. Seed and Mike laughed, but Devin didn't find it funny. He felt partly at fault for bringing Meagan here.

"Man, I'm going to the restroom. I'll be back," he announced.

He walked down the hallway back to the club's packed floor, and William stood to his feet to follow him. Once they were both in the restroom, he joined Devin in a piss at the urinals.

"You good, man? I saw the ruckus out there," William said.

"Yeah, I'm good. Just a bitch that doesn't understand that's 'It's over' means 'I'm done.'"

Devin was too caught in his feelings to realize the man next to him was the same man he had watched fuck Meagan in the kitchen and the same man whose pictures covered the walls in Meagan's house.

"What about the other one? She seemed pissed too."

"She is, but that's wifey right there. I'm going to give her some time to cool off, and then I'll make things back right with her."

"Yeah, I saw all the girls flocking around y'all's table. She's fine, but it has to be hard on her for women to constantly throw tail at you like that."

"Nah, man, it's not like that with her," Devin said, shaking his meat and putting it away. "She has her own fame, with the big-ass house and all. Them hoes out there don't bother her."

"Oh, I thought you said she was your wife? Y'all don't live together?" William knew he was cutting it close with the questions he was asking, but they had never seen each other before. He was just another nosy nigga in somebody else's business.

"No, not yet. She's in this fucked-up situation she's trying to handle right now, but that shit is coming to an end soon too," Devin said, looking at the man for the first time. "You have a good one."

"You too, young nigga."

Devin left the restroom and walked up to the table where J. Seed and his baby's mama were and handed her the keys to his rental car. "Go ahead and take the rental home, Mimi. Me and my brother got some shit we need to handle real quick."

She looked at J. Seed for the okay, and once he gave it to her, she bounced without asking any questions.

"Let's go," Devin said a few minutes later.

J. Seed followed Devin out of the club, and they got into his car.

"Go park behind the building," Devin instructed after J. Seed started the car. "Meagan's husband just rolled up on me in the restroom. We're going to follow him."

"For what? Let's go back in there and beat his ass. Did the nigga say something to you?"

"Nah. He didn't know that I knew who he was," Devin said, popping the glove compartment open to retrieve the gun he was sure J. Seed had in it. "But I'm ending this shit with him tonight. That's *my* bitch, J."

"Then let's go make that shit official. It's time to dead that nigga."

Chapter Eleven

Angelo Sr. walked into the hospital to pick up his wife and take her home. He never expected to find Clara checked in under critical care. Normally, she waited for him in the waiting room of the hospital, but today she couldn't be found. After questioning everyone he passed in the hospital corridors, he got the answers he needed.

"We found her unconscious, Mr. Hurley . . ," a nurse practitioner informed him at the nurses' station.

"Bishop Hurley. My son is Mr. Hurley," he corrected.

"My apologies, Bishop Hurley. She was trying to use the restroom and must have fallen while getting out of her chair. She pulled her oxygen port out, and she's been unconscious for hours. Another patient found her on the floor, locked in the stall. We have her on life support, but she's not doing too well. She flatlines every time we take her off."

"Then take her off. She's DNR."

The nurse practitioner found it strange that he would come in and instantly request his wife be taken off the machines that were helping to keep her alive. She had lost oxygen to her brain, but the doctors still agreed that there was hope for her.

"Do you have any documentation stating that she's DNR? We can't just take your word for it."

"She's a patient here. You should have it somewhere in her charts."

"I'm sorry, sir, but this is becoming confusing. She isn't a patient here. We've checked multiple times."

"Yes, she is. I bring her to the cancer center here every week. She has stage four lung and throat cancer."

The nurse practitioner quickly jotted down the information he provided, and invited him to wait in his wife's room while she went to look it up. He did as she had asked.

After checking to make sure his wife was still out of it, he dug a small piece of paper out of his pocket and used her bedside phone to place a call. "I want my money back, with interest, Patrice," he said into the phone.

"Why, big dog? I did the job. Call the hospital. Her body should be chilling in the morgue by now."

"Well, it's not. Somebody found her and saved her. I'm looking at her now."

"I'm not paying you back," the woman said into the phone. "I told you to let me put a bullet in her or slice her ass up into pieces, Bishop. You wanted the shit to look like she died from natural causes."

He had devoted hours to brainwashing her, and it was failing him right before his eyes. He had worked hard to get Irene, the daughter of a member of his church, sent to a locked-down mental facility for the criminally insane for murdering her husband and children, instead of spending life in a prison cell. He had worked even harder to sneak her the instruments that she needed to break out of it too.

After listening to her talk for hours about how she had enjoyed torturing her family and how she longed to kill others, he had felt like a padded room would suit her better than four cement walls. Once she'd moved to the institution, he'd begun having follow-up visits with her to try to help her make right with God, but as of late, his frustrations with his wife and son had made him understand how the woman could kill those closest to her.

Clara was back to her old tricks of lying and keeping secrets. One Monday after dropping her off in Savannah, his pickup truck wouldn't turn over. His alternator had gone out, and instead of paying the high cost to have the pickup towed, he walked five miles to the nearest auto-parts store to get the parts and tools to fix it himself. As he took the alternator off, a flashy Cadillac Escalade limo pulled up to the hospital entrance. It was the same limo he had spent hours praying to God for to replace the ones he had at his mortuary. Angelo Sr. headed over to the limo to see if the driver would allow him to take a peek inside and was stopped in his tracks by a familiar face getting out of the backseat.

It was William, Clara's ex-husband and the same William who had caused him to sin by committing murder. Only his sin had ended up being committed against the wrong person. It was William he had tried to kill by filling the windshield-wiper fluid reservoir and the oil reservoir of his car with gasoline. He had even gone as far as coating the car in gasoline to ensure William didn't walk away alive, but that wasn't how it had played out. Instead of William being the one to get in his car, Clara's best friend, Rita, had walked up to it. Angelo Sr. had been hiding too far away to stop her from getting in it, and when he'd seen Clara turn the corner with a cigarette in her mouth, he'd known it was already too late. Seconds later, the car had exploded, and he'd fled the scene, believing he had killed them both.

He wanted William dead because he felt that William was the one keeping Clara from building a bond with their son, and also that William was standing in the way of him reuniting the family he and Clara had made together. With William out of the way, Angelo Sr. would have the leeway he needed to try to rekindle what he and Clara had had so many years ago.

She was his first, and even at that time, she'd been the only woman he made love to. The opportunity to stray had presented itself on many occasions with the women in his congregation, but he had refused to commit the same sin of sexual immorality twice. If he lay down with another woman, she would be his wife first.

Repeatedly praying to God over it wasn't working, and the only solution he could find was doing away with William for good. As the car had exploded, so had his heart, and for days after the accident, he hadn't left the mortuary. Heartbroken from his crime, he'd gone to check his mailbox, and there he'd found love. Clara had made it out alive, and although she had had to hide for a while, she had promised to come back to be with him, and she had. Watching William help Clara into the backseat of his limo had been the last straw for them both, and their murders would be the only sin he was willing to commit twice.

"If you're going to keep the money, I need you to produce me a body. I missed him in Atlanta because he was walking out of his lawyer's office and I was too far for accuracy. Get him instead, and we're even," Angelo Sr. said as he watched Clara's eyes flutter like she was trying to open them.

"I'll do you one even better, big dog," she said, barking, and he hung up the phone, not in the mood to listen to another one of her psychotic breaks.

Angelo Sr. dashed into the hallway and started screaming for the nurses to come to Clara's room, but they were already headed in her direction. Her vital signs had been picked up over five minutes earlier on the machine they had been monitoring her with, and the nurses were waiting for her doctor to return before they walked in.

"She's trying to open her eyes," he yelled excitedly, and for the first time since his arrival, the nurse practitioner felt that he genuinely wanted what was best for his wife.

She asked him to step out of the room as the doctors hovered over Clara, and she followed him out.

"I did find information on her in our cancer unit, but she hasn't been a patient here in years. Her records were transferred to a hospital in Atlanta, but under the name of Clara Jones. Do you have a copy of your marriage certificate? We need to request that they send over her recent records, but we need your permission to request them."

"You're a hospital, for Pete's sake, and this is an emergency situation. Can't they send them over, anyway?" he said, exasperated.

Before the nurse practitioner could answer, he remembered the records he had watched the doctor hand William after each of her appointments as he'd safely hidden behind magazines and newspapers. She was a cash-only customer and had William listed as her medical power of attorney. There was no way the hospital in Atlanta would release anything to him. He decided that he needed to break into William's house or the condo and retrieve the records himself.

"I'm sorry. I just love my wife and am freaking out over all of this. I have copies of her medical treatment records from the past six years outside in my truck."

"You keep her medical records from the past six years in the car?" Something about the man in front of her wasn't adding up.

"Of course I do," he said with a smile. "Just in case something like this happens. I'll be right back." She watched him walk to the elevator, wondering if he'd really come back.

It took him seven days to return with the information after breaking into William's house, but as it turned out, that was a waste of his time. The hospital already had what they needed by then. Clara had both eyes open when he returned and the electrolarynx in her hand.

"Who's the crazy bitch you hired to kill me?" she asked through a series of struggling breaths.

"I don't know what you're talking about," he lied, looking over his shoulder, as if expecting the police to come in and arrest him. Clara must have read his mind.

"No one knows you put a hit out on me but me, so stop looking for the police. I heard you on the phone. Funny thing about that is it was your voice that woke me up. If that isn't irony, I don't know what the fuck is."

"Clara, I swear—"

"You swear what to who, demon seed? You called the psycho bitch from my room's phone, and I heard your lying ass request a refund. Then the crazy bitch called back, asking to speak to big dog because the phone got hung up in her face. Apparently, her crazy ass got the front desk and asked to be transferred to my room. I told her you weren't here, and she asked if I could take a message for her. She wants you to call her back so you can hear her new plan and who she was going to murder for you instead. She wanted you to know she is sorry that she couldn't kill me and make it look like I died because my lungs failed. To hire a fruit cake like that to kill me, you have to be the dumbest motherfucka I know."

"I'm sorry, baby. I didn't mean to."

"You didn't mean to hire someone to kill me? Then tell me how this rare accident happened."

"I was working at the—"

"Shut the fuck up!" she demanded.

Angelo Sr. rushed over to her bed, fell on his knees, begged her for forgiveness, and tried to explain why he had tried to have it done, but it didn't matter now, because Clara knew she wouldn't be released from the hospital. Death had finally wrapped her in its veil, and she was holding on to her painful life only to speak with Angelo one last time.

"Hush. Save the begging for forgiveness for judgment day, you false prophet. I'm not going to ruin Angelo Jr.'s life more than we already have. Your little secret will die with me, but please get in contact with him and make him come and see me."

"Why should I believe you when you've still been sneaking away to go see William?" The confidence had returned to his voice, and the anger too. He prepared himself for the lie he thought she would tell, but she took another route.

"Sneaking to go see my husband? The man I left you and our son for the first time and the same man who could afford to save my life without stealing from his congregation to do it? You are officially the dumbest motherfucka I know. Tell my son to come and see me before my next call is to the police."

"I'll reach out to him, but I can't promise you he will come."

"Well, you better make sure he does. I'm ready to check into that upper room the old folks used to talk about. I'm fighting until I see him."

"Don't say that. Let's pray."

"You won't be praying over me, Lucifer. And why shouldn't I be truthful? Hell, if I don't die soon, you will kill me, anyway. That crazy bitch did a damn good job of shortening my time, but God said I had something I needed to make right first, and it doesn't have shit to do with you, Azazel." She pressed the button on the side of her bed to put herself in a seated position before she continued. "When I came back, I really hoped things would work out between us. I tried hard to fall in love with you again, Lord knows I did, but it wasn't there. I guess you know that I've been using William for more than money to pay for my hospital treatments?"

He nodded his head, acknowledging that he did know this.

She went on. "Well, I was still in love with him but didn't realize it until after I said, 'I do,' to you. Do you know that nasty muthafucka married our goddaughter? He's walking around Atlanta with Rita's baby girl, as if he wasn't one of the people that used to change her diapers." She laughed and shook her head. "When I found that out, it broke my heart in two. I'm sure you were planning to kill him next, but you don't have to. Once I talk to Angelo and tell him the truth about my past, which he has been working so hard to find out, William will be doing life in jail for Rita's murder."

He shot his eyes up at her and wondered if he should confess to his wrongdoings but decided against it.

"I know William didn't kill her," she said. "There was gasoline leaking from his car, and when I threw my cigarette down, thinking it was water on the ground, the motherfucker blew up. You're the only person that knows the truth about it too. Let that pedophile rot in jail for breaking my heart twice, and don't worry about Junior. Once I'm gone to glory, he won't have to work another day in his life. Now get your ass out of my room, Bishop. Take this as our last goodbye. Like you said, I'm going to rest in peace again."

"I never wanted it to end this way."

"And you never wanted us to *begin* the way we did, either. Now leave, and please get you some pussy besides mine. I took your virginity, but there's a lot better than this worn-out pin cushion I got. You already headed to hell. Might as well get you a good nut first."

Angelo Sr. walked over to her and kissed her lips one last time, and to his surprise, she didn't try to stop him.

***

William got in his car and held his heart. He was sure Meagan had just broken it. He needed to talk to someone, and the only person he wanted to talk to was missing in action. He called the hospital that her driver had told him he dropped her off at.

"Can I be transferred to Clara Jones's room, please?" he said when someone answered.

After a brief delay, the woman on the other end asked him to hold while she transferred him. He let out a sigh of relief and then realized someone was trying to reach him on the other line. He picked up. It was Meagan.

"Is everything okay at the house? I really want to come back home," she said.

"I got the window fixed, but the alarm company won't come out until the morning." Remembering he had Clara possibly waiting on the other line, he put Meagan on hold.

"Hello . . . sir? Are you still there?"

"Yes, I'm here."

"There was no answer in Ms. Jones's room. You may want to try back in the morning. She might be asleep."

William had forgotten that it was close to two in the morning and thanked the lady for her time. He switched back to the call with Meagan.

"Stay the fuck there, like I told you to, until everything is okay at home, understand me?" He knew he needed some time to figure things out and to drive to Savannah to check on Clara in person. Meagan remaining at the hotel would provide just that.

He didn't feel safe at the house, either, and decided to get himself a hotel room for the night, which was a smart move, because Devin was on his tail. He pulled into the hotel, gave the valet his keys, and then vanished through the doors.

***

"I'm going in," Devin said, unbuckling his seat belt.

"Hell nah! They have cameras everywhere. If you're going to do this now, you'll have to play it smart. Let's call it a night. We'll get that bitch in the morning," J. Seed instructed as he followed the valet to see where he had parked William's car before they drove off. He promised Devin they'd be back by six in the morning.

An hour later Devin lay on J. Seed's couch, his mind whirling with thoughts of Meagan. He wondered if she had made it to her hotel safely and if she was okay. He sent her a text but got no answer. He called her number and got her voicemail. He knew he was making a stupid move, but he wanted her to know that everything would be all right. He left a message.

"I know you're mad at me, so you're sending me to voicemail, and I don't blame you. I'm sorry she hit you, and I'm even sorrier that I took you there. I wasn't thinking straight. Tomorrow I'm getting rid of all my problems, starting with your husband. He's standing in our way, and I know after I do it, you might hate me or even tell the police, but I got to do what I feel in my heart. However the shit turns out, just know that a nigga loves you and only you. Good night, baby."

He hung up the phone and got a sick feeling in his stomach. It was the bitch in him from playing Mama to his siblings whenever their mother was too stressed out to handle all seven of them. His intuition was trying to tell him something, and he chose to ignore it, but it wouldn't turn off. It was telling him to get his ass off that couch, head over to Meagan, and have her erase his message, but if this was the way the cards were supposed to play out, then so be it. If he ever believed in anything, it was love, and that was exactly what he had for Meagan. Nothing mattered but her, not even the baby growing in Tesha's stomach, one that carried his DNA. He was sure it was his child. That was why he didn't mind giving her the abortion money after signing his contract and depositing his check.

"What's this for?" Tesha asked as she stared at the stack of money he had placed on her nightstand.

"The money to go handle that tomorrow."

"Handle what?"

"That," he answered and nodded at her stomach.

"Big badass, famous Diablo scared to use his words, but he's supposed to be a rapper. Nigga, please. You fuck me raw almost every fucking day and nut in me like you're saying you hope I get pregnant, and now you stroll up in my place, talking about, 'Handle that.' Handle what, you sissy bitch? Say it if you mean it." She climbed out of bed and stood in his face. "Say it, Devin. What do you want me to do with that money?"

"I want you to cut the rest of my ties to you the right way, so I don't have to pay to have it done the wrong way."

She slapped him.

"Who is this bitch? And don't say there ain't one. You've never talked that shit to me. That new pussy has you tripping. I'm the bitch that split that burger and fries with you because you couldn't afford to feed us. It was me reading you the fucking dictionary because your dumbass struggles with pronunciations but wants to be the biggest rapper alive."

"Why do y'all hoes always do that shit?"

"I ain't no ho."

"Me and a few niggas I know from around the way beg to differ. You want to debate it?"

Her silence gave him his answer, and once it became awkward, she asked, "What am I doing?"

"You throwing shit in my face that you accepted while we were together. You think I've forgotten how you rode for me, because I'm calling it quits with you? Hell nah, I haven't forgotten shit you did with or for me, and I appreciate that shit from my heart, but let's be real. I ain't forgotten about them niggas I caught you with, either, or the lies you told so you could creep with them because my ass was broke and they had a few dollars. Answer this for me. Why is it that now that I have finally made, it means that I'm supposed to stay stuck with you because you were there during the struggle, and when you let my struggle force you to break bad on me at least once a week? I don't owe you shit but that abortion money."

He escorted himself out of her house, and she followed behind, calling him every foul name she could think of. If he had been any other dude from their neighborhood, she would have been slapped for half the shit she said, but he wasn't them, and the truth was, he loved her too. She was second on the list, and first place was becoming available, and he wouldn't let anything or anyone stand in his way of being with Meagan. Tesha had to go, and so did the baby she was carrying.

After he drove off, leaving Tesha standing in the middle of the street, crying, she began blowing his cell phone up. He read a few of her text messages, one in which she confessed to be fucking with a "real man" on the side, and the one where she lied about being pregnant by someone else. But after she threatened to tell the police about all the robberies she knew he had committed over the years with his boy J. Seed, he tossed the cell out of the car window on Interstate 75 heading south. Vowing to crush her soul was what made him walk into her job with Meagan on his arm.

Meagan, that was all he wanted, and after getting signed, he knew she was all he needed. Her husband, the suspicious-ass limo driver, and anyone else who thought they could cause her pain would die by his hands.

He forced himself to fall asleep on J. Seed's couch, at peace with the decision he had made.

Meagan saw her messages and missed calls from Devin, but he was dead to her at the moment. His immature decision-making had gotten her hit in the face. There was nothing he could say right then that would allow her to forgive him for it.

She wanted to go back home and lie in her bed, but William had killed that possibility, and now she was alone in her hotel room. The strawberries had sat out for too long and had gone bad, but both bottles of champagne were still there to keep her company. After drinking a bottle by herself, she called her secretary, Stacey.

"Hello. Are you busy?" she said when Stacey picked up on the fourth ring.

"No. I was sleeping. Is there something wrong, Mrs. Tolliver? It's late, and I don't think you've ever called me outside business hours," her secretary said, turning on her bedside light, feeling slightly irritated by the call.

She hated Meagan. There wasn't a nice way to put it, and she had earned the right to. Meagan made her the fall guy, the one who took the blame for every mistake Meagan made. If she didn't get one of her models a gig, it was Stacey's fault. Royalty checks sent out late? That was Stacey's fault too. And if William beat her ass and sent her to the office with shades on her face, Stacey caught the attitude for his abuse too. However, her employer paid her a very nice salary to be that fall guy, and for that alone, she had reported to work every day for the past five years with a smile on her face. But Meagan calling her house phone at three in the morning was more than a surprise: it was as rare as a confirmed UFO sighting.

"I really apologize for waking you, and you're right. I've never called you outside work or attempted to, but I really need someone to talk to."

"Is it about the agency?"

"No. This is more of a personal call."

"Oh, okay. Then I'm hanging up. Good night," Stacey told her. She ended the call, turned her light off, and left the phone off the cradle so Meagan couldn't call back and wake her up again. She didn't care what Meagan wanted to talk about. If it wasn't job related, she didn't want any part of it. In five years the most personal conversations they had had were thirty-second greetings at the start and the end of the workday.

Stacey wanted to give Meagan the same dry, callous treatment she had dished out at the office, but she couldn't. Stacey's heart was too big, and she had been able to tell on the phone that her boss was drunk. She waited another sixty seconds and then dialed Meagan's cell number. When Meagan picked up, Stacey was the first to speak.

"What is it that you want to talk about? You treat me like shit, blame me for every fucked-up thing that happens at the agency, and now you want to have a girl talk. If your mind is that fucked up to make you think I'd be willing to listen, go ahead. I think this is going to make for a good laugh."

"I'm sorry," Meagan mumbled into the phone.

"What? I couldn't hear you."

"I said I'm sorry. I'm sorry for being a bitch, and you have every right to feel the way that you do, but, honestly, I need you. I don't have anyone else to talk to, because I'm a horrible person who doesn't have any friends."

"You are a horrible, controlling little bitch, but that isn't why you don't have friends. William is the reason you don't. He controls you, and then you come to work and take the shit out on me. Go ahead, drunk and friendless person. I'm all ears."

Meagan wasn't sure if she should continue after hearing the way Stacey felt about her, but a part of her knew she needed to hear it, because it was the truth. She wanted to ask Stacey to refrain from calling her out of her name, but her secretary wasn't on the clock, and it was Meagan who was intruding on her personal time. If Stacey thought she was a bitch, Meagan would have to hear it.

"I don't know what to do, Stacey. Everything looks so perfect from the outside looking in, but it's not, and *I'm* not. I'm married to my godfather, the man who raised me and who also slept with my mother, and a man who thinks it's okay to beat his wife whenever she doesn't say or do as he tells her. I've been with William since I was a little girl, and now that I'm forty, I don't know why I've wasted so many years invested in something that isn't real. His love for me isn't real." Meagan paused to keep the tears from falling, and Stacey took the silence as her turn to take the microphone.

"Well, first of all, your shit doesn't look anywhere near perfect. I don't know who's lying to you, but I'm not going to. He's been beating your ass and fucking up your face, and you say you don't know why you're wasting time staying with him? Let me help you out. You're stuck with him because that's all you know, and that's all you *want* to know. Secondly, don't tell nobody else that perverted-ass nigga is your goddaddy. That shit sounds sick and makes me want to beat his ass for taking advantage of you all those years ago."

Meagan broke out in laughter. She had heard Stacey on the phone with her friends many times and had always admired how she never bit her tongue. From their bad choices in men to their fucked-up hairstyles, if they brought it to her, she dished the truth out, and that was what Meagan wanted right now. She wanted to hear the truth from a woman who she knew cared nothing about her, just like she had heard the same kind of truth minutes before saying, "I do," to William. She thought back on that now.

The vineyard was packed, as expected, given the success William was enjoying from his restaurant chain. Georgia Peach's wasn't the first African American– owned and operated franchise; however, it was the first of its class.

Meagan stared out the window in the bride's suite at the guests piling in to share her special day with her and felt empty. Neither she nor William had family alive to join in their celebration of love. His parents had both passed away before he made it to forty, and being the product of two only children, there weren't any cousins for him to grow up with. It wasn't the same for Meagan, but her mother had burned every bridge she had with her family years before Meagan's birth, and although she knew the exact house her grandparents lived in, they had never made an effort to be in her life, so she didn't waste the invite.

The wedding day was supposed to be one of the happiest days in a woman's life, yet somehow for Meagan, it was making the list of one of the worst. The caterers were late. The pastor was unreachable. There was a quarter-sized stain on her wedding gown, and how it had gotten there, no one seemed to know. Not one of her bridesmaids was a true friend, and it was proven when they excluded her from her own bachelorette party by

*giving her the wrong address and time for the event.
They even went the extra mile of talking about her
behind her back as they dressed in the suite three doors
down from hers.*

*"This is the prettiest and most expensive wedding I've
ever been in and to. Why is it that the people who know
they shouldn't be together are the ones who go all out
of the way for their weddings? This is the type of shit
I want when it's my turn, but I know that bullshit-ass
salary I'm getting won't cover half of this," one of the
bridesmaids said behind the closed door as Meagan
eavesdropped from the hallway.*

*Meagan didn't know any of the six well enough to be
able to recognize their voices. Each was a manager at
one of William's restaurants and had volunteered to
stand in if she needed spot fillers. If it was her choice,
she wouldn't have any bridesmaids, but seeing that
William had close friends, she had felt obligated to find
six fill-ins to complement his single groomsmen.*

*"It's always like that because they know everyone in
attendance knows they ass shouldn't be getting married,
and let's be real, especially not these two. The way
William beats her ass—"*

*"Girl, you ain't never lied," another bridesmaid inter-
rupted. "She fucked up on our order when they came to
Houston, and, baby, when I tell you he took his belt off
and beat her like she was seven, I ain't lying. I was like,
'Damn! What's next? A punishment?' If he had pulled her
pants down and she had on day-of-the-week panties, I
would have fell out."*

The room roared with laughter.

*"The beatings are one thing, but I'm sure all of y'all
know he ain't right in the faithful department, either. He
flirts, and he will go as far as you let him. I've had to let
go a few shift supervisors at his request for some bogus*

reasons, because I found out why he went over my head and gave them bonuses. That fool is crazy to jeopardize all this for some pussy, and neither girl looked better than Melba," Miss Houston said.

"She called that bitch Melba. Her name is Meagan. LOL," said another of the bridesmaids.

"Melba, Meagan . . . Shit, that bitch ain't my friend, but I tell you this. I'd marry his ass in a heartbeat, too, if I was that much younger than him. I heard she was his goddaughter, and he used to molest her. That bitch's life is pathetic. I hope she was smart enough to get insurance on his nasty ass."

Laughter filled the room once more, and Meagan ran back down the hallway with their thank-you cards in hand, to be disposed of after she removed the thousand dollars she had planned to give each one of them. In truth, it was actually payment for them agreeing to pretend they were close and for posing in some pictures. The bitches were well-paid actresses that had no acting experience, and it showed, because they couldn't wait until the wedding was over before they dogged the bride, their temporary friend.

How do you walk down the aisle, knowing everyone is hiding their laughs with fake smiles? *she thought as the door to her room flew open.*

"Are you ready, baby? I want to see you," William said, looking as good as he always did in his tux.

"I thought it was bad luck to see the bride before the wedding?"

"That's a myth, baby. You know that you and I make our own luck." He looked into her eyes and saw signs she had been crying. "What's wrong?"

"It's nothing," she lied.

"It's something. You have tear tracks in your makeup. What's wrong?" He crossed the room and closed the door.

"I'll be okay." She turned to fix whatever flaw he had noticed with her makeup and was met by his hand encircling her neck and closing around it tightly.

"Are you having second thoughts about marrying me, little girl? Because if you think you're going to get out here and embarrass me in front of all those people, you have another thing coming."

"I can't breathe," she said, placing her hands on his.

"Yeah, yo' ass can breathe, or you wouldn't be talking. Now answer me. Are you trying to embarrass me?"

"I c-can't," she managed to say as his grip tightened and he began tugging on her neck, causing her to twitch. *"I can't embarrass you. We are already married."*

"What?"

"I can't embarrass you. We are already married, remember? The courthouse."

William was caught up in the beauty of their wedding day and had forgotten they were already legally married. When they'd gone to file for their marriage license, he and Meagan had just made up from a spat the night before, and he had been able to tell that she was debating leaving him. Out of fear of possibly losing her, he'd turned the trip to the courthouse for their documentation into their legal wedding day by having them married on the spot by the justice of the peace.

The door opened once more. *"You know you're not supposed to be in here, William."*

When Miss Houston's accent carried her words across the room, William slowly released Meagan's neck, and he pushed her out of arm's reach.

"Go on and get out of here. It's bad luck for the groom to see the bride. That's Texas tradition," Miss Houston continued, as if she hadn't seen what was going on.

"I don't want to break tradition," William replied. With his eyes locked on Meagan, he spoke his next words. *"I'll see you shortly at the altar, baby. I love you."*

"I love you too," Meagan *said through tears and a deflated throat.*

When the door was fully closed, Meagan's fill-in bridesmaid rushed over to lock it, then ran to Meagan and hugged her tight. Rocking her, she said, "You're so beautiful, Melba. I don't know why you are putting up with his shit, and it's not none of my business. I'm here only because William said he'd pay me after this. I'm not your friend, and I don't want to be, but look me in my eyes and promise me one thing."

She turned Meagan's face until they were eye to eye. *"Promise me that you won't let death do you part. Don't die by his hands, and don't spend your days locked up because you got tired of the beatings and killed him. Kill his wallet, murder his dreams, and beat him at his own fucked-up game. Take your fifty percent of his empire and make sure your lawyer works on getting a piece of the fifty he has left. There ain't nothing better than having a husband besides having a life insurance policy paid in full upon a husband's death."*

Meagan snapped out of her reminiscing, and when she could no longer laugh at the truth in Stacey's words, the tears began to fall.

"So how do I get unstuck?" she squeaked.

"Do something you've never done. Call the police on his ass and leave. Fuck his prestige and his fame from that good-ass food he's overcharging the city for. I mean, damn, thirty-eight dollars for a plate of oxtails, greens, runny macaroni and cheese, and those extra-buttery potatoes. That shit taste good or whatever, but why don't I get a discount for putting up with your shit for eight hours a day?"

Meagan remained quiet, listening,

"But seriously, you have to make a choice. Do you want to leave or stay? Counseling or a trip to jail? I'll tell you this. If you were my friend, I'd be the one going to jail for trying to whip his sorry ass. A man who puts his hands on a woman is a bitch. There's no debating it. And that's who you are married to, an old, rich, handsome bitch. Leave him alone, file your divorce, get as much of his money as you can, and then come up with your own dreams. He made you model. Then he made you stop. You don't even know what it is you want to be when you grow up, and your ass is a few days away from applying for Social Security. Bitch, that's sad."

"I hear you, but it's not that easy."

"Why isn't it? I mean, do you want to live or die? Because right now, your ass is living dead." Stacey yawned and then said, "There's my fifteen minutes of friendship. Hope it is reflected on my bonus check, or at least the next time you think about talking to me like I ain't shit, you remember this call. Good night." Stacey hung up the phone again and grabbed her cell phone to send a text.

This is my cell-phone number. Never call my house again. And I'm praying for you, because I don't have to like you to love you. Leave his ass.

Back to the bottle Meagan went, and when the next two glasses of champagne were gone, she made another call.

"What are you doing, sexy?" she said into the phone, her drunken state apparent, when someone picked up.

"I'm not doing anything. I was asleep, until you called."

"Then come do me and bring some weed. I want to get fucked up, and then you fuck me. Do you know what I was just thinking about?"

"No. What were you thinking about?" he asked, getting up to check his slim supply of weed.

"I was thinking about us and what you said to me at the nail shop. I think we could work out, and I think you were right. You might be the one for me."

"Is that right?" he asked, knowing she had to be fucked up already.

"Yep, you're a real man, but you do have some childish ways. I'm starting to think all men do, and your head . . . oh, your head is off the chain. Your head alone could make me pack up and leave his ass. I love my pussy eaten, but I want more of that dick. Can I have some more?"

"Yeah, I got you."

"Can I have it all the time? Whenever I want it?"

"Sure," he said, turning the key in the ignition. He had been sleeping in his limo for months and living out of the trunk of his Chevy Impala. He needed to grab himself some clean clothes and take a shower, but his car was parked on the other side of town, at the truck stop.

"Do you want kids, Angelo? I can give you some pretty-ass babies, but we have to start working on them now. I'm getting old, and I already got arthritis. Don't know if it will affect my pussy one day, so we need to put that plan in motion."

"Look, I'm going to go get my car and a cigarillo. I'll be there shortly." He hung up, not wanting to continue with her drunken conversation.

There was one more call Meagan wanted to make, and it didn't require a phone. Actually, she wasn't sure what it required, because she wasn't sure of the location she was making the call to, but she had watched enough movies to get an idea.

"Mama, I don't know if you can hear me in hell or if you can see me in heaven, but I hope you are listening. I have questions that only you can answer for me, and I'm hoping there's a way that you can get those answers to me. I don't know what happened in your life that turned you into the bitch that you were, but why didn't you swallow me? I wish you had. However, I'm here, and I want to know why. It was you who took the time to teach me how to do my own abortions at home using three different methods, all dangerous but fail proof, so why didn't you use one of them when you got pregnant with me? Out of all the abortions you had, I want to know what made you decide to skip it with me?

"You see, I'm forty now, and I don't know why I was given flesh. Look at my life. I didn't have a childhood, I was fucking grown men before I had my first period, and I ended up marrying my godfather. I married a man who used to dog fuck you as you pretended to be his wife's best and only friend. I wonder what would have happened if I had opened my mouth and told Clara that you were in the diner's office that day, fucking her husband. If I had told her crazy, 'two packs of cigarettes a day smoking' ass in that same moment that I was also fucking him. I wonder if she would have dug in that big, ugly purse she carried, pulled out her gun, and done us both a favor by killing us.

"If she had, she would still be alive, because we both know it wasn't that explosion that killed her. It was us. You, *William*, and I—we killed Clara, because we all pretended to love her as we dogged the shit out of her behind her back. I'm not saying she was perfect. Hell no, she was fucked up in the head, like you. But she never crossed the lines, nor did she backstab us. She loved William, and seeing that we both knew that, he should have been off limits. The men she chose had no tie to you or me, but we can't say the same.

"And look at how my life turned out because of it. Ass beatings, no friends, rich, but with no life. I'm William's wife, but she was Clara, a strong woman with a purpose. I'm just here with no purpose, and now I want one.

I want that real thing people call love, too, but I don't know what that is. Let me ask you another question. Why didn't you take one day of those fucked games and lessons you felt were mandatory to teach me what to do in a relationship? I refuse to believe you've never had a real love, because I'm here. There had to be one man that you loved, and in my heart, it was my father. Nothing about you screams that you wanted to be a mother, and even if you decided to have me, why didn't you give me away?

"You made the decision to raise me, and I believe I know why. You couldn't have my daddy the way you wanted him, because he was probably married, with a family of his own. You always preferred to play your ho games on married men, and I believe it backfired on you, didn't it? You found a good man, he fucked you good during one of his weak moments, and when his love for his wife returned, he dropped you. I was your piece of him, wasn't I? You loved and hated me because I was your constant reminder that you didn't cut the mustard, you weren't the best option out there, and you couldn't hold a candle to what he had at home. You loved my daddy, and you would have done anything for him. The same way you were with William . . .

"Wait! Is William my biological father?"

Chapter Twelve

Angelo made it to the hotel in time to prevent Meagan from being put out. She was in the hallway, in her panties and bra, singing, "Giving Him Something He Can Feel," by En Vogue and acting out the video. The front-desk agent was trying to get her to go in her room and stay there, but every time she got her back in the room, Meagan walked right back out, singing another verse.

"If you don't go in your room and sleep it off, ma'am, we're going to have to call the police and have you escorted off the property."

The Asian lady looked beyond frustrated when Angelo walked up, picked Meagan up off her feet, and carried her into the room. Once he got her on the bed, he ran to the door, apologized, and promised they wouldn't hear a word out of her for the rest on the night.

"Did you bring the weed? I need to smoke," she announced, standing on the bed, as if it were a stage.

"Man, sit your drunk ass down! If you want me to roll this weed, you have to chill out some."

"Yes, William's lapdog," she said, flopping down on the bed. "Whatever you say, William Jr." She fell out laughing, as if it was the funniest thing she'd ever heard.

Angelo quickly broke down the weed and rolled the blunt. The NO SMOKING sign on the back of the door caught his attention before he sparked it up.

"What are you waiting for? Fire the reefer up."

"We can't smoke in here," he snapped.

"Oh yes we can."

She got out of the bed and ran into the bathroom. When she came back, she had a soaking wet towel, which she placed under the door. She repeated all the moves Devin had made on their first trip to Gilligan's Island. When she turned the shower on, she realized what she had been doing and became determined to erase the memories of Devin by replacing them with the ones she was about to make with Angelo.

Maybe it was the champagne, but in that moment, she decided that she was done with Young Diablo. It was time to stop playing with young boys and making nursing-home visits with the old man she'd married. Unbeknownst to Angelo, she was about to give him a shot to prove himself worthy of her. If he passed, she'd be all his, to construct a future with. If he failed, she'd take a break from men altogether and focus on herself.

"Let's smoke Mr. Hurley," she said, peeking out the bathroom door.

"Let's smoke so this weed can mellow your ass down," he said, making his way to her. He fired it up and closed the door behind him.

"You know what I like the most about you, Angelo?"

"I don't, but I'm sure you're about to tell me."

"Damn, right," she said after taking the weed into her lungs. "I like how you're not afraid to speak your mind, and you don't give a damn if you hurt my feelings. As long as you're being honest with me, I don't give a damn about you hurting them, either." She passed the blunt back to him and unsnapped her bra. She began twirling her nipples in between her fingers. When he handed her back the blunt, she said, "Suck on them while I smoke. You didn't touch them at all the last time."

He didn't have to think about it as he pulled her into him. He sat down on the rim of the tub, making the

breast-to-mouth distance perfect. He knew she was cumming when her knees shook with each nibble he planted
on her nipples. She passed him back the blunt.

"Stand up. Now it's my turn to suck on you."

He assumed she was talking about his pole as he
pointed it in her face, but she ducked under it and
hummed the song she had been singing in the hallway.
Angelo's meat began to deflate. The whole act felt juvenile, so he stopped her in her tracks.

"Let's wait until we get in the bed, baby. This blunt is
smoking itself," he lied, passing it back to her.

By the time the blunt was too small for either one of
them to hold, she had calmed down a lot. Now they could
play pussy and get fucked. He wrapped his arms around
her from behind, and they penguin walked to the bed
After laying her down like a piece of silk, he put his face
between her thighs and went to work. She moaned softly
and locked her hands on the comforter. When her thighs
clapped against his face like cymbals, he knew she had
gotten off her first one. Kissing her slowly up to her belly
button, he extended his arms until his hands could feel
her nipples and pinched them softly over and over again.

He replaced his hands with his mouth, and he sucked
on one breast, then the next. Seeing that he had drizzled
his spit in between her breasts, he mopped it up with his
damp tongue and continued licking her up the middle
until he reached her chin. He devoured it, as if her
chin were a third breast. Her breathing changed, which
let him know she didn't find having her chin sucked a
turn-on as much as he did, so he stopped and made his
way to her lips. The lip-lock turned into a tongue dance,
and she took the lead. He caressed her face with the palm
of his hand and felt the knot on her forehead.

"He beat you again?" he asked, exasperated.

It was like the imaginary sex music that was playing in her head instantly cut off as he hovered over her body to see the war wound.

"No, William didn't do that. Devin's stripping high school sweetheart decided to reclaim her property."

"So you're telling me that you let a child knot you up, and he didn't do shit about it?"

"It wouldn't have mattered if he'd done something about it or not. When she walked up to our table and questioned him about me, I knew I was done with him."

"You should never have started something with that little boy in the first place." He leaned down and kissed her swollen forehead. "But I see you've learned that the hard way."

Angelo was about to reset the mood he had taken them out of, but just then his phone rang. It was his father calling him. He picked up.

"You never call me at five in the morning. What's the emergency?" he said into the phone as he got out of the bed.

"It's your mother, Junior. She's at St. Joseph's/Candler Hospital in Savannah. She's holding on until she sees you. She says there's something you need to know."

"Don't think I'm going to be able to make that trip, but let me know when I need to come do my job."

"What job, son?"

"Pallbearer."

"I need you to listen to me and hear me clearly, because I don't want to say too much on the phone. Your mother—"

"My mother abandoned me," he interrupted, to finish his father's sentence. "She walked out on us and—"

"And you don't know shit, boy," his father said, interrupting him right back.

Angelo heard the word but didn't believe that it had come out of his father's mouth, and before he could question it, there were more.

"You think you know every fucking thing, but you don't know shit. Yes, that bitch left us, but I loved her, and I love you. Whatever you've been doing in Atlanta, she already knows, and now there's some shit you need to know. Are you going down there to get the fucking truth from the horse's mouth, or are you going to keep letting me lie to you because I'm clergy?"

"No. I'm on my way, Pops. Can you meet me there?"

"Well, son, your mother is upset with me about a few fucked-up things I've done, and we've said our final goodbyes. If you need me to be there with you, I'll meet you there, but she wants to talk to you alone. After the shit I pulled, I have to agree with her."

"Yeah, Pops, I need you up there with me, because I'm not leaving until she's said whatever it is she needs to and she's gone."

"I'm getting up now."

"Okay. I'll see you shortly," Angelo said, about to hit the END button on his phone. But then he heard his father say something.

"And, son . . . ?"

"Yes, sir?"

"I love you. And if I've said or done anything to hurt you, I apologize. I've hidden behind these robes, but they are filthy, son. They are as dirty as your mother's, but she was strong enough never to hide hers."

"You haven't done or said anything to me that I didn't deserve. I love you too, Pops."

"I wish that were true, son. Oh, how I wish that were true."

Angelo quickly ran into the bathroom and jumped in the shower. He let the water hit his face as his salty tears of heartbreak mixed with it. He had had hate in his heart for his mother all his life, and now her life was ending.

You get only one mother, even if she isn't fit to be a mother, he thought to himself and then fell into prayer. After bathing and getting dressed, he walked back into the room to grab his bags so he could leave. Meagan had gotten fully dressed to go with him.

"Let me wash my face and brush my teeth, and I'll be ready to go," she said.

"You can't go with me. I have personal shit I have to handle, but I'll be back. And when I am, all the bullshit you have going on here will have to stop. I'm making you mine." He hadn't decided on moving forward with Meagan until that very moment. She had potential, because she had put a small crack in his heart that permitted her entrance. It was not love, but care and concern. And that was more than any other woman had gotten him to feel. He was tired of the shit William and Devin were putting her through. Although he felt she was allowing it, seeing how immature she was in her drunken state had made him realize that there was a small girl trapped inside of her that hadn't gotten the opportunity to grow up. It was the same child that lived within him, and he knew they could mature together.

"Well, if you're making me yours, then I need to be with you through whatever it is you're going through," she said as she headed into the bathroom, with him following her.

"No, you can't go this time. But once this chapter of my life is closed, I promise I won't stop you from being there for me."

"I'm going with you, Angelo," she snapped.

"No you're not. Now, sit your hardheaded ass down somewhere. I'll see you as soon as I get back."

"Who are you supposed to be? William? You want me to sit back and let you dictate my moves now? You're not William, and I'm done playing Clara." She ended the exchange of words there and began brushing her teeth.

"What did you just say?" He was confused about what his mother had to do with anything she was saying.

She finished brushing her teeth and washed her face before she turned to face him. "I said that you're not William, and I'm done playing Clara."

"Clara who?"

"William's dead wife. Her name was Clara."

Angelo's legs turned into mud, and he fell back onto the toilet. His mother was William's ex-wife, and now everything made sense in a weird way.

"Clara was your mom's best friend?" he asked.

"Yes, she was my godmother too. But I told you, they died in that car accident in Albany."

"Wait. That makes William your godfather, doesn't it?"

Meagan chuckled. "You put that together fast. I guess I can't slide anything past you." She was being sarcastic, but she ended her sarcasm by rolling her eyes. "Yes, he used to be my godfather, but he took advantage of that too. The day both of my mothers died, he was about to divorce Clara to be with me. It probably was a blessing that she died not knowing the truth, because William was sleeping with my mom too. He had all three of us hoping that he'd spend forever with us because he was a good man, but I'm sure I'm the only one he ever beat. My mama was a slut that he wouldn't waste time trying to help, and Clara was firm. When it came to her marriage with William, she ran the show. It took him forever to decide to leave her for me, and in my opinion, the delay came from his fear of her." She laughed and then added, "My godmama didn't take no shit."

Angelo was taken aback by the stomach-cramping information she was giving him. William was more of a dog than he had originally thought. He had been fucking his wife, her best friend, and his goddaughter like he was the man, and Angelo would do anything to show him that he wasn't, including stealing his current wife.

He stood and walked out of the bathroom. Meagan trailed behind him. "Grab your purse. I've changed my mind. You are coming with me. There's something you need to see," he told her.

"Wait, there's something that I need to tell you before we go," Meagan said, taking a seat on the edge of the bed. She instantly felt completely sober at the thought. "My mama told me she had over nine home abortions before she decided to have me and at least four more after me. She never wanted kids. When I asked her why she decided to keep me, she never gave me an answer. She would rub my face and give me a smile, as if she could see my father's face. The only other person I can recall her looking at like that was William."

"So, what are you saying?"

"I don't know what you know, or why you asked the questions about my mama and godmom, but I need to add an unanswered question to that list. Is William my . . . ?"

"Hey!" Angelo yelled to prevent her from asking the question. "This shit is already a daytime soap opera. We will find out, and if that sick shit is true and he knew it all this time, I'm gon' kill him."

William couldn't sleep at all that night. He kept being awakened every hour on the hour by dreams of Meagan's wedding to the younger man he had met in the strip club. He didn't find it weird that she was trying to build a new life with a man who was obviously younger than she was, because that was what he had done with Meagan. What did bother him was the fact that she was ready to end what they had without talking to him and trying to work it out.

He had pushed her to this point—that, he couldn't deny—but he was doing a lot better. Now that he could

see the checkered flag marking the end of their relationship, there was so much that he wished he hadn't done
and even more that he wished he had. Like disclosing to
her that Clara was back.

Clara had threatened to put them both in jail, which
was information he should have shared with Meagan.
Maybe if he had, they could have worked with his lawyer behind Clara's back to find a solution to the problem.
If he had, then maybe, the rips in their bond would have
healed themselves. There had been motive to kill Clara,
but if he had paid a detective, he would have uncovered
the motive she had had to fake her death. *If I had han-
dled the shit differently . . .* , he thought.

Tired of thinking about what he should have done,
could have done, and wishing what he had done, he
checked out of the hotel at four in the morning to wait
on the security company to arrive at the house at seven.
The technician arrived at seven o'clock on the dot and in-
stalled the video-surveillance cameras. He also replaced
the faulty system that they currently had with the latest
and greatest home security on the market.

"That should do you, Mr. Tolliver. I expected to come
down here and see a burnt kitchen in the process of being
remodeled." He laughed. "I guess Mrs. Tolliver made it to
the kitchen in time."

"What? What are you talking about?" William was lost.

"Your fire alarm went off not too long ago, and I had to
call and check if everything was okay. You know we get
fined if we send the fire department out for a false job.
Mrs. Tolliver said she had been cooking and burnt the
food. It was funny to me that a master chef's wife couldn't
cook, but she had an idiot talking to her, so she was probably distracted." He grabbed his work kit and was about
to leave, but William stopped him with more questions.

"She was on a three-way call when you talked to her?"

"No, she had some crazy guy with her. I could hear him talking crazy to her in the background when she put the phone down. You know the guy. You were home while he was here. I heard you say something that sounded a little sexual, so I hung up the phone to give you some privacy. You're like me when it comes to my missus. I want it anytime, anywhere."

William knew the exact day that he was making reference to. It was the day he had walked into a smoky kitchen and got himself a welcome home present.

"The guy in the background, what was he saying that you felt was crazy?"

"Well, I thought he was joking with both of you once I heard your voice, but he said something about killing you and the limo driver. That was all I made out, because their voices had moved away from the phone, and then yours came blaring in."

"You heard someone in my house with my wife, talking about killing me and my driver, and you didn't report it to me or the police? What sense does that make?"

"I would have reported it to the police, Mr. Tolliver, if I had thought it was a serious threat, but I heard your voice. You had to have been there while he was, because this all happened in a matter of minutes and—"

"The potato chips," William said, running to the pantry. He opened the pantry door and looked around the room until he spotted the broom closet. He snatched open the door and thought back to the youngster at the club. He knew he could fit into this closet.

"Greg, are your calls still recorded?"

"Yes, sir. We can't make a call without it being recorded for our insurance purposes," he said, now taking the situation more seriously than he previously had.

"Look, I have to go to Savannah for a day or two, but when I get back, I'll need that recording for the police and my lawyer. You just helped me in ways you'll never understand."

"Glad to be of service. And I hope this here video surveillance helps if there's another break-in."

"I'm no longer feeling like it was a break-in. It's starting to smell like an inside job. You have a good day, and don't forget to get that recording together for me."

William closed and locked the door behind the clueless good ole boy and said aloud, "If Meagan wants out of this marriage, she's free to go, but she won't be taking a dime of mine with her plotting my murder."

He took his phone out of his pocket and called Tommy.

"Meet me at your office now. I have something I need to tell you face-to-face," he told his lawyer.

Part Six

Disrespectfully Ours

Chapter Thirteen

Devin was awakened at five thirty in the morning by J. Seed standing over him, dressed in all black, with a ski mask over his head. He had it rolled up to his forehead, so Devin could see his face.

"Here. Put this on. Are you ready to go handle this business?" J. Seed said.

"Hell yeah, I am," Devin said, taking the matching clothes from him. He got dressed quickly, and they were out the door by 5:40 a.m.

"Listen, I know you're ready to move off your feelings. You're mad, and that's cool or whatever, but we moving smart," J. Seed announced once they were seated in his car. "We can't run up in the hotel. It's full of cameras, and so is the parking lot. We are going to have to stalk the nigga until the right opportunity presents itself."

"Fuck all that. When I see him, I'm shooting."

"Then you need to make this a solo trip. You my brother, but I have sons that need their daddy, and after getting hired as your security, I don't have to get my hands dirty anymore to provide for my young niggas."

"If you don't ride with me, J., and I get popped, there won't be any legit money coming in. You can't do security if I'm doing life in jail. I'll move on your word."

"Smart man."

They drove at a high speed until they reached the hotel, and then J. Seed circled the parking lot twice, but William's car was gone.

"Go by their house," Devin demanded. "I'll catch the nigga slipping there."

J. Seed threw the car in reverse and whipped out of the hotel's parking lot backward. He wanted to tell Devin that maybe he should give it a few days to think it out, but if Devin said the shit had to be done now, he wouldn't question him about it. He drove them straight to Meagan's house, and he passed by as they watched William drive out of the gate.

"Follow that bitch, but don't let him see us."

"I got this, little bruh. Just sit back and ride," J. Seed said, trying to calm down his overly excited homeboy.

They stayed two cars behind William the entire time. The only time they couldn't maintain that distance was when William exited the interstate. He made a left off the ramp, and J. Seed purposely missed the light.

"You should have run that bitch. I don't want to lose him."

"Hey, you need to calm down. If we're going to do this, we got to move smart. We're in Buckhead. We'll catch his ass sitting at the next red light. I told you, I got this."

He was right; they were three cars behind William at the red light on Peachtree. When William signaled to make a right, Devin screamed, "Pull up on the nigga to the left, and I'll pop his ass through the driver's-side window."

"Yeah, and then your ass will be sitting in Fulton County Jail before sundown. They have traffic cameras all over this bitch. It's nothing but money over here. They have to keep watch on the area. We'll follow him until he leaves from over here, and I'll let you know when you can get at him."

Devin was becoming frustrated with J. Seed's extra show of precaution. He had already fucked up by telling Meagan on her answering machine that he was going to kill William. He didn't have to worry about them getting caught, because she was more than likely going to snitch on him, anyway. J. Seed didn't know it, but Devin had sent them on a mission from which they might not return with their freedom. He couldn't tell his boy now, after hearing him mention he had to get back to take care of his sons.

They watched as William pulled into a heavily populated business center and parked. They passed the entrance and hit the block twice before pulling into the parking lot. J. Seed parked at the far end of the lot, but they had a good view of William's car.

"So what do we do now?" Devin asked, feeling antsy.

"We wait until the nigga comes out, and then we follow him to his next destination. He'll fuck up and go somewhere where we can get his ass. These cameras won't be able to keep saving him."

"It ain't the cameras that's saving him," Devin mumbled.

"You're right, but it's the cameras that determine our freedom. I know you don't have kids, but you're acting like you don't even want the bitch anymore. If you're not doing this shit to be with her, why are you doing it?"

There was only one real reason he wanted to kill William now, and that reason was to bring his shit with Meagan to an end. He didn't like how William talked to her in the kitchen like he was ruling shit, or the way she responded after treating him, Devin, like shit, and this was how he had chosen to redeem himself. Meagan was William's little girl, and he was Meagan's little boy, but if he killed the granddaddy in the picture, he'd always be remembered as the man. To be the man that killed William would keep him in Meagan's mind, and that was enough for him, since he knew she'd never let him in her heart. But he couldn't tell his boy that now.

"I'm doing this shit to marry her and help her spend that insurance check. I thought you were in it for a piece? If I marry her, you won't have to rob her, because when I eat, my family eats too. Let's get full, my nigga."

"I like the sound of that shit right there, Diablo. Yo' bitch about to be a widow."

"Wait. Repeat all of that again," Tommy told William as he handed his client a cup of coffee.

"It wasn't Clara who had me shot at. It was Meagan."

"And you know this to be factual because . . ."

"Because Greg from the security-alarm company heard her with a man in my house and they were plotting to murder me. He even has a recording of the conversation."

"Meagan doesn't seem dumb enough to plot a murder in your house or to be recorded doing so. Have you heard the recording?"

"No, I haven't, but last night I went to have a drink at the strip club, and she walked in hand in hand with some young guy. I watched them kiss and everything, and then his real girlfriend punched Meagan in her face."

"Meagan was in a fight at a strip club and was there with a younger man? None of this sounds believable. She's too classy a woman to be fighting in a strip club. I can believe the younger man part, because she doesn't look a day over thirty, but come on. We're talking about your Georgia Peach. She worships you, and if she doesn't, then she stays through all the beatings you give her."

No matter what William said, Tommy was ready with a rebuttal. He had been around Meagan for years, both on and off the clock. When Georgia Peach's became a franchise, she and William went on a seven-day cruise to the Bahamas to celebrate. He knew Meagan, and nothing William was saying sounded like her.

"Well, she was, Tommy, whether you believe it or not. She looked like an ex–hip-hop dancer's side piece from the early nineties. I didn't think she'd ever wear anything like that, but she did, and I'm guessing it was to make her little boyfriend comfortable. After the fight, she left, and I got a chance to talk to the man in the restroom. He hadn't a clue of who I was, but he mentioned our house and called Meagan his wifey. When I questioned their marriage, he said she was in a fucked-up situation that she was working on getting out of. I'm that fucked-up situation." William held back tears as his last words choked him up. "I think she had her little boyfriend break into the house and steal all the records that prove my infidelity with Clara. I'm not certain, but that would make sense."

"Okay, William, if all of that is true, we'll need that recording to turn over to the police. Meagan will be arrested for conspiracy, and she won't get a dime of your money in the divorce, not like she'd have her freedom to spend it, anyway. We have records that it was your money that was used to launch her companies, which, we will say, was a part of her plot to kill you. Financially, you will be fine, but what about emotionally? You're old, my friend. You'll never find another Meagan. Maybe you should start seeking counseling or, in your case, God."

"I'll worry about all of that when I get to Savannah. Clara was admitted to the hospital, and I need to check on her."

"As your lawyer, I have to advise you legally to cut ties with her. She could come up in your divorce, and if Meagan can prove infidelity on your part as her motive, it will make the battle longer. Depending on the jury selected, they might have sympathy for her, which could translate into a reduced sentence for her."

"At this point in my life, Tommy, I don't give a fuck about any of that. If Meagan is smart, she'll say that I raped her and forced her into the marriage, seeing that our relationship started long before she was eighteen."

Tommy's mouth dropped at the news, but William wasn't done spitting out surprises.

"Oh, and before I go, there's one more thing I think it's time for you to know. Clara is my wife, too, and, um, Meagan's godmother, and Meagan believes she is dead. My wife and Meagan's mother were best friends, and I kinda slept with all three of them. Anyway, I thought Clara had died in the accident that killed Meagan's mother, but she came back and proved she hadn't. I do love her, and I want to make things right by her, since she's not dead, but I love Meagan more." He stood up.

Tommy ran around his desk and barricaded the door, preventing William from making his great escape.

"You need to sit your ass back down. You can't drop a bomb on me and call it fireworks, so start talking now. You've played innocent for too damn long. I let you lie to me about the physical abuse you've been subjecting Meagan to, and *now* you tell me of a possible history of sexual abuse?"

"She fucked me. She wanted this dick. So did her mother," he snapped.

"That might be true, but I think a jury would love to look at your rich ass as a rich, sick pervert who took advantage of a child, and since everyone who knows the two of you knows how you like beating on your wife, it makes it real easy to make the case that she's been kidnapped all these years. Hell, you beat her with a belt at a photo shoot for posing with a male model, and then she announced her retirement at the peak of her career. You better start talking, or find yourself a new lawyer."

"She was my goddaughter, Tommy. I didn't see her as anything else. Clara couldn't have kids, and her best friend was having a baby, so we lucked up."

"Stop there. The best friend that you had a sexual relationship with, right?"

"Right."

"When did you start fucking your wife's best friend?'

"I don't know, Tommy. We all grew up together in the church choir. When we got bored, we played these little 'touch and kiss' games, so I'd say the first time I actually poked her was when we were fifteen."

"Fifteen. Are you sure Meagan isn't your child?"

"Tommy."

"Don't *Tommy* me. If it's possible, I have to ask."

"When Rita announced she was pregnant, I asked her about this possibility, and she said no. Meagan isn't my child, man."

William said it, but for the first time in forty years, he felt like Rita could have been lying. He hadn't seen another man in her life back then, but whenever he'd told her he couldn't spend time with her, she had always said she'd go hang out with her other fuck. He hadn't believed her then, either, but she had never sweated him about it. Clara and he hadn't been together yet, and they had barely known each other outside church. She hadn't been the barrier keeping William and Rita apart. It was William's slutty ways that had stood in the way. He had loved pussy, and he had loved it from multiple sources. Not knowing what was real in his life anymore,

William told Tommy everything except the part about Clara threatening him. He needed to leave, and if he told his lawyer he was being blackmailed, Tommy would never let him go.

"Is there anything else you should be telling me, William?"

"No. Okay, yes. I also paid my limo driver to fuck Meagan, to befriend her, and to give me updates on her. He'd make a good witness, if necessary."

"Angelo? You're paying Angelo to sleep with your wife? This shit is a soap opera," Tommy said, hitting his forehead against his desk, as if it would cut off the daytime show.

Once William left the emergency meeting, wishing he had put it off until he made it back to town, he headed to the gas station to fill up for his ride to Savannah, and on the way to get the gas, he noticed that two men were tailing him. He pulled into the yellow gas station, and they swooped into the green gas station that sat directly across the street. With Devin's eyes on him, they both filled up their gas tanks.

The ride to Savannah was spent quietly as Meagan slept off the alcohol she had consumed the night before, at Angelo's request. She didn't wake up until the car cut off in the parking lot of the hospital.

"What are we doing here? And where are we?" she asked wiping the sleep out of her eyes with her hands.

"We're in Savannah. I'm taking you to meet my mother," he answered as they climbed out of the car.

"Your mother? I don't think we are ready to be doing parent introductions. We decided only hours ago that we were going to pursue this."

"If I knew then what I know now, you would've met her," Angelo told her as they walked through the sliding glass doors and entered the lobby. He pointed to the ladies' room. "Now go to the restroom and wash your face. You have dried-up drool on the side of your mouth, and that shit ain't sexy."

Meagan walked into the restroom but bypassed the sink to relieve her bowels. The liquor left in her system didn't mix well with the news that in minutes she would be meeting Angelo's mother. If they were meeting in a hospital, Meagan knew she was sick or, even worse, she had been hurt in some kind of way. The meeting would be awkward, to say the least.

She wiped until the toilet tissue came back clean and then washed her hands and face as she looked at herself in the mirror. Her once slicked-down ponytail was now fuzzy, and she refused to meet his mother looking that way. It was bad enough that she was still wearing the immature clothing Devin had bought her, but she wouldn't make it worse by meeting his mother while looking like something he had brought home from the club. She freed her ponytail from the holder and then washed her hair in the sink. When she cut the water off, someone handed her a stack of napkins with which to dry her face and neck.

"Thank you." Meagan laughed as she took the napkins, feeling slightly embarrassed. Once she had dried her face, she turned to look at the woman standing behind her. She had a psychotic smile on her face and a visitor's tag taped on her all-black sweat suit that read LION.

The woman was so close behind her that Meagan couldn't make a move. "Excuse me," she said, trying to get by her, but the woman kept her feet planted in that spot and looked unmoved by Meagan's words. She continued to display her psychotic smile as she stared at Meagan. "I'm sorry, but I'm trying to get by you," Meagan said, speaking louder this time.

Finally, the lady took a step back, allowing her to pass, and Meagan left her wet curly hair as it was and exited the restroom.

When she walked out, Angelo gave a smile at her new hairdo, and they made their way to the elevator. He grabbed her hand as they exited the elevator, and took a deep breath. The woman at the information desk informed him that his mother was on the second floor, in room 208, and he saw that they were standing near room 206. He thought about asking Meagan to wait in the waiting room until he told his mother what was going on, but with all the lies and secrets floating around, he needed it to be a shock for them both. He and Meagan walked down the hallway and came to a stop at room 208. Angelo opened the door and was met by the sounds of the machines working to keep his mother alive and a closed curtain in front of her bed.

Meagan came to a stop when she heard the sounds that occupied the room, but Angelo tugged at her hand and encouraged her to walk behind the curtain first. When Meagan strode past it, her heart stopped. She threw up the alcohol that remained in her stomach, and tears filled her eyes. Clara's reaction was completely different, as she grabbed her electrolarnyx to curse Meagan out . . . until she saw her son walk in behind her.

"Hey, Mama. I take it that the two of you already know each other," he said, picking up a clean gown that sat next to Clara's bed in order to wipe up the vomit.

"Yes, we do. That's my Georgia Peach and William's wife. What is she doing with you, though?"

"Well . . . ," Angelo started, but not until he could look at Meagan's face. She was crying, but he could still see the shock on her face through her tears. "I brought Meagan with me to see what you thought about her. I'm thinking of stealing her from that bitch William, and something is telling me that you love my idea."

A smile as wide as the Atlantic Ocean spread across Clara's face. "Yes, I love that idea. You're more like me than I thought. You have my blessings, if that's what you came for, and I'm glad you brought her, actually. It's time that both of you knew the truth."

"But . . . you're supposed to be dead. I watched you and my mama die," Meagan protested.

"No, Peach, you saw your mother's murder. Get her a chair, Junior. She'll need to sit down for this."

"What happened to your dementia?" he asked, laughing, as he cleared the area to make room for the chair.

"I guess it stopped, like you must have stopped working for William, if you're stealing his wife," Clara countered.

"Touché," Angelo said as he grabbed Meagan a chair.

Clara began telling them the story she had made up in her head. "William had filed for divorce, but he didn't have the balls to go through with it. Instead of divorcing me and watching me take half of everything he had, he took the coward's way out and decided to kill me. He was always a bitch to me, but I didn't think the bitch was that scared of me that he'd find it easier to kill me than to get me to sign some papers that would call it quits." She looked at Meagan. "Do you remember when he left, lying about going to get gas for his car?" she asked.

Meagan nodded. "He spent the entire day talking about his car. First, it was his tire and then gas. I've always thought about it."

"Well, I found it to be strange that it would take him so long to return with some, seeing that there was a gas station less than three miles up the road. So I stepped outside to smoke and caught him covering the car with gasoline. I ran back inside to tell your mother. She had said she was going to the restroom to find out what was going on with you, but when I got back to our table, she had taken the keys off of it and left. I went back outside to find her, and she was already sitting in the driver's seat of William's car and was about to turn the key in the ignition. When she cranked the car, it blew up, and I watched William jump back into my car and drive off."

"So he knew you weren't in the car?" Angelo asked.

"No, son. I wondered about that at first too. You see, Rita and I stuck together like Siamese twins, so if she cranked up that car, that meant we both were in it. Whatever was said between Meagan and her mother must have upset Rita, because she tried to drive off and leave me."

Clara continued to tell her story, mentioning her stay in Savannah and her being diagnosed with cancer. "When I came back for help, he almost shit his pants to see me alive. Before I could blackmail him to pay for my treatment costs, he volunteered to help so I wouldn't tell what he had done to us."

"He killed my mother, Clara. You should have told on him," Meagan said through sobs.

"You're right, but at the time I needed his help, and I was still hurt that the two of them had been having sex behind my back and the two of you."

"So, you knew about him and my mother too?" Meagan asked, not wanting the spotlight shone on her own wrong-doing.

"Hold the fuck up! This nigga was fucking all three of y'all, and all of y'all knew it, and nobody decided to do or say shit to him about it? That's why he thought it was okay to ask me to ho for him. The nigga felt like a pimp," Angelo cut in.

"When did he ask you to ho for him?" Meagan asked, but Clara started talking again, and Angelo apologized for interrupting her.

"To answer your question, Georgia Peach, no, I didn't know about him and your mom at first. I was in denial, but the truth came to light. I knew your mother was a ho . . . ," she said, then waited for Meagan to become offended at her show of disrespect for her mother. When Clara saw that she hadn't offended Meagan, she continued, "But I never thought she'd backstab me like she had done. Anyway, I came up with another plan, and, Junior, this is why I asked you to come."

Angelo walked closer to his mother's bed and grabbed her wrinkled hand softly so he wouldn't disturb the IV she had in it.

"I not only had William pay for my treatments, but I also made him buy me property as compensation for what he had done to me."

"The condos," he said.

"Not only the condos, but a few other properties, too, and there is also a bank account with close to a million dollars in it from the income I generated from the properties. All of them are yours. Your aunt Camille has everything in her name and will sign it over to you once I'm gone. I'm sorry I wasn't there for you when you were little, and when you contacted me when you were all grown up and handsome like your father. William was out to kill me, and I couldn't bring harm to you," she lied.

"It's okay. The shit has been hard on me, but I love you, anyway. But that nigga William has to die," Angelo said with determination in his voice.

"Oh no, we're not letting him off that easy, nor will I allow him to consume your freedom like he has done mine. When I die and the coroner gets ahold of my body, they will discover who I really am, so I wrote a letter telling all of this in it. Your aunt has a copy of the letter too. You need to meet with her to get it before my body turns cold, and then you need to take it to the police station. All I want you to do for me is to make sure he dies in jail. That way me and Rita's souls can rest in peace." She turned her attention back to a weeping Meagan.

"Georgia Peach, I'm sorry he took advantage of you, and even sorrier that I let your nothing-ass mother bring you into our deadly childhood game, but you will benefit from all of this. With him being sentenced to murder, you'll get everything that bastard has, so get your affairs in order. I know you love him, but he wasn't just disrespectfully yours. He was all of ours. Rita is dead because of him, and I was forced to spend my life in hiding. Don't let him do it to you too. You grew up to be more beautiful than I ever imagined, and I know my son will do right by you. I wouldn't want either of you with anyone else."

Clara squeezed Angelo's hand with the little strength she had left. "So, Junior, is this the information you wanted to know? I know you took the job working for William to find out about me."

Too embarrassed to answer, he nodded his head before asking, "What's up with you and Pops? He said you're mad at him right now."

"Married life, son, and if you and my Peach exchange those vows, you'll understand exactly what I mean."

Angelo Sr. was standing by the door, listening. He had been waiting in the waiting room when his son and the young woman he had never seen before went walking by. And then he had stationed himself by Clara's door, His only reason for listening was to see if Clara would keep her word and not tell their son about his attempt on her life. Once he was sure she wouldn't, he made his way to the elevator. He decided to let Angelo live his life, and if Angelo wanted him to be a part of it, he'd have to come to Albany to see him.

"Clara, why didn't I know about your son?" Meagan asked.

"Nobody knew I had a child by the pastor's son but his father, my father, and the father. The rumor spread that the pastor found a baby on the church's step and that his son got a word from God telling him to raise him. Your mother thought I was working a married man out of some money by going to the hospital. She didn't bother to visit or check in on me. I never told a soul, nor did his father, until the day he introduced me to our son."

"And what about my father? I know my mom grew up with you and William, but the two of you didn't really know each other until you were grown. Is it possible that William is my father?" Meagan asked.

Clara didn't answer, because the truth was, she didn't know. She had given birth to Angelo and had been keeping her distance from the world. She hadn't been dating William at the time, and he and Rita had been known as best friends. They could have been fucking, but why would Rita have introduced them and gassed them up so they would date if she had had William in her pocket? Clara's heartbeat sped up at the thought, and she wanted William dead in that moment. She answered Meagan the best way she could.

"When you're tracing the steps of hoes, the footprints will cross over one another, but in my heart, I believe William is not your daddy. He's your goddaddy only. He loved you in a different way back then, and he would have killed anyone that put a hand on you. That's the only relationship I want to remember the two of you having. He isn't your husband. My son is. That's the way it would have been if we, the parents in your life, had loved you right. Y'all were destined for this. It's your birthright."

When Clara was done talking to the new couple that stood before her, she closed her eyes, having finally made peace with her son. Less than five minutes later, with Angelo and Meagan watching, she flatlined, and the doctors and nurses weren't able to revive her. God must have forgiven her, because she died peacefully in her sleep.

Chapter Fourteen

Angelo stayed with his mother's body until they moved her to the morgue. He tried to call his father, but he wasn't answering his phone. His mother had given him directions to follow and the information he needed to contact the auntie he hadn't known he had. After meeting up with Meagan in the waiting room and picking up the possessions his mother had on her person when she was admitted to the hospital, which was about three thousand dollars' worth of blank money orders and the normal junk women carried in their pocketbooks, they got off the elevator on the first floor, only to walk into a crime scene.

Two security guards had tackled the woman who had helped Meagan in the bathroom, and they were putting plastic wrist restraints on her as she lay on the floor. Not more than fifty feet away from the huddle was a body lying facedown in a puddle of blood. A doctor kneeled over the body, shaking his head. When Angelo saw the overalls on the dead body, he instantly knew that it belonged to his father.

He pushed the doctor out of the way and turned his father over on his back. There was a hole in his head and chest. Anger surged through as he ran over to the killer and struck her in the face with his left and then right fist. He was quickly restrained.

"Why?" he yelled, tears and snot covering his face.

"The dog chased the cat, so the cat hired a lion," she said over and over again.

"What in the fuck are you talking about, crazy bitch?"

"Bishop said to kill Clara because she was already dying, but Clara was smart and had more money, so I killed Bishop instead," she said and then began roaring like a lion. Using her mouth, she went into her shirt pocket and pulled out a check for twenty thousand dollars, written by Clara. "I visited the cat to kill her, but she was nice and talked to me like a lion. She said she'd give me more than he gave me, so I killed him. The lion killed the dog." She roared again and then mixed dog barks and roars.

The police arrived and locked down the scene. They questioned Angelo for thirty minutes or so and then told him that he was free to go.

The three-hour ride from Atlanta to Savannah seemed longer this time to William, because he spent his time thinking about Meagan. He didn't want what they had to end like this, and he had decided he would sit her down, tell her everything, including that Clara still was alive, and see where they would go from there. He was sure his lawyer would advise him not to do it, but it was his life, and he was too old to play games with it.

He pulled up to the front of the hospital, and police cars were everywhere. One of the officers stopped the car in front of his, and seconds later the driver made a U-turn and drove back out of the hospital's parking lot. As William pulled up, the officer flagged him down and walked over to his window.

"Is it a life-or-death emergency?" the officer asked him.

"No. I'm here to visit a patient."

"Sir, the hospital is on lockdown at the moment. You will have to come back in an hour. We should be done by then."

"Hey, man, listen. I drove down here from Atlanta. I don't know anything about Savannah. Can I just park at the rear of the building and wait in my car until you all clear out?" William begged.

The officer inhaled deeply and shook his head. "Go ahead and park on the side of the building, by the emergency entrance. Do not exit your car for any reason until you get the clearance to."

William nodded his head in understanding and made a U-turn. He rode past J. Seed and Devin, who had been in line behind him, without looking their way. He parked and sat in his car, listening to Meagan's Teena Marie greatest hits album. Before long he began singing along with each track, like Meagan normally did. The singer's words were infectious, and the song "Déjà Vu" hit close to home. He had been there before and was circling back to that place where love would end and a fresh start would begin, but he didn't want it. If he couldn't mend what he and Meagan had, he'd focus on his health and his business.

Starting over with anyone this late in his life would be a waste of time, but what hurt him the most was the notion that once he was gone, so was his bloodline. He didn't have any children with Meagan by choice, and now that he had time to reflect on his decisions, he regretted not starting a family with her. If Meagan decided to pursue the younger man, he had no choice but to put her in jail, and that meant that everything he had worked for in his life would die with him, given that he had no one to leave it to.

A single tear rolled down his face—but there wouldn't be another that he'd let fall from his eyes—as he watched Meagan walk out through the emergency-room exit alone. If he found out that she had been in cahoots with Clara this entire time, he'd kill them both.

***

J. Seed didn't roll down his window, as they had watched William do. Instead, he made a U-turn and drove out of the parking lot before the officer could reach them.

"Where are you going now?" Devin asked, at the peak of his frustration.

"Do you see all the police cars? I'm not about to stay here. Let's grab something to eat and then come back. It's too hot up here."

"What if he leaves? We don't know shit about Savannah. How are we going to find him?"

"If he leaves before we get back, we'll just have to try to catch his ass back in Atlanta."

Devin squinted. "Catch him back in Atlanta?"

"Yeah, remember we have to play this shit smart. Look at where he went. What business does this nigga have at a hospital in Savannah?"

"I don't know, and I don't care. I want the nigga dead. I don't need to know what he came out here for."

Devin hadn't followed William this long to wait until they got back to Atlanta, and when they passed the side of the hospital as they drove along the street, he glanced over and happened to see William with his hands on Meagan and acting aggressively. Instinctively, he jumped out of the moving car and ran in their direction, gun in hand.

"Let me go, murderer!" Meagan yelled, hoping that Angelo or the detective he was talking to would hear her and come running.

"Murderer? What in the hell are you talking about? The only murderer I know is you," he countered. "You thought Greg from the security-alarm company wouldn't tell me about that nigga you had in the kitchen? Yeah, I know all about y'all planning to kill me and Angelo, so y'all could be together."

"That's not what happened. And, anyway, Devin was just talking. But—"

"Oh, is that the name of the little boy that got your ass whupped at the strip club last night? Devin?"

Meagan's jaw dropped as he supplied information that he shouldn't know anything about. "You know what, William? None of that matters anymore, because your wife, Clara—or should I say your dead wife, Clara?—told me how you killed my mother and tried to kill her before she died for a second time. I won't give you the opportunity to kill me too."

They swapped facial expressions, and William was now the one left with his mouth open, in shock.

"Yes, I know everything, asshole, and we're over. Once you're in jail for life, I hope the thought of me being married to Clara's son, Angelo, makes your days in there harder."

She turned her back to him and headed back inside to get Angelo, but William snatched her up by her dangling hair.

"Angelo is Clara's son, huh? That makes sense," he said, nodding his head. "You're so smart, but your ass is stupid. You can't see the setup? Clara and Angelo were playing us both."

"Let me go!" she yelled. "You're the only muthafucka that's playing me."

Angelo and the detective had finally heard Meagan's yells and ran out the door. When the detective saw what looked like a domestic dispute taking place, he pulled out his Nextel device and sent a chirp that would be heard by all the uniformed officers throughout the hospital. Before Angelo could yell for William to let her go, a figure dressed in all black came running through the parked cars, as if they were a maze.

"Meagan, watch out!" Angelo yelled, and she and William both scanned the parking lot and caught sight of the masked figure running toward them.

William let her go. Meagan, thankful that she was wearing Jordans, took off running toward Angelo and the detective, while William took off running through the parked cars when he realized the masked man was coming his way. Two shots were fired at William, but both missed him. The detective pulled out his gun and let off two shots at the masked figure, but he missed the moving target.

Meagan was now in the safety of Angelo's arms as a group of police officers made their way through the emergency room's exit doors. Two officers pulled Angelo and Meagan to safety, and the rest went flying across the parking lot, giving the masked man chase.

"Damn, Devin. Damn," J. Seed muttered aloud. He didn't know what to do as he watched his hardheaded little brother hit the ground running after his target.

Cops began to appear, and with all the attention on Devin, J. Seed realized he could hit the highway back to Atlanta without being seen. He had kids, and the intention of proposing to their mother on his next big payday. He had promised his makeshift family that he was done with the dumb stuff, and that from that moment on, he'd put them first. He was done robbing mama-and-pop stores and niggas he felt were slipping. He'd be the man that his family needed. But how? How could he be in this moment with Devin and not do shit but run? He had made a promise always to be his brother's keeper, although they were strangers by blood. But Devin *was* his little brother, and that was written in his heart, especially after losing his big brother, Calvin, the way he had.

J. Seed's palms were clammy like cocoa butter on dirty hands. His heart beat harder than normal, but under

these conditions, it would have been charted as stable..
Death was certain, he was sure of it. Life in jail wasn't an
option, and dying under another man's control by lethal
injection or the electric chair didn't make the list of ways
he wanted to go out, either. If death was going to lie on
his chest like his bitch, it was going to be God's way or his.
Those were the only acceptable methods by which to die.

Clutching the steering wheel tighter, hoping his firm
grip would be the action that would ultimately save his
life, he desired to live. At this current moment, in the
space between life and death, incarceration and freedom,
he began to value life fully. The reality of it should have
made him vomit, and he would have vomited if the urge
to shit wasn't controlling the contents of his stomach.
The fried bologna on nearly moldy bread that he had
smothered in leftover mayonnaise from little packets
he found in the back of his utensil drawer hadn't been a
good idea. It became edible only when he realized it was
his last day eating scraps for the entirety of his being.
It was his farewell to the bottom, and he had hurriedly
swallowed it in two greedy bites. Punishment for his
greed was the meal flipping around his stomach as he
pressed on the gas pedal and flew through red lights. The
task was done now, and all he had to do was get away
with the shit.

"Here I come, D," he yelled. Then he said softly, "I'm on
my way, Calvin. See you soon."

He hit the gas and ran over the detective who was hot
on Devin's tail. Once he was sure he had turned the man
into roadkill, he jumped out of the car and shot at the
group of police who were headed their way. He wanted
to put a bullet in one of them before the series of bullets
pierced through his body from the neck down, but he
didn't get the chance. J. Seed hit the ground, dead.

Devin ducked between the cars, taking a different direction to catch up to William. He heard the bullets sound off behind him. Some headed toward him, and the others headed at his boy, who had taken out the detective who was closing in on him. From the sound of the new civil war that was taking place around him, he had just lost his brother. The thought made his chest tighten as he rolled over the back of a Lincoln to dodge the shots headed his way, but he'd known there might be casualties even before they arrived in Savannah. He refused to be killed before he got his prey.

It must have been meant to be, because two cars ahead of Devin, William came darting out from behind a car. Devin let off the rest of the rounds in his gun. It didn't matter that out of four bullets he sent toward William, only one hit him, because Devin had met his goal. The bullet went diagonally through the back of William's neck and came out his right eye. William was dead. Devin quickly dropped the gun and threw his hands up in the air before the approaching police officers could kill him next.

He was tackled to the ground, and the ski mask he was wearing was snatched off his head. With handcuffs on his wrists, he was brought back to the emergency entrance and thrown in the back of a squad car, but not before passing J. Seed's dead body. Devin wanted to run over to him, scoop him up in his arms, and cry, but something about pulling the trigger and killing William had made him numb to everything. His mission was accomplished.

One of Devin's arresting officers took a picture of him with his cell phone as Devin sat in the backseat of the police car, and then brought it over to Meagan and Angelo.

"Do either of you know this man?" the officer asked.

"Yes. His name is Devin," Meagan said, speaking up when Angelo didn't. She couldn't tell what he was thinking. But with all the death that had hit him directly and indirectly, she was sure that he was feeling a combination of anger and pain.

"I'll need both of you to stay here for a moment. Then you'll be brought in for questioning and a written statement."

Angelo pulled out his phone, retrieved the telephone number his mother had given him, and called his aunt.

Meagan's mind couldn't comprehend the conversation he was having, because she couldn't take her eyes off Devin. The longer she stared at him, the more she could tell he was losing his soul. He never looked at her; nor did he seem sad about the turn of events. He just sat there, unbothered, like she was invisible. She broke down in tears.

William was dead. Clara was dead. J. Seed was dead. And even though she had never met him and knew nothing about him, Angelo's father was dead too. All the lies of the past had resurfaced, and she was left to cope with the traumatic effects on her mental health that the terrifying events had produced.

When the crime-scene investigators arrived, she and Angelo were taken down to the police station and placed into two separate rooms. Before the detectives could say a word to her, she asked for her lawyer. They let her call Tommy back in Atlanta, and he promised that he was on his way. She sat in the room for close to four hours before the detectives returned with him.

"Mrs. Tolliver, I'll advise you which questions of theirs to answer. Otherwise I urge you to stay silent," Tommy said as he took a seat next to her.

The detectives introduced themselves. She had already met Detective Hollenback at the crime scene, but this was her first interaction with Detective George. Judging by the scrunched-up facial expression she wore, she was a pissed-off black woman who was in need of a good fuck.

Detective Hollenback started their questioning session by showing Meagan crime-scene photos. He asked her to identify all the individuals she could. They started with a picture of Angelo Sr.

"Can you identify this man?"

She looked at Tommy, who nodded for her to speak.

"No, I cannot. I was told by Angelo, my limo driver, that he was his father. The first time I saw him was when we exited the hospital's elevator, and he was dead," she said and then waited for the detectives to move on. Next, they showed her a picture of Patrice.

"What about her?" the female detective asked, speaking up for the first time since she had entered the room.

"No, I cannot identify her. I saw her in the restroom when we first arrived at the hospital this morning. I was washing my hair, and she handed me a stack of napkins to dry it with. The next time I saw her, she was being held down after killing Angelo's father."

"Did you see her murder him?" Detective Hollenback questioned.

"No. As I said before, he was already dead when we got off the elevator."

Detective George went through the photos again and laid J. Seed's picture in front of her. "How about this man?"

"I've met him twice. He was Devin's friend. The only thing I know about him was that they called him J. Seed from College Park."

"I'm glad that you mentioned Devin Montgomery. At the crime scene, you told my partner here," she said, making reference to Detective Hollenback, "that you knew him. How?"

Meagan looked at Tommy, knowing that once she answered the question, all the respect he had for her would instantly dissolve.

"Devin . . . Devin is my ex-lover. We had a sexual relationship that lasted a little over eight months."

"Is that why he killed your husband, William?" Detective George asked, placing a picture of William's dead body in front of her.

That was the first time Tommy had been told that William was dead, and the news sent him to his feet.

"I'm sorry, but I wasn't informed that Mr. Tolliver is dead until now. I need to speak with you both in private." Tommy didn't wait for the detectives to walk out of the room. He was standing in the hallway before they could get out of their chairs.

Tommy disclosed to the detectives the conversation he had had with William hours earlier, and provided them the telephone number for the security company so that they could hear the recording themselves.

Meagan wondered what was going on outside the door to the room, and worry struck her when she realized that they had been gone for more than an hour. When the door opened, Detective George walked back in by herself.

"Due to a conflict of interest, Mr. Hunt has declined to take you on as a client. I can take a written statement from you now. Or perhaps you would like to take some time and get a lawyer?"

Meagan didn't understand why Tommy was refusing to be her lawyer, but she assumed the death of his close friend was the cause of it. She stood up. "No. I prefer to give a statement once I have a lawyer."

"Whatever you feel is best," Detective George said as the door opened and a uniformed cop walked in. "Meagan Tolliver, you are under arrest for conspiracy and solicitation of murder—"

Meagan cut off the detective. "What? I didn't hire Devin to kill William. He did it—"

"I gave you the opportunity to give a statement on your behalf, and you refused," the detective said, talking over her. "You will have the opportunity to tell your side of it in court, and you will be judged by a jury of your peers. Please take Mrs. Tolliver away."

Through teary eyes, Meagan devoured the beauty of the scenery on her way to getting booked. She knew it would be months, maybe even years, before she'd see the beauty of freedom again.

Part Seven

Disrespectfully Yours

Epilogue

"Today marks the two-year anniversary of the case that is known throughout the world as Disrespectfully Yours, and it is also the day that Devin Montgomery will be sentenced for his hand in a murderous, almost three-decades-long bloodbath in southern Georgia. If you haven't been following the case, it started back in the fall of nineteen ninety with what was ruled at the time as the accidental deaths of Rita Glover and Clara Tolliver." A photo of Rita was displayed for TV viewers before one of Clara was shown.

The crime reporter continued. "The two women were reported to have died in a car explosion, which the detectives determined was caused by a gasoline leak, but two decades later the world would learn differently. Although Ms. Glover was killed in the explosion, Mrs. Tolliver did not perish. She fled to Savannah once she realized that an attempt had been made on both of their lives by her husband at the time, William Tolliver, who was known for his famous soul-food restaurant chain, Georgia Peach's." A picture of William standing outside his California restaurant was shown.

"Mr. Tolliver wanted his wife dead so he could pursue a relationship with Meagan Tolliver, Rita Glover's minor daughter at the time, whom you may remember from her modeling days. Here is a picture of her from her layout in *Kings Magazine* in two thousand five. It took twenty-one years of marriage between William and Meagan Tolliver before Clara would return to tell what really happened on the day she fled for her life. Dying of cancer, she wrote out her confession in what investigators are calling a bestselling nonfiction novel, if it ever was published, giving details as to what led William to soak the car's engine in gasoline before setting the vehicle on fire.

"But this nonfictional tale doesn't end there, as Clara's return marked the beginning of a new string of murders. Her new husband, although there aren't any legal documents to verify their marriage, Bishop Angelo Hurley, who Clara secretly birthed a child with in her late teens and gave away at birth, had his own murderous intentions in mind. He hired a hit man to murder his wife so he would no longer have to struggle to pay for her cancer treatments. The contracted murder attempt failed, but not before Clara found out about the attempt. She prevented her own murder by writing a check to the hit man for twenty thousand dollars to kill Bishop Angelo Hurley instead, which the hit man did successfully. On the same day that Bishop Hurley was murdered on the first floor of St. Joseph's/Candler Hospital here in Savannah, Georgia, Clara Tolliver lost her battle to cancer, but not before disclosing the truths of her past dealings with William to his new wife and her goddaughter, Meagan." The reporter paused for effect.

"But not-so-innocent forty-year-old Meagan Tolliver had secrets of her own, as she had been engaged in an eight-month sexual relationship with twenty-five-year-old Devin Montgomery," the reporter revealed. Devin's mug shot was displayed. "Devin was on his way to stardom, as his first rap single hit the charts with a bullet, but his jealousy and frustration from being a boy toy got the best of him and turned him into a cold-blooded killer. With detectives and police officers covering the floors of the hospital after Bishop Hurley's murder, the rap star had his close friend, thirty-year-old Jason Seed, distract the police with a shoot-out, one that cost him his life, as Devin chased William Tolliver down with a gun and killed him in the hospital's parking lot."

The reporter took a second to take a breath and shake her head. "I know it sounds like I'm reading a movie script, since this story seems too unreal to be true. But all the events are factual, and William knew they would unfold. He had contacted his lawyer before making the trip from Atlanta to Savannah. He had provided his lawyer with information hours before his death that pointed a finger at Meagan as a conspirator to his murder. But after months of incarceration, the subpoenaing of phone records and voice messages, and Devin Montgomery testifying that she had no involvement in the murder, the conspiracy charges were dropped. She was later sentenced to seven years of supervised probation for not reporting the conspiracy to murder her husband. The jury felt that although she was not involved, the recording the security company had of Mr. Montgomery saying he would commit the crime against her husband and limo driver Angelo Jr., the son Clara had given away, proved she had reason to believe her husband was in danger and chose to do nothing to stop the tragedy that would follow." The camera then panned around the outside the courthouse.

"As you can see, we and other media sources were not permitted entrance to the courtroom for Mr. Montgomery's sentencing. He was found guilty of first-degree murder for killing William Tolliver, and under the felony murder rule, he was found guilty in the murder of Detective Mark Thomas, the detective who was run over by Mr. Montgomery's accomplice, Jason Seed. We will report Mr. Montgomery's sentence as soon as it comes in. We know the question on everyone's mind is: Will all the lies and murders cause Mr. Montgomery to die by lethal injection? We'll have the answer to that for you soon. I'm Samantha Whiterspoon, reporting live from outside the criminal courts building. Now back to Kim Miles in the studio."

Kim Miles of Crime TV had a few questions of her own. "Samantha, as you mentioned earlier, we here at Crime TV have been following this case for the past two years, and we've heard rumors about a paternity test being included in this case. Do you know anything about it?"

"Well, there were actually a few paternity tests surrounding the case, but they have nothing to do with the crime or the sentencing itself. The most buzzworthy of the three tests in the case was the one done on William Tolliver to determine if he was not only Meagan Tolliver's husband and godfather but indeed her biological father as well. The world held its breath for those results and didn't release it until it was confirmed that he was not her father. I'm sure waiting for those results to come in kept Mrs. Tolliver on the edge of her seat.

"Kim, there was another test done on a stripper that attacked Meagan Tolliver, because of her relationship with Devin Montgomery, but that, too came back stating that he wasn't the father. But if you recall, Kim, we showed footage of a five months' pregnant Meagan Tolliver being released from jail months back. We were privileged to interview Mr. Montgomery after he was found guilty, and he wasn't at liberty to speak on the murders until sentencing, but he did inform us that he underwent DNA testing with a few other men to determine who fathered Meagan Tolliver's child . . ."

Meagan turned the television off because she couldn't take any more. Devin's trial and all the media coverage had prevented her, her now one-year-old son, Denali, and Angelo from moving on with their lives. Once she had been acquitted of her conspiracy to murder charge, she had received what was rightfully hers from William and had quickly sold everything she could, including Georgia Peach's. Then she had packed up and moved back to Albany, Georgia, with Angelo.

The months she spent in jail had been easy on her, seeing that they'd been spent mostly in the infirmary. There hadn't been any problems with her pregnancy, but due to her age and her mini bout with post-traumatic stress, her doctors had felt she was at a high risk for a miscarriage and other complications. Surprisingly, treatment for her PTSD had started in the holding tank the first day she was arrested. She thought back on that day.

"So what did you do, pretty girl? You don't look like the jail type," the stud said as she twirled a lock of Meagan's hair. They had been sitting in the holding tank together for close to an hour, both adjusting to their new loss of freedom.

"I really don't know. One moment I'm visiting my dying godmother, and the next I'm a witness to murder and then headed to jail for witnessing it. I really don't know." She paused. *"But can you please stop touching my hair?" she demanded, finally noticing her surroundings.*

Meagan was zoned out. Nothing about her arrest felt real. Honestly, nothing felt real once she left Atlanta. All those years of thinking her mama and Clara were dead, to find out one of them wasn't and that she was catching feelings for her godmother's son Meagan didn't know she had birthed. Pain, that was all she felt, and it was all that she was left with. Everyone she was close to was dead or in jail, and she felt like she was the cause of it.

Her mother would still be alive if William hadn't called that meeting so many years ago. Clara wouldn't have had to hide if William hadn't fallen in love with Meagan and decided to end his marriage. The truth that bothered her the most was, none of this would have ever happened if she hadn't flirted with William the night of her prom. Being hot in the ass was what had caused her grief since that day. There wasn't anything good that had come out of her union with William. He had been beating her ass before he said his vows and had never stopped.

"I don't know why I'm here, either," the stud revealed. "My bitch hit me and called the cops, saying I hit her, when she knows she's the only one doing the fighting in our relationship. I told myself to leave her alone a long time ago. Fight, fight, fight. That's all her ass ever does, and guess who ends up in jail? Man, look at my face."

"Oh my God. Did they arrest her too?" Meagan was instantly thrown out of her rumination by the word *fight*. Looking at the scratches that covered her cellmate's face caused her to jump. The skin from her hairline to her chin on the left side of her face was scratched up. "It's clear she hit you."

Her cellmate shook her head and said, "In a perfect world with a fair system, she'd be sitting somewhere in the building with us, but this shit is too fucked up for that to be facts. Her ass probably at home, wondering why I haven't called her yet."

"What?"

"You know, she's one of those insecure types. If I'm not with her, I'm somewhere fucking off on her."

"You must have got caught cheating before."

"Once. I got caught cheating once, and she has held it over my head for two damn years."

"And you think she's wrong for that?" Meagan's guilt had surfaced.

"Hell yeah, if she decided to stay in the relationship with me. If you're unhappy in the relationship you're in and you decide to stay or do nothing about it, who can you be mad at but yourself? Deciding to stay means deciding to forgive, and if you thought you could and can't, then you don't owe your time to explaining shit to nobody. If my girl couldn't handle what I did, she should have left."

"I hope you don't think it's always that easy to pack up and leave. I was in a relationship where he beat me if I thought about it."

"Did you have a job?"

"Yes, of course," Meagan answered.

"Did he work with you?"

"No, he was living his own dreams."

"So he didn't work with you, and you decided to come home every night out of fear, right?"

Nervously, she answered, "Yes."

"Then that was a choice that you made. You had eight hours to run, hide, and get away. An eight-hour flight from Georgia would land you somewhere in or near Germany," she said with a laugh. "I'm not saying it's easy to leave. I know there are different levels to this shit, but guess what? If we let someone else dictate our lives, we have to deal with whatever comes from us giving them consent to."

Meagan didn't want to hear her, but she heard her loud and clear. There wasn't any finger pointing she could do for what she had allowed to happen. Going to jail wasn't a punishment; it was a reality check. And she'd never forget the reality she'd find in it.

Angelo never received the property and money his mother blackmailed William for, because everything was in his aunt's name, and he couldn't provide any proof that they belonged to him or William. Clara had trusted her sister to do the right thing, but it was too much money for her sister to give up willingly, and there was no one that could force her to do so. However, Angelo still came out on top. He inherited his father's four-bedroom house, which used to belong to his grandparents, the church, and the mortuary. He moved his new makeshift family into the house and sold everything else. Between him and Meagan, they had enough money to never work another day in their lives, and if Denali chose not to work, he wouldn't have to, either.

Angelo watched now as Meagan played with her son in the living room. He wished the DNA results named him as the child's father, but upon reading the letter he had received in the mail moments earlier, he learned that he wasn't.

"Did they give him the death penalty?" Angelo asked, praying the answer would be yes.

"They haven't announced it yet, but does it really matter? He'll die in prison either way."

"How do you feel about it?"

"You know how I feel about it, Angelo. He's a cold-blooded killer, so whatever comes his way is well deserved. Can you grab Denali for me so I can go check the mail?"

Angelo had the paternity letter she had been waiting on in his back pocket. He didn't plan to give it to her until the sentencing was done, but if Devin's sentence really didn't matter to her, he'd give it to her now.

"I think this is what you're looking for. Here."

She ripped open the letter and scanned through the lines like a professional speed reader. When she was done, she balled the letter up and kissed Denali, with tears building in her eyes.

"So . . . is he William's or Devin's?" Angelo asked. "I got my letter saying little man isn't mine on paper, but he's mine, anyway."

"Then it doesn't matter whose blood he has." She shrugged. "What do my men want to eat for dinner?" Meagan asked, changing the subject, but Angelo still wanted to know.

"You're right, baby. It doesn't matter, but I'd still like to know."

Meagan handed the letter to Angelo and began busying herself in the kitchen, with the child on her hip. He flew his eyes past the DNA analysis results to the part that mattered to him the most.

"The above alleged fathers, William Tolliver, Angelo Hurley II, and Devin Montgomery, are excluded as the biological fathers of the tested child. Based on the testing results obtained from analysis of the DNA loci listed, the probability of paternity is 00.9996 percent," he read out loud. "Wait, so who is little man's daddy?"

"You are. We've already established that."

"Yes, we have, but you said it could be only one of the three of us. Unless you got pregnant by Jesus, yo' ass lied. Who else were you fucking?" he snapped.

Meagan had had a feeling the test results would reveal a side of Angelo she had yet to see. He'd played cool about the paternity thus far, but that was because there was a possibility he could be named as the father. She knew he'd heat up if he wasn't.

"You want a list of who I was fucking so you can count who's been in my pussy or a list of his possible fathers?" she countered, rolling her eyes.

"Damn. There's a difference? How many different lists do you have for your pussy?"

Angelo wasn't trying to start an argument, because there was only one person he prayed wasn't the father, and that was William. If the courts named William as the father, it would make it hard for the couple to forget their past each day they spent raising the child. In a fucked way, William had a father role over both of their lives. He was technically Angelo's stepfather and Meagan's godfather, although he didn't perform the duties of either title correctly for different reasons.

Angelo prayed that if he wasn't the father, Devin was. He had always liked the young man, and the fact that he had killed William made him all right in Devin's book. He hated what Meagan had caused him to turn into for her love. His career and his freedom were gone, and possibly his life, because he had fallen in love with the wrong bitch. That had always been a fear of Angelo's and the sole reason he hadn't dated. He had watched his father go through the same thing over his mother and had never liked the taste it left in his mouth. On the bright side, with Devin spending the rest of his life in prison or possibly being put to death, Angelo could adopt Denali and raise him to be the man he wanted him to be.

"I thought you said we weren't going to spend our lives consumed with who Denali's dad is?" she asked as she walked over to him and placed both of his hands on her stomach. "You said he was your blood no matter what, just like our baby growing in my stomach. Did you change your mind?"

Angelo kissed her stomach and then placed his ear on it. He didn't say anything until he heard his baby move around in its temporary home.

"No, I didn't change my mind. I just want to know. We will never have this conversation again."

"I know we won't, because you are the only father he will ever know, but if you mean by blood, I'm guessing it's one of those other two youngsters I was messing with that you cut off. My guess would be the delivery driver, because he had a lot of kids, and there were times we got caught up in the moment and protection wasn't used."

"And you're good without ever knowing? You know you're doing him like your mother did you when it came to your father."

She shrugged nonchalantly, and Angelo decided he should leave well enough alone. There wasn't any reason to go flipping over mattresses to find the man Denali shared DNA with, because Meagan was right. Angelo was his father, and that was that. He wouldn't allow another test to be done on the child to prove to anyone what he already knew to be facts. At first, he had felt like every man was owed the right to know if he had introduced a child into this world, but when Meagan pushed one last time in the delivery room, he became the only father that mattered.

What if they did track down the biological father and he rejected Denali? he thought. After his experiences with his own mother, Angelo vowed that his son would never experience the same pain of rejection, and he would spend the rest of his life ensuring that.

The End